ERINDIPITY
RIDES AGAIN

DAVID KENNY

MENTOR
BOOKS

This Edition first published 2007 by

Mentor Books, 43 Furze Road, Sandyford Industrial Estate
Dublin 18

Tel. +353(0)1-295 2112/3   Fax. +353(0)1-295 2114
email: admin@mentorbooks.ie
www.mentorbooks.ie

ISBN: 978-1-84210-427-9

Cover: Kathryn O'Sullivan
Cover Illustration: Brian Fitzgerald
Editing, Design and layout: Nicola Sedgwick

Printed in Ireland by ColourBooks

1 3 5 7 9 8 6 4 2

Foreword

You may be wondering how a second volume of **Erindipity** has come to find itself nestling between your fingers. How can the author justify doling out more information about Ireland when 2006's **Erindipity, The Irish Miscellany** claimed to be the definitive book of its kind? You may be wondering if you've been cheated. Or you may not be wondering anything at all. You may have closed the cover and not know I'm still talking to you. Permit me, anyway, to explain how this book came to be written.

In 2005, publisher Danny McCarthy asked me to expand on his colleague, Nicola Sedgwick's, idea of a book of Irish extremes: highest, lowest etc. I wasn't that inspired. The shelves are crammed with books offering the reader little naked snippets of Irish facts and figures. So we agreed that for every superlative, I would stuff in a load of other unrelated, sometimes rude, very occasionally untrue, bits of information and observations. The book would both celebrate and lampoon all things Irish. Happily for us, **Erindipity** got great mileage in print and on the airwaves, and the whole experience was hugely enjoyable. However, there were still a lot of questions, like little urchins tugging at my sleeve, begging to be answered. How long was the longest queue for ice cream? The best place to avoid getting your knickers bombed by the Jerries? And what was the best-ever miracle on the 7A bus?

So we decided to pull on our wellies, get back in the saddle and do one final round-up of facts. Some pieces are thinly-veiled attempts to vent my spleen, such as The Worst Song. Some are historic oddities, like the English soldiers who céilí-danced all the way to meet Rommel. There are two extra-long, extra-detailed entries to cater for hardcore factologists (nerds): Longest Road and Longest Stretch of Railway. For the rest of you, there's the Best Place To See Drew Barrymore In The Nip, and much more.

Enough explanations: let's get Erindipping . . .

Dave Kenny

Dedication

With all my love to my gorgeous wife Gillian
And a hug to my little godson, Nicholas O'Sullivan

Acknowledgements

This bit is always fraught with dangers – it's not who you put in, it's who you leave out that causes the trouble. Here goes, if my memory can be trusted:

Erindipity Rides Again would not have been out for Christmas if it hadn't been for two very decent, understanding human beings: Nicola Sedgwick and Danny McCarthy.

The former calmly tolerated my tardiness and did a fantastic job fine-tuning this book. Her quick-wittedness kept me on my toes and I am deeply indebted to her. I also happen to be very fond of her. Danny, you're some man for one man, as you culchies like to say. Apart from being a bit of a genius, you also happen to be a very nice man and a good friend. Thank you both.

I'd also like to thank the following for their encouragement: my mum, Gráinne, sisters Deirdre and Niamh, brothers Rory and Murph, the Carrolls – Paul, Carmel, Sophy, Baby Ben and Dominik Lewis. Then there's Cianan and Sophie O'Sullivan, Andrew and Gabrielle Flood, Lance and Suzanne Hogan, John and Louise Thomas, Clio Carroll, Joe Garde, Michael Clyne, Gareth and Charlie O'Connor, Maurice ('Rusty') Haugh, Tony and Aoife O'Donoghue.

The sources of information for this book are too many to mention, they include newspaper archives, the internet, RTÉ, The National Library and my own stack of history books and periodicals. Damien Corless' great book on Irish politics, **Party Nation**, deserves special mention for the Anthem and the **Irish Press** headline stories. A special word of thanks goes to Nóirín Hegarty for being so flexible about my working arrangements. And the final word goes to the late Mark Ashton: we all miss you.

Contents

WITHDRAWN FROM STOCK

Shortest and Longest

Shortest Stretch of Coast

GAA nickname aficionados will already know that Clare is the Banner County, Meath the Royal County, Cork the Rebel County, Armagh the Orchard County, Kerry is the Kingdom, Waterford the Decies and **Leitrim** is . . . any guesses for what Leitrim is? Leitrim is 'Lovely'.

No one, not even its own inhabitants, could be bothered to dream up a sporting name for this pretty, but lonely, lump of Connacht. So they called it 'Lovely Leitrim'. Can you imagine a worse monicker to be inflicted with as you race out onto the pitch with your ball or your ashplant in your hand, fired up, baying for blood and the announcer roaring: 'Here come the Lovelies!'?

'Lovely' is what you reply when someone asks you how your cup of tea is. It's how you describe the beige socks you got as a Christmas present. It's the code word for someone or something that's insipid, forgettable, uninspiring – but not too boring to be annoying. It sums up someone who is not interesting enough to be irritating, but dull enough for you to start spring-cleaning the inbox of your mobile phone while they're talking to you. 'He/she's really lovely,' you say to a mutual friend because you can't recall the person's presence as offensive, but neither can you recall them having any discernible features. Think Mr Potato Head from the movie *Toy Story* (1996) – denuded of his plastic nose, eyes, mouth, ears, hair and brows. Leitrim is 'Mr Potato Headless'.

Someone once said, uncharitably, that if Leitrim was a colour it would be taupe. Apart from being unfair this is also untrue – it would be grey. 'Leitrim' is the Anglicised version of *Liath Druim*, the 'grey ridge'.

That's not to say that Leitrim does not possess many wildly interesting facets, it's just that the rest of Ireland couldn't be bothered looking for them. And here are those facets: the county is 1,526 sq km and divided into two parts by Lough Allen – the northern bit being mountainous, the southern half being level. There's some industry (textiles, car parts, electrical goods and the like) and oats are grown. As are potatoes. And there's a pig farm somewhere. And there's lots and lots of grass. And rain.

So you see, Leitrim has a lot going for it.

It also has some wonderful scenery, but seeing as how scenery isn't edible its population declined from 155,000 in the Famine years of the nineteenth century to 28,950 in the present one. According to the 2006 Census Leitrim has the **Lowest Population Density** (that is, the number of persons per square kilometre) in the State at eighteen. To put this in context, Dublin has the highest with 4,304 and the overall figure for the country is 60 per sq km. This figure of eighteen is an increase on the previous low of sixteen, but is still rather diminutive.

But it's not all doom and gloom in Leitrim – it can boast a very high per capita number of world-class authors. First there's the late, brilliant son of Aughawillan, **John McGahern.** Okay, so it is all doom and gloom. Then there is, of course, the local drug-loving Australian-Mexican Booker Prize winner.

DBC Pierre – or **Peter Warren Finlay** as he was Christened in Oz – landed in Leitrim in 2000 after a colourful youth spent dabbling with chemicals and chasing various dodgy schemes, including attempting to locate the lost gold of the Aztecs. He was raised in Mexico by his wealthy English parents so the transition to life in crazy, out-of-control old Leitrim can't have been too hard. It was here with the rain dripping down the windowpane that he edited his debut novel, *Vernon God Little,* which won the stg£50,000 prize in 2003.

If DBC (Dirty But Clean) came to Leitrim looking for solitude he may not have been impressed to learn that the underpopulated county is split down the middle on gender lines: there are 14,903 chaps to 14,047 ladies. On top of that 33.1% of the population is under twenty-five. With that frisky, young 1:1 ratio Leitrim is seeing plenty of love action and should, in no time, be bursting at the seams with families bringing their kiddies to the only beach in the county. That beach also happens to be the

Shortest Stretch Of Coast In Ireland – 3.21 km of Donegal Bay, 14.5 km to the southwest of Bundoran. If it ever gets overcrowded, the inhabitants could always spend their holidays on Ireland's . . .

Longest Beach

Erindipity Rides Again is delighted to be the first book of its kind – or any kind for that matter – to reveal that there are nineteen rhyming counties on the island of Ireland. Most of them are pretty ropey, and five of them share the same end words, but rhyme they do. They are: Dubli(n), Monagha(n); Wick(low), Car(low); Wex(ford), Long(ford), Water(ford); Meath, West(meath); Kild(are), Cl(are); May(o), Slig(o); Lei(trim), An(trim); Ferman(agh), Arm(agh). If you rule out the Meaths, as they're really just the same name repeated, then the counties with the most rhyming letters are Kerry and Derry with four apiece. Incidentally, the non-rhyming letters D and K also happen to be the author's initials. The latter means very little but does hint at a grotesque, bloated ego at work on this book.

Derry and Kerry are not only the most rhyming counties in Ireland, they also share another unique boast. Benone/Magilligan Strand, from Downhill to the mouth of Lough Foyle in north Derry is considered one of the finest beaches in Ulster and is said by the good folk of that part of Ireland to be the longest in the country. They're not alone in this claim. A quick Google of 'Northern Ireland Longest Beach' will throw up gazillions of sites saying the same thing. Even the excellent *London Independent* newspaper of 26 May 2001 and Irish News.com back up the claim (see http://travel.independent.co.uk/news_and_advice/article245973.ece and http://www.irishnews.com/tourism/derry/dyquick.html).

However, if you swim around the coast to the other end of the island you'll hear the same claim being made in Kerry. So who's right, the Foylesiders or the citizens of the Kingdom?

The answer is: Kerry. The longest beach in Ireland stretches 19.5 km from Maharees through Castlegregory to Cloghane village and can kick sand in the face of Benone/Magilligan Strand, which is only 11 km. However, (or 'highandever' as they say in Derry), the northern beach has an even more interesting claim to fame than its Kerry cousin – it was here that **Harry Ferguson** earned his place in the history books by making the first powered flight in Ireland back in 1909.

Ferguson (1884–1960) travelled a full 118.5 metres in a monoplane that he had built himself. This intriguing man went on to drive racing cars, started his own motor business in 1911 and during the First World War designed and introduced tractors to rural Ireland, revolutionising farming. Motor giant **Henry Ford** was so impressed with Harry's achievements that he offered him a job (which he turned down), and in 1938 undertook to manufacture Ferguson's machines in America for the latter to sell. The deal was a 'gentleman's agreement', based on nothing more than a handshake and Harry would live to rue it. After Henry Ford passed away he became embroiled in a dispute with the Ford Motor Company and eventually walked away with $9.25million compensation in 1952. Similarily a 1953 merger with the Canadian Massey-Harris company worked out unhappily for him and he decided to retire, leaving an extraordinary legacy around the farmyards of the world.

Fergie was a real gent and his dream was to raise living standards all over the world. In 1943 he stated that agriculture 'should have been the first industry to be modernised, not the last'. Think of Bob Geldof on a tractor but with better personal hygiene.

Happily, Harry was not the first Irish transport pioneer with a heart of gold – there's also the charitable Mr Robert Dowling who's coming up in the next section. Now hurry along and read the following interesting facts.

INTERESTING FACTS

- Carlow has the bizarrest GAA nickname in the country. Its players are called The Scallion Eaters (pronounced 'Ayters').
- Ireland has one-third of the world's coastal links courses and two of them are based in the same County Clare townland – Lahinch.
- Kerry was once the centre of communications between Europe and the States. The first

transatlantic cable was laid between Valentia Island and Hearts Content, Newfoundland on 14 July 1865. The first commercial message sent from the Kerry station was from Queen Victoria to the American people and it read: 'Glory to God in the highest, on Earth peace, goodwill to men'. The island is also home to the oldest footprints in the northern hemisphere. The pre-dinosaur tetrapod tracks, which form a trail about 15 m long, were made between 350 and 385 million years ago. Endless gabbing and primitive life forms in Kerry? Who'd have thought it?

Longest Stretch Of Road

Forget the Romans – when it comes to road building, the Irish have always been top of the rubble heap.

Generations before Julius Caesar and the boys had the good sense to criss-cross their empire with highways and byways the Irish had shouldered their shovels, packed breakfast rolls in their satchels and headed off into the mushy peatlands to carve out our ancient bog roads. And while Custer and his men were getting free haircuts from battle-axe-wielding Indians, who were swinging their pickaxes to get the American railways up and running (well, they *are* a type of road)? That's right, the Irish, of course.

And when her Britannic Majesty, Queen Victoria, was

ruling the waves, or waiving the rules or whatever, who was it that was out digging her streets of London in the belief that they were paved with gold? Poor **Paddy Navvy**, that's who (while also offering to tarmac her driveway as well).

Is it any wonder then, that the Irish love their roads so much? In terms of recent history this love affair has become more of a wild, steamy-session-in-a-layby as our wealth and status in the world has grown. 'You can never have too many roads', the ancient proverb goes and it was this that prompted our politicians to go begging to Europe in the 1980s for money to build more of them. If we were all unemployed (which we were), then we might as well look busy, the logic went. Then as more people started working on the roads the unemployment figures went down and then the house prices started to rise because the New Navvys, as they were called, needed somewhere to live. Then the Old Navvys came back from Birmingham and London and got jobs working for the New Navvys and they too bought houses. 'Hello,' said the Americans, catching the scent of a fast buck, 'Those roads look mighty fine, and we were wondering if you guys would like to build us some factories for making stuff for erectile dysfunction and the like . . .' and the New Navvys

> In terms of [Ireland's recent history with roads] this love affair has become more of a wild, steamy-session-in-a-layby as our wealth and status in the world has grown.

said, 'We'd love to, pals, but all our Old Navvys are busy working on the roads', and the Americans said, 'You should get some Polish Navvys, because they're cheap, they work hard and they only want Sunday morning off to go to Mass' and the New Navvys replied, 'Great idea', and went off to sell their Hiaces and buy state-of-the-art Jeeps to drop their children off at the childminder's because

A): they had loads more money and

B): only Navvys drove Hiaces and they didn't want to look like Navvys any more.[1]

Now there were more Hiaces and Jeeps on the roads than ever before, so the New Navvys created what became known as 'traffic jams' and used to spend hours sitting on their beloved roads honking their horns happily until someone else came up with an ingenious plan. 'Let's make some money out of these traffic jams,' they said, and they built toll booths in the middle of their new roads, which meant that the traffic jams were worse and they got to make money and buy more Jeeps and everybody was happy. And that is how the Celtic Tiger was born.

Fact. Now where were we?

The longest highway in the country is also the oldest and is called the **Esker Riada**, which traverses Ireland from Lucan in County Dublin to Galway in the west. It is approximately 246 km long, which is 313 km short of the famous Appian Way in Rome (563 km), but 9,300 years older as the Romans only turned the first sod on their road in 312 BC.

---

[1]You may be interested to learn that this is The Longest Sentence in This Book. Try reading it in one go, out loud, without pausing for breath.

The early inhabitants of Ireland knew the Esker Riada as *An Slí Mór*, which translates as The Great Way, and to them it was the island's most important thoroughfare. The Esker Riada also bisects Ireland and the two halves are roughly equal in size. After the Battle of Maynooth in 120 BC, Conn of the 100 Battles and Owen Mór agreed that the country would be divided into two parts either side of the Esker Riada, to be called *Leath Cuinn* and *Leath Mogha* – Conn's Half and Mogha's Half respectively. Dividing the country north and south isn't such a new idea after all.

Many travellers on *An Slí Mór* would have been heading to places like Tara and Newgrange (*Brú na Bóinne*, built 3,100 BC) and might have stopped off at Ireland's biggest crossroads for a jig or cup of tea. This crossroads is located at Clonmacnoise which was founded by St Ciaran in AD 548 and is (tape measures aside) roughly in the centre of island. The dead centre of Ireland can be found at 53N and 8W, should you be inclined to locate it. For many years people believed it to be hiding in Emmet Square, Birr, County Offaly, but *Erindipity* successfully disproved this and destroyed the town's tourist industry. Please don't sue.

(It's in Tipperary near an area known as Kilcunnahin Beg, not far from Cloughjordan and 0.6 km ESE of The Pike).

At either end of *An Slí Mór* lie **Galway** and **Lucan**. Galway is famous for wild, beautiful scenery and stag parties while Lucan is famous for a big spa and a famous general (not the same person).

In 1758 a sulphur spa was discovered on the bank of the Liffey at Lucan village and the subsequent Spa Hotel became a favourite meeting place of the Dublin set who came to take the health-giving water and be entertained. Some visitors, however, left the hotel in an altogether unhealthier state than when they arrived. In 1825 Mr Owen O'Fisher from the Irish Society in London ingested more than the water at Ireland's **Most Famous Health Spa** for his breakfast. In his report to the society he wrote that his meal was composed of fried lamb chops, boiled tongue, eggs, cream, freshly churned butter, a variety of breads, griddle cakes and tea and coffee. He washed all this down, not with a glass of Liffey water, but a half balloon of white cognac. Presumably he went for a run on the treadmill afterwards.

Eventually drinking sulphuric river water went out of vogue and the spa building became a school for Protestant clergymens' sons. Then in 1883 the Lucan steam tram arrived, reviving interest in the spa, and a new hotel was built near the old one. This hotel is still there and will still supply draughts of the waters if you ask nicely.

Lucan is also famous for being the demesne of **General Patrick Sarsfield**, the man who signed the Treaty of Limerick with England in 1691. Sarsfield, the first Earl of Lucan, was born around 1650 to Patrick Sarsfield Snr and Anne O'Moore, daughter of Rory O'Moore. He was educated at a military college in France and built up an impressive career as a soldier. He was made MP for County Dublin on 7 May 1689 and a commissioner for raising taxes the following year. It was in arms, however, that

Sarsfield made his name because when William of Orange landed in Ireland he found himself guarding Athlone. Later that year he was made Baron Roseberry, Viscount of Tully, Earl of Lucan and Colonel of the Lifeguards.

He went on to be commander-in-chief of the forces in Ireland and after the disastrous Battle of Aughrim led his men in an orderly retreat to Limerick, an action that saved a lot of lives. He then brokered the terms of the Treaty of Limerick on 3 October 1691. But perhaps all the years spent drinking Liffey water had softened his brain so much that he trusted Perfidious Albion[2]. The Treaty consisted of two parts: military and civil. The military articles allowed Sarsfield and other members of the Irish army to join the French or Williamite armies. Most opted for the former and left Ireland for France on twelve ships carrying 2,600 men in the Second Flight of the Earls. So far, so okayish.

The civil part of the Treaty dealt with the treatment of Catholics and the property of those who had fought for King James. This part was ultimately broken and after 1691 the Catholics were penalised and their lands confiscated. As a result Limerick is sometimes called the City of the Broken Treaty. Or, in more recent years, City of The Broken Bottle On The Head of a Saturday Night.

Sarsfield died at the head of a French division at the Battle of Landen in Flanders on 29 July 1693.

As this is fast becoming the **Longest Stretch of Text in This Book** let's return to the Esker Riada. While being Ireland's **Longest And Oldest Highway**, is not, however, Ireland's Longest Stretch of Road. This is

[2] An old derogatory term for England

because it's not man-made. The esker is a natural range of rocky mounds which were deposited by a retreating glacier about 10,000 years ago at the end of the last ice age. Therefore it's not the Oldest Road either. That distinction could well belong to the Iron Age road on display at Corlea in County Longford, which was built around 150 BC across boglands close to the Shannon. The 18 metre-long oak road is the biggest of its kind to have been uncovered in Europe, and is on permanent display in a purpose-built hall with special humidifiers to protect the wood. The part of the road that remains buried has been carefully preserved by Bord na Móna and the Heritage Service. We say it may be the oldest, but old bog roads are constantly being uncovered as the country's lust for flyovers and underpasses rages unabated.

But it's not just bog roads being discovered. In May 2007, just twenty-four hours after the Minister for Transport turned the sod on the €850million M3 motorway in County Meath, it was confirmed that a site of major archaeological importance had been discovered in the Tara-Skryne valley. The circular enclosure, clearly visible on a hillside at Lismullin, was most likely used for rituals in either the Iron Age or Bronze Age. For years campaigners had unsuccessfully attempted to stop the 60 km M3 going through the area, which is one of the most archaeologically rich in Europe. The argument that it would destroy the soul of the place and inevitably ruin major historical sites failed to impress the men with the concrete mixers. 'Find ancient settlements/temples/ whatever at Tara? Go on out of that', had been the response. Didn't they look foolish when they had to tell the New Navvies that construction was being put on hold? To say that work on the motorway has since progressed at a snail's pace would be correct and would also provide a pithy little segue into the following few paragraphs.

It's not just archaeologists who drive road builders around the bend. In 1999 work on the €160million, 13.2 km M7 Kildare Town bypass ground to a halt because of a complaint to Europe about the plan to solve one of the country's main traffic bottlenecks. The culprit in this case was a snail.

It wasn't just any snail, however. It was the rare *Angistora vertiego* which lives in Pollardstown Fen, just 4 km from the bypass. Fans of the whorl snail claimed the new road would devastate water supplies to the marsh area, draining away nearly two and a half million litres as the bypass was dug near it. The fen is considered to be unique in terms of its flora and fauna – as well as for its most famous inhabitant.

True to its nature, the snail dragged out the row for over two years before it won its case. Engineers went back to the drawing board and eventually used an impermeable liner or 'tanking' in the construction of a 3.5 km section of the motorway, which finally opened in 2003. It was the first time that this method had been used in Ireland, so the little snail had made road building history as the **Shortest Campaigner to Halt a Roadworks**. This is all very nice but doesn't get us any closer to revealing the Longest Stretch of Road, which is . . . but before we get to that, you might be interested to know that the **Longest Stretch of Road To Be Snubbed By Everyone** can be found in County Cork. The M8 bypass of Rathcormac, Fermoy and Watergrasshill in the north of the county was opened in October 2006 on budget (€300million) and eight months ahead of schedule. It had taken 400 construction workers twenty-seven months to build and the Government boasted that it would remove 17,000 heavy goods vehicles from the traffic flow through the villages. The good motorists of Ireland's largest county were delighted and understandably proud of their achievement – until they learned the road was to be tolled at €1.60 per car. Soon afterwards the unfortunate residents of Watergrasshill were complaining that the bypass had actually increased traffic through the hamlet by 6,000 vehicles per day, including around 1,100 trucks, which were all avoiding payment of the tariff.

In early 2007 the toll operators admitted that only 11,000 vehicles per day were using the stretch of road. Indeed, the toll proved so unpopular that drivers from Cavan began making weekend round trips to Watergrasshill just for the enjoyment of saving some money.

And finally, the unveiling of the Longest Stretch of Road ever built in Ireland. According to the National Roads Authority, 'the M8/N8 Cullahill to Cashel road project, which commenced in October 2006 and is due for completion at the end of 2009 is the longest road project ever to be undertaken in the State to date and comprises approximately 40 km (10 km motorway and 30 km high-quality dual carriageway). The M4

Kilcock/Kinnegad motorway which was officially opened in December 2005 comprises 39 km of motorway'. So now you know.

INTERESTING FACTS

- Roscommon is the Pothole Capital of Ireland. On 2 May 1985 Fianna Fáil's Bobby Molloy told the Dáil in Private Members' Time that 'there are LITERALLY millions of potholes in County Roscommon'. He went on to implore the transport minister to act, as he had told Mr Molloy on 'two recent occasions that he was the man who was going to fill the potholes'. The minister was good to his word, but decided that for him to personally fill in 'literally' millions of potholes might take up too much of his time. So he had them transported to Monaghan instead.

- There are approximately 97,000 km of paved roadways in the Republic of Ireland. All of it pristine, unclogged and well-maintained.

- Lentil-eating, tree-hugging crusties are frequently responsible for holding up roadways etc., but planners in County Kerry have to contend with an altogether different type of protestor – the hooligan fairy. In February 2007 the Little People were roundly blamed for sabotaging one of the major national primary routes in the southwest. A mysterious dip which appeared on the N22 at Curraglass near Killarney baffled engineers and led to suspicions by one councillor that angry fairies were behind it. The road passes through a wide area of standing stones and ancient monuments on the foothills of the Paps Mountains. The locality is steeped in folklore and a number of place names refer to fairy forts or 'lioses'. In 2005 the road suddenly developed a big dip several metres long, and extensive repairs were carried out by the council. Two years later the road dipped again and county councillor Danny Healy-Rae demanded a detailed report into the matter. In a formal motion put before the council Councillor Healy-Rae asked: 'Is it fairies at work?' The council's road department later replied that it might be due to 'a deeper underlying subsoil/geotechnical problem'. This being tourist-conscious Kerry – where one can make a Crock of Gold out of a Crock of Crap – the former explanation was favoured by many of the good burghers of Killarney. Apparently the fairies were just laying the foundations for a troll booth on the motorway.

Longest Stretch Of Railroad Opened In A Day

Prior to the arrival of the railway in Ireland the primary mode of transport was either by donkey and cart or penny-farthing bicycle. The latter was particularly popular in County Roscommon as the big front 'penny' wheel was generally too large to get stuck in the 'literally millions' of potholes which were commonplace there until the late twentieth century (see Interesting Fact page 18). This bicycle's successor, the High Nelly Old Black Bike only caught on in that county after the potholes were exported. But this is a digression.

On 17 November 1834 the *Hibernia* – or Iron Horse as the ancient inhabitants of The Noggin used to call it – became the first train to steam down the 8.8 km track between Westland Row station in Dublin's city centre and Kingstown in south Dublin (now Pearse to Dun Laoghaire) at the official opening of Ireland's first passenger line. It made the journey in 19.5 minutes – just 30 seconds slower than it takes today.

The railway was intended to be opened in June of that year, but due to technical hitches and a massive storm which demolished the bridge across the Dodder at Lansdowne Road, it saw more false starts than Sonia O'Sullivan. The *Dublin Penny Journal* of October 1834 described one of the test runs:

> Connection between the engine and carriages was at first by means of chains, which as may be imagined, produced very unpleasant results when starting or stopping – the carriages crashing together again and

again before they came to rest. The spring buffer to some extent remedied this, but it took some time before a silent and satisfactory method of coupling[3] was evolved.

The excitement around the project outweighed the initial objections to wasting stg£300,000 so that a 'few nursery maids' could descend from 'the town of Kingstown to the sea at Dunleary, to perform the pleasures of ablution'.[4]

The *Dublin Evening Post* was delighted with the opening of the 'splendid work' but was unimpressed at the early start the first passengers had to endure without their MP3 players, mobile phones and free newspapers to help them avoid making eye contact with their fellow commuters:

> Notwithstanding the early hour at which the first train started – half-past nine o'clock [sic] – the carriages were filled by a very fashionable concourse of persons, and the greatest eagerness was manifested to witness the first operations of the work. Up to a quarter-past five the line of road from Merrion to Salt Hill was thronged with spectators, who loudly cheered each train that passed. The average rate at which the trip was performed yesterday was nineteen minutes and a half, including the delay of about two minutes at the Rock, where passengers were taken up. Much confusion was occasioned at starting by the want of proper arrangement, but this inconvenience will be very easily obviated.

Some things never change.

[3] Yes, yes, he said 'coupling'. Choo-choo trains going in and out of tunnels, woo-woo, dirty sniggers etc. and so forth. Now that we've got the phallic symbolism out of the way, may we proceed?

[4] Old Dunleary, as it was called in the nineteenth century, is situated about 1 km north of Kingstown, or modern Dun Laoghaire. The ruins of High King Laoghaire's original dún (fort), built around AD 429, survived there until the early 1800s, when a Martello tower was built on it to protect against Napoleon's navy.

Trains may have been run at intervals throughout that inaugural day, but there was no set service until the following January when they were run every half hour, both ways, from 9–5 p.m. On Sundays the trains ran every twenty minutes, with a lunch break from 12–2 p.m., a single fare setting you back 1s, 8d and 6d for first, second and third classes. The William Dargan-constructed line was a great success with the well-to-do, as they realised that they didn't have to risk life or limb or irritated haemorrhoids using their penny-farthings or donkeys to get out to Kingstown for a 99 cone outside Teddy's ice cream parlour (minus the Flake as they hadn't yet been invented). 1834 also saw the emergence of the **First Train Spotters**. At the beginning there were only a handful of these hanging out at the stops along the route, and they had to share the one anorak, but five years later their numbers swelled as the Ulster railway line opened from Lisburn to Belfast. The descendents of these pioneering anoraks might be interested in the following statistics (everybody else look away now): The Dublin Kingstown track was 4 ft 8 $\frac{1}{2}$ in gauge or 1.4 m if you prefer metric. The Ulster line was 6 ft 2 in gauge (1.8 m). The real growth of the Irish railways only started to happen in the 1840s when the

> 1834 also saw the emergence of the First Train Spotters. At the beginning there were only a handful of these hanging out at the stops along the route, and they had to share the one anorak . . .

standard gauge had been fixed at 5 ft 3 in (1.6 m). Earlier lines were altered and in 1844 Dublin and Drogheda were linked, followed in 1846 by Dublin and Carlow.

In 1850 the total track lengths measured 885 km and ten years later this had more than doubled to 2,173 km. Today that figure stands at 3,312 km, of which 46 km is electrified.

Non Train-Spotters rejoin us here. While rail travel grew in the 1800s bike sales fell off, as did the fortunes of one Charles Bianconi – Ireland's **First Ever Bus Driver**.

Joachim Carlo Giuseppe Bianconi was born in Tregola near Como in Italy to a small farmer (a mere 1.6 m in his stocking feet) on 24 September 1786. The area was renowned at the time for the cultivation of mulberries and silkworms, which is apropos of absolutely nothing whatsoever to do with this piece.

Young Carlo loved to help out on the farm and go hunting with his friends and, as his dad Pietro had his own silk mill as well as cows and pigs and the like, one can presume that he had a few decent ties in his wardrobe. At the age of ten he went to live with his granny and was educated by his uncle, the Rev. Giosue in Caglio. Being the outdoor type he didn't excel at his scholarly pursuits. When he was thirteen he was sent away to another school near Asso where he also failed to shine but did manage to find himself a girlfriend whose wealthy father didn't approve of him. Life was not a bowl of cherries for young Bianconi.

After all this shunting around his father reckoned he needed to be shunted around some more and so asked an artisan print framer, Andrea Faroni, to take him as one of his apprentices to England where he intended to set up shop. And so young Carlo went from farmer to framer and, true to form, there was even more travel on the cards.

Faroni decided against London and headed to Dublin instead, opening his business in the Temple Bar area in August 1802. It was here that Carlo and the other boys were sent out onto streets to sell their prints to the *bon viveurs* and stag parties of Olde Dubline Towne. As his English was lousy, many of the revellers thought Bianconi was selling pints and gave him a clip around the lughole for misleading them. Actually, that bit's not true. But it could be. If it was true then it would explain why his English improved so quickly and he and the other boys were so successful that they were sent off every Monday with a stack of prints, returning the following Saturday with pockets full of brass. Soon they were ranging further outside of Dublin and Carlo began taking note of the poor state of transport across the country. His apprenticeship ended in 1804 and he decided to stay on to start his own print-selling business. He bought a big valise for his wares and traipsed around the countryside with it on his back. Business was good, he was liked wherever he went and he started to use the English form of his name, Charles.

Eventually he tired of tramping the roads and settled in Clonmel, County Tipperary as a 'carver and gilder of the first class' at No 1 Gladstone Street. It was here that Charles the gilder struck gold (metaphorically, of course) in 1815.

The end of the Napoleonic Wars meant thousands of horses bred for the conflict came onto the market at knockdown prices of £10–£20. Forage was also reasonable so Bianconi seized the opportunity to set up Ireland's first cheap public transport system. On 6 July 1815 the first Bianconi car ran from Clonmel to Cahir and back, carrying six passengers and mail 35.4 km at 12 km per hour. The fare was one farthing a mile and the service became so popular so quickly that Bianconi branched out to Tipperary, Limerick, Wexford, Waterford, Cork and Kilkenny. Other places clamoured for their own 'Bians' too.

Over the next forty years an unprecedented communications network was built up with Clonmel at its centre. By 1825 Carlo's routes covered 941 km of countryside and he employed a huge workforce of drivers, agents, stable hands and guards. He even had his own factory to build his coaches which, from 1833 on, were producing the famous four-wheeled 'long cars' which could carry up to twenty passengers at a time. Bianconi had gone from being an itinerant peddlar to become one of the richest men in the land. Then came the age of the railway in 1834 (remember the railway?) which threatened to wipe out his business. Undaunted, Bianconi developed his system around the rail network, meeting the trains and carrying people to the more remote areas of the country. Before he died in 1875 at the age of 89, Charles Bianconi had twice been elected Mayor of Clonmel, helped establish the Catholic University of Dublin (now UCD), bought the stately Longfield House and 1,600 hectares of land in various parts of the county, married his daughter off to Daniel O'Connell's nephew and witnessed the opening of the Longest Stretch of Railway Line on a single day.

This was the 122.3 km run from Mullingar to Galway on the MGWR (Midlands Great Western Railway), launched on Friday 1 August 1851.

INTERESTING FACTS

- In 1840 1,280,761 passengers travelled on the Dublin–Kingstown train line. In 2006, 27 million people used the Dart (Dublin Area Rapid Transit) service along the same route. The following are the stations servicing the Dart: Greystones, Bray, Shankill, Killiney, Dalkey, Glenageary, Sandycove, Dun Laoghaire, Salthill and Monkstown, Seapoint, Blackrock, Booterstown, Sydney Parade, Sandymount, Lansdowne Road, Grand Canal Dock, Pearse Street, Tara Street, Connolly, Clontarf Road, Killester, Harmonstown, Raheny, Kilbarrack, Howth Junction, Bayside, Sutton and Howth.

- Dalkey Dart Station is an anagram of Yank Ate Tart's Dildo (a favourite southside dessert) while Harmonstown Dart Station is Hoots Mon! It's Drawn Tartan, which is just plain gobbledygook.

- Bianconi once spent a night in the cells in Passage East, outside of Waterford, when he was caught flogging a print of Napoleon Bonaparte during the height of the war. This meant he was either very brave or preternaturally stupid.

- Bianconi invented the *long* car, lived in *Long*field House and appeared in this book in the section '*Long*est Stretch Of Railway'. No, it's not a coincidence. Much.

Longest Distance Travelled In A Bathtub

Here follows an interruption by the author: the following two entries should, arguably, be included in the People section of this book as they deal with a number of very interesting and unusual characters. However, it would be wrong not to mention the diaspora and those places they have Hibernicised through their sheer audacity or, in some cases, pure nuttiness. South America is one of those places often overlooked by students of Irish history as they gaze westwards across the Atlantic. For example, many are aware that Admiral William Brown of Foxford, Co Mayo founded the Argentine navy but may not know that the great cattle ranches of the Pampas are practically all owned by the descendants of emigrants who left these shores in the nineteenth century. These people, many of whom have never set foot in Ireland and for whom Spanish is a native tongue, speak English with their forebears' regional Irish accents. Similarly, how many could tell you that Che Guevara was of mixed Spanish and Irish ancestry and could trace his roots to the Lynchs of Galway? With this in mind, I beg your leave to include the following two Erindipitous pieces, both based around the Amazon and coincidentally the Peruvian town of Iquitos.

Actually, ignore all of the above. It's my book and I'll write what I want. *DK*

The longest distance ever travelled in a bathtub is 804 km, give or take a few metres.

Dubliner **Robert Dowling** set this pioneering benchmark in naval history when he set off down the Amazon in a customised household bathtub. Yes, that does say 'Amazon' and 'bathtub'. The Donabate man challenged himself to single-handedly sail 5,471 km along this mighty waterway (the Nile is its rival) in his singular craft to raise money for Temple Street children's hospital.

The idea came to Robert when he was chatting to friends about what mad thing they all wanted to do before they died. Twenty-five years – and a large dollop of his own money – later, the dream became reality when the forty-eight-year-old salesman-cum-sails man set off from the Peruvian town of Iquitos in May 2006 (possibly humming 'rub-a-dub, three, sorry, ONE man in a bathtub'. Or possibly not). His course was downriver with the flow to the border of Colombia and Brazil, covering 400 km and then on through the latter country, finally reaching the town of Almerim close to the coast.

His bath – should you ever wish to attempt this yourself – was housed in a steel frame supported by side tanks for extra stability and powered by a 15 hp Suzuki outboard engine. The journey, undertaken with tinned food, a GPS unit, satellite photos and various charts and maps, started off well. The Peruvians had taken a shine to our naval hero and Robert enjoyed a relatively trouble-free journey until he reached Colombia. There he had to contend with the threat of running foul of the infamous, ruthless rebel group FARC. Travelling as quietly as he could by night he stole by their campfires and continued to negotiate the river into Brazil. It was here, sadly, that his plans went down the plughole. But it wasn't a rebel armed to the teeth or even a shoal of hungry piranhas that ended Robert's journey – it was a bureaucrat. After travelling 804 km through the jungle he was told that he couldn't continue because he didn't have a licence for his bathtub.

Picture the scene: hardy Irishman in a bath in deepest Brazil accosted by little man with a clipboard and a peaked cap . . .

Robert: Morning.

Bureaucrat: Morning.

Robert: Looks like rain. (*smiles*)

Bureaucrat   (*sarcastically*): Well, you *are* in a rain forest. Do you have a licence for this . . . (*waves clipboard in direction of bathtub*) . . . vehicle? Sub-section C, Paragraph One of the Amazonian River Code clearly states that all motorised bathtubs must be licenced. It's the law, you know.

Robert: No.

Bureaucrat:	Would you mind stepping out of the vehicle, sir?
Robert:	Yes, I would mind.
Bureaucrat:	Why?
Robert:	Because we're in the middle of a river . . .

And so ended – if not exactly in those words – Robert's incredible journey.

However, the adventure didn't end there. In November 2007 Robert was making plans to return and retrieve his tub from the small town in Colombia where he had been forced to leave it. He was also planning his next trip down the Amazon to raise funds for disadvantaged South American children – on a jet ski.

This extraordinary, kind-hearted Dubliner won a Best of Irish Award from the *Irish Daily Star* newspaper in 2007 and *Erindipity Rides Again* believes Dublin City Council should erect a statue in honour of him.

We could nickname it 'Rob-a-Dub-Dub-in-a-Tub'.

Longest Distance Sailed Up A Hill

0.8 km (or half a mile). Whatever about the sanity of travelling down the Amazon in a bathtub, sailing a 340-tonne steamboat up a small mountain in order to build an opera house in the Peruvian jungle is clearly cuckoo.

This is what Mr Brian Sweeney Fitzgerald did at the end of the nineteenth century to entice the tenor Enrico Caruso to perform for him, according to German movie director **Werner Herzog**.

His 1982 movie classic, *Fitzcarraldo,* tells the tale of an Irishman who lives in the Peruvian back of beyond selling ice to the local Spanish rubber barons. Unlike Fitzcarraldo, these chaps know how to run a business – exploiting the Indians, not paying their pensions and whatnot – and he is considered a bit of a gobdaw, unremarkable but for his obsessive love of opera. Oh, and he's shacked up with the local madame which doesn't go down well either. (That reference to a lady of easy virtue and 'going down' is purely coincidental). Determined to build an opera house in the town of Iquitos (where Robert Dowling started his Amazon journey), Fitzcarraldo tries to prise financial backing from the tight fists of the local millionaires. After being laughed out of town, his hooker with a heart, Molly, backs him and he buys a boat and steams upriver to an unclaimed land parcel that he intends to exploit for its rubber. If he gets rich he'll be able to build the opera house and Caruso will sing there. 'If you build it he will come', a dreamy voice tells him at one point in the movie when he's standing in a cornfield. Or was that *Field of Dreams* (1989)? Yes it was, but something similar happens because the Fitzcarraldo of Herzog's flick is definitely hearing voices and could do with being connected to a couple of electrodes.

The only river access to his potential rubber plantation proves to be unnavigable due to a series of rapids and waterfalls. However, Fitzer is undaunted and tells no one of his secret plan until he reaches a spot in the river that runs parallel with the upper tributary and his prospective plantation. How is he going to get his steamboat 0.8 km over the mud mountain that separates the two rivers? With pulleys, ropes and a lot of Indian sweat, of course. Despite winding up broke – mentally and financially – Fitzcarraldo achieves his dream of opening an opera house.

Herzog's story of obsession and insanity, starring fellow German Klaus Kinski (perhaps they should have called it Fritz*carraldo*) is loosely based on fact, but the making of the movie was stranger than anything his fevered brain could have dreamt up. After the original leads, **Jason Robards** and **Mick Jagger**, were forced to pull out due to illness and tour commitments he got Kinski on board and then reshot the entire movie, which was already 40% complete. Robards and Mick had a lucky escape as filming proved to be an extraordinary ordeal, and involved hauling Fitz's 340-tonne steamship at a 45 degree angle over a small mountain – without camera trickery.

Herzog also shot several scenes onboard the steamer while it ploughed through the rapids, injuring three of the film crew. Kinski, Herzog's longtime friend and collaborator, was also something of an insurmountable obstacle as he fought with director and crew and seriously cheesed off the natives. At one point a local chief offered to murder him for Herzog, who turned down the kind offer as he needed him to complete filming.

The life of the real Fitzcarraldo was no less interesting than that of his fictional namesake. **Isaias Fermin**

Fitzgerald was born in 1862, the eldest child of an Irish naval officer who had settled in the mining district of San Luis de Huari, in the Central Andes of Peru.

The young Isaias was a bit of a firebrand and got up to all kinds of shenanigans including getting near-fatally wounded in a gambling quarrel just after finishing school. He was also accused of being a Chilean spy during Peru's war with that country in 1879, forcing him to change his name to Carlos Fernando Fitzcarrald. Still in his teens, he ran away into the jungle and took up work as a rubber tapper. By the age of twenty-six he was the richest rubber man in the Ucayali region of Peru, exporting his bouncy product all the way to London. At thirty-one the enterprising Fitzcarrald founded a city and had an isthmus named after him (who wouldn't want an isthmus named after them?), opening up a new transportation route which made him even wealthier. It was during the discovery of this new route that he hauled his steamboat up a mountain. Unlike Herzog, however, he chose to dismantle the ship and carry it up piece by piece to lighten the Indians' load.

This was not to say that he wasn't an utter swine to the indigenous people of the Amazonian forests. His brutality was as legendary as his brilliance as an explorer and his choice was

His brutality was as legendary as his brilliance as an explorer and his choice was simple: 'Work for me under horrible conditions on rubber tapping expeditions that will last for years – or be put to death.' Nice man.

33

simple: 'Work for me under horrible conditions on rubber tapping expeditions that will last for years – or be put to death.' Nice man.

Despite achieving so much in his short lifetime, many today regard Charlie Fitzgerald as just another greedy cog in the wheel of English imperialism and a destroyer of native cultures displacing, as he did, various tribes from their territories. On 9 July 1897 the thirty-five-year-old Fitzcarrald/Fitzcarraldo/Fitzgerald was drowned in the Urubamba river, when the boat carrying him to his isthmus was wrecked.

Perhaps if he had chosen to travel by bathtub . . .

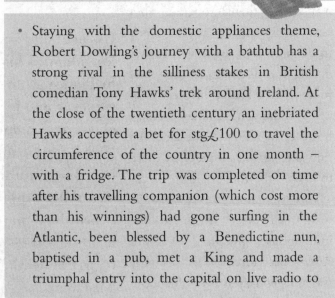

INTERESTING FACTS

- Staying with the domestic appliances theme, Robert Dowling's journey with a bathtub has a strong rival in the silliness stakes in British comedian Tony Hawks' trek around Ireland. At the close of the twentieth century an inebriated Hawks accepted a bet for stg£100 to travel the circumference of the country in one month – with a fridge. The trip was completed on time after his travelling companion (which cost more than his winnings) had gone surfing in the Atlantic, been blessed by a Benedictine nun, baptised in a pub, met a King and made a triumphal entry into the capital on live radio to the strains of a bagpiper. Which is pretty cool. Even for a fridge.

- The Irish are not only fans of bathtubs and celebrity fridges, but are the world's top purchasers of Aga stoves. Thirty percent of all the iconic cookers/heaters sold across the globe in 2006 and 2007 made their way into Irish homes.

- Old rubber lips, Mick Jagger, has acted in two movies about larger-than-life Irishmen. *Fitzcarraldo* – where he had to pull out of filming – and 1970's *Ned Kelly* where he played the part of the rebellious bush ranger. Kelly was famous for wearing a bucket on his head . . . it wouldn't be a bad idea if Mick did the same.

Longest Queue For A Bath

The residents of conspicuously middle-class Dun Laoghaire, like Robert Dowling, love their baths. However, unlike Robert, the denizens of this seaside burgh are not renowned for having an adventurous streak (as they tend to vote for Fine Gael). They are certainly not rebellious. Blue-rinse grannies and spotty accountants (nobody else lives there) taking to the streets, storming the barricades and terrifying the powers-that-be? Ha! Never!!, you cry, snorting and hooting with derision.

Well, you're wrong.

On 18 September 2005, 2,500 locals stamped their feet in anger at a proposed €140million redevelopment of their decaying coastal swimming baths and gave town planners the fright of their political lives. **Dun Laoghaire-Rathdown County Council** had decided that the public didn't need or want the amenity to be restored and planned to give the green light to private developers to build an eight-storey apartment and shopping complex on the site. The venerable baths had served the town and surrounding county well for a century and a half. The first pools on the rocky escarpment opposite the People's Park were the Royal Victorian Baths, constructed in 1843 and rebuilt between 1905 and 1911. Previously, the spot had been occupied by a military battery. The battery had never seen active service, unlike the baths during the summer of 2005.

The proposal would have destroyed sea views, added to traffic congestion and privatised a large portion of a public seafront that is famous throughout Ireland for its promenade. The Save Our Seafront group, with local activist and son of actress Sinéad Cusack, **Richard Boyd Barrett**, at the helm, persuaded the normally reticent residents of the town to find their vocal chords and march along the coast to get the council to do a U-turn. The protestors gathered at the People's Park and tramped through the town and back along the seafront, passing the doors of the baths which were closed in 1997.

At the end of the walk the majority of the crowd joined hands and formed a queue either side of the baths that stretched for 0.8 km.

The council were thwarted and the plan was put on ice. As it was a beautiful sunny day and someone used the phrase 'put on ice' many of the protesters got a subliminal hankering for a 99 cone across the road in Teddy's Ice Cream Shop which can boast having the . . .

Longest Queue For Ice Cream

Teddy's Ice Cream Shop is as well loved a Dublin institution as the sea baths and has been selling its creamy confection, with optional chocolate Flake, since 1950. Despite all the changes to the city and coastal town of Dun Laoghaire, Teddy's refuses to relinquish its place in the hearts of the devotees that queue patiently along Windsor Terrace for their turn at its famous window. It's one of the few shops that still sells boiled sweets, clove rock, acid drops and iced caramels by the quarter pound from jars. The owners refuse to use syrups or flavourings on their ice creams and the emphasis is always on the traditional – down to using the original weighing scales to measure out their sweets.

Teddy's was founded by Edward Jacob of the famous biscuit family who decided that the seafront needed an ice-cream shop, tea rooms and souvenir 'boutique' selling Aran sweaters and all the usual googaws. He sold the business in 1996 along with bequeathing a ghost and his long-term employee Rita Shannon who has worked in the shop for over forty years, which has to be some kind of record.

The ghost is of her fellow ice-cream swirler, Bridie, who was so devoted to the place that she used to sleep there. She went to the Great Parlour in the Sky in 1990 and they do say that on quiet, moonlit nights . . . (etc. and so forth).

The ice cream season runs from April to October – although with global warming this may soon change. With some extremely complicated mathematics involving the science of proxemics (explained later) it's possible to add up the lengths of all Teddy's queues since it first started trading. Ordinarily this would involve counting the number of cone purchasers since 1950 and making various allowances for spatial relationships etc. Unfortunately there is no exact figure for the amount of customers who have lined up outside Teddy's over the years.

Indeed, Ice Cream Queue Measuring itself is not an exact science and is only in its infancy.

There is also the Inter-Ice Cream Sociability problem to deal with. This . . . states that nobody except a very lonely or fat or fat and lonely or lonely because they're fat person ever eats an ice cream cone on his or her own.

There is also the Inter-Ice Cream Sociability problem to deal with. This, in layperson's terms, states that nobody except a very lonely or fat or fat and lonely or lonely because they're fat person ever eats an ice cream cone on his or her own. 99% of 99 purchasers are families, couples and groups of friends. This means that, as a rule, one person is chosen to buy ice cream for two or more people (mums or dads buying for the kids, boyfriend for girlfriend and so on). As such, the amount of cones sold at the window doesn't reflect the number of people in the queue. Any figure arrived at would be wildly inaccurate.

Therefore we will endeavour to calculate a measurement for the Longest Queue For Ice Cream based on the length of the average queue over the past fifty-seven years – a much more modest, yet eminently more provable, figure.

The word 'proxemics' – as mentioned above – was first used by a chap named **E.T. Hall** back in 1963 when he investigated our use of personal space to deal with various individuals and circumstances. This zone, or body bubble, constitutes an area that we protect from the intrusion of outsiders. For example, the body space we use for hugging or whispering is 16–45 cm (6–18 in), for conversations between good friends is 45 cm–1.2 m (1.5–4 ft), for conversations between acquaintances 1.2–3.65 m (4–12 ft) and for public speaking, over 3.65 m (12 ft). For ice cream-queuing our space bubble is 45 cm, front and back, plus the width of the average cone lover's body (also 45 cm) giving a total of 135 cm.

The average line of people at the window, based on a study of busiest and off-peak periods (Teddy's used to regularly stay open until 2 a.m.), is 18 bodies deep. Taking all this information together we get the following equation: 135 cm multiplied by 18 (people) multiplied by 183 (days per season ignoring variations for leap years) multiplied by 57 (seasons by the end of 2007). The equation is worked out as follows:

135 x 18 = 2,430 x 183 = 444,690 x 57 = 25,347,330 cm

Therefore the Longest Queue for Ice Cream is 253.4733 km. Let's round it up to 253.5 km. QED.

Shortest Explanation For How The 99 Got Its Name

Have you ever wondered why an ice cream with half a Flake stuck in it is called a '99' and one without is a plain 'cone'? This troubling question has vexed many great minds on the islands of Ireland and Britain for almost a century. Various theories abound:

1. The Flake bar is 99 mm long.
2. They used to cost 99p.
3. 99 is 66 upside down (don't worry, this will be explained).
4. The Flake is stuck into the cone at a 99 degree angle.
5. It takes 99 seconds to eat.
6. There are 99 layers of chocolate in a Flake.

Let us discuss these one at a time:

1. No, it's not, and even if it was nobody used the metric system on these islands back in the 1920s or 1930s when the 99 first appeared.
2. 99p in the 1920s would have bought you a house and put your children through college.
3. A Cadbury price list from 1935 reads:

    > 99 CDM Flake (For Ice Cream Trade) 1 gro[ss]
    >   singles 6/6. One price only.

    If you subscribe to the notion that 99 is 6 shillings 6 pence upside down then you are, indeed, flaky.

4. Yes of course it is, that's why the vendors use protractors when they're making them. You really should get out more.

5. Possibly if you're a greedy pig with a stopwatch.

6. Even Cadbury's says it doesn't know where the name came from. A calculated guess would suggest they know how many layers go into their own products.

It's possible the name came from the previously mentioned price list, but others believe that the monicker originated from the cones and not the chocolate. Back in the 1930s a company called Askeys made a cone stamped '99' but that may have been in response to the name rather than being the origin of it.

One colourful explanation is the Italian Theory. Some believe the 99 was dreamed up by Italian ice cream sellers in honour of the last wave of conscripts to head off to the First World War in 1917. These eighteen-year-olds were born in 1899 and referred to as the Ragazzi del '99 – the Boys of '99. They were so highly regarded that some streets in Italy are named after them. In the early twentieth century, Italian ice cream vendors were very numerous in Ireland, Britain and especially Scotland, and may have brought the tradition with them.

That country's capital, Edinburgh, has its own claim to the name. In 2006 ice cream maker Rudi Arcari told the BBC that her grandfather Stephen invented the cone in 1922 and since then the family has been selling them from their shop – at 99 Portobello High Street.

Whether this is true or not remains to be seen. Even the *Oxford English Dictionary* has 'origin unknown' in its entry for the tasty treat. *Erindipity Rides Again*, however, is only interested in the Shortest Explanation For How The 99 Got Its Name, and that is – IC.

IC are Ice Cream's initials and also one possible way of spelling 99 . . . in Roman numerals.

INTERESTING FACTS

- Dun Laoghaire was bombed by the Germans during the Second World War. The shell, which damaged buildings but caused no fatalities, landed next to the People's Park at Rosmeen Gardens. The Nazis obviously thought 'People's Park' sounded a bit too Commy.

- The greater Dublin area has over 50 Italian-owned chippers. The first Italian families came to the city mainly from Scotland and the north of England and were originally ice cream sellers. With the Irish weather being as previously mentioned they realised they needed another way to make money through the winter months, so they began selling fried fish and chips. If they couldn't harden our arteries with confectionery, they were going to do it with our beloved spud. Back in Scotland these ice cream sellers/chippers' relatives went one step further and created a hybrid incorporating the best of both worlds – the deep-fried Mars bar. The Scots love eating them after the pub, even though they look like a turd dropped by a dehydrated camel after it's gorged itself on toffee.

Longest Main Street

Dublin's O'Connell Street has been likened to many things, including the Champs-Élysées in Paris, but on a more petite scale. Stroll along it on a warm summer's evening and savour the fragrant, oily, bull farts of the buses as they set down outside the many fine restaurants – Supermac's, MacDonald's, Burger King etc. Observe the urbane boulevardiers as they beat each other up with their crutches over who gets the last swig from the Buckfast bottle. Eschew the gaucheness of a game of chess outside a bijou café in favour of playing the slots in Doctor Quirkey's Good Time Emporium,

. . . and later in the evening run the length of the street trying to avoid getting mugged (skangers generally don't like moving targets). Dublin can, indeed, be heaven.

and later in the evening run the length of the street trying to avoid getting mugged (skangers generally don't like moving targets). Dublin can, indeed, be heaven.

O'Connell Street is not the Champs-Élysées, but it is the **Widest Street** in Ireland, and one of the broadest in

43

Europe. It measures 46.04 m on average, is 44.34 m at its narrowest point and 46.96 m at its widest point. The widest street in Europe is the aforementioned Parisian boulevard, at 71 m wide and 1.9 km long.

The area around O'Connell Street is relatively young in comparison with the rest of the city and was only reclaimed from tidal flats from the seventeenth century onwards. The upper end of the street was first laid out around the end of that century and was named Drogheda Street. In the late 1740s, banker **Luke Gardiner** (of Gardiner Street fame) tore it down and rebuilt the modern Upper O'Connell Street, which was extended to the Liffey in 1784 and renamed Sackville Street. As the political and financial life of the city was centred on the southside of the river (Dublin Castle, the Bank of Ireland etc.) the northsiders began looking for a couple of landmarks of their own and so were given Nelson Pillar (1808), the General Post Office (1818) and Abdul's Kebab House (1820).

Northsiders seldom like to be reminded that southsiders live in the real, old, original Dublin. After more non-stop whinging a few statues were shipped across the Liffey to keep them quiet. They are:

- **The O'Connell Monument**, designed by John Henry Foley, completed by his assistant Thomas Brock and unveiled in 1882. Daniel O'Connell (1775–1847) was the great Liberator and is credited with winning Catholic emancipation for Ireland. He was a great man for the ladies as well and it used to be said that 'you couldn't throw a stone over the poorhouse wall without hitting one of O'Connell's bastards'. The practice of throwing stones at unfortunate children born out of wedlock was quite common back then.

- **The William Smith O'Brien statue** by Thomas Farrell. This was originally placed on a traffic island at the O'Connell Bridge entrance to D'Olier Street in 1870 and was shifted to O'Connell Street in 1929. O'Brien (1803–1864) was a politician and revolutionary and was transported after his part in the 1848 rebellion.

- **Sir John Grey's statue**, again by Thomas Farrell, unveiled in 1879. John Grey (1816–1875) brought a water supply to the city in 1868. Not personally, of course – he got someone to lay the pipes etc.

- **Jim Larkin's statue** by Oisín Kelly, unveiled in 1980. Big Jim (1876–1947) was a giant of the trade union movement and at the centre of the action during the 1913 Lock Out.

- **Father Theobald Mathew's statue** by Mary Redmond, unveiled in 1893. Fr Mathew (1790–1856) was a towering figure in the teetotal movement. He was the man who invented the Pledge, which Catholics take to foreswear alcohol.

- **The Parnell Monument** by Augustus Saint-Gaudens, unveiled in 1911. Charles Stuart Parnell (1846–1891), also known as The Chief and the Uncrowned King of Ireland, was the driving force behind the Home Rule movement of the nineteenth century. He looked nothing like Clark Gable (see Interesting Fact on page 49).

Nearly all of the buildings on O'Connell Street date from post-1916 as the street was devastated during the Easter Rising and damaged again in July 1922 at the start of the Civil War, when 'irregulars' under Oscar Traynor occupied it after the bombing of the Four Courts. The battle lasted from 28 June until 5 July, when Free State troops brought their artillery up to point blank range to blast the IRA-held buildings. The entire terrace north of Cathedral Street to Parnell Square was destroyed and a number of buildings on the northwest side of the street were reduced to rubble.

O'Connell Street is approximately 600 m (1,968 ft) in length and as has been pointed out is the widest street in the country, but it is not the longest. To find that street you have to go a bit further up the northside and veer westwards. Stop when you hit County Donegal and head for Letterkenny, for it is here that you will find the **Longest Main Street**, which runs for an impressive 1.2 km (3,960 ft).

Letterkenny may be the biggest town in Donegal, it may be surrounded by some of the most beautiful countryside in Ireland and may even boast the most hospitable people in the country, but it doesn't have the one thing the northside of Dublin can lay claim to: the Shortest Street Name.

Shortest Street Name

As mentioned in the previous passage, O'Connell Street was originally called Drogheda Street before businessman Luke Gardiner started pulling it down and rebuilding it in the eighteenth century. It was so called because it was originally owned by the Moore family, who were the Earls of Drogheda. One illustrious member of this family was a bit of a wag and decided that the streets off O'Connell Street should bear his name and so Dublin was given Henry (Street), Moore (Street), Earl (Street), Of (Lane) and Drogheda (Street). If it is not enough for you that 'Of' is the shortest street name in Ireland, then how about heading back to Ulster to find the . . .

Shortest Street

On the evidence of Michael Street in Omagh, the builders of County Tyrone must be the laziest or most forgetful on the island of Ireland. The street contains just one house, mysteriously called 'Number 10'. Were the other houses demolished? Washed away in a storm? Swallowed up during an earthquake? No. The fact is that there were never any other houses on the street. Laurence Rush, long-time occupier of Number 10, is on record as saying he thinks his house was the first to be built, and although the contractor intended building one to nine later, it never happened. Still, the street parties must be pretty cheap to organise.

Longest Time Trading
As A Department Store

Here we are again on O'Connell Street. Try as we might we can't avoid returning to it in this section. So let's try to leap back out of it as quickly as we can, shall we?

One of the world's first purpose-built department stores opened its doors on the city's main thoroughfare just in time for the Dublin Exhibition of 1853 – Delany's New Mart 'Monster Store'. This shop was pre-dated by about a year by Aristide Boucicaut's Parisian *Le Bon Marché* shop which actually started trading in 1838 but didn't grow into a full department store until 1852. What made Delany's different, however, from *Le Bon Marché* and other shops of its day is that it started life as a department store – it had not evolved gradually from a smaller retail outlet. It was built on a grand scale, as was befitting Dublin's position as second city of the Empire, and was the envy of many other major European capitals. It also housed the Imperial Hotel in its upper floors and was bought by the **Clery family** in the 1880s. The building was destroyed in 1916 and reopened in 1922, modelled on Selfridges of London. With all this chopping and changing and shelling and rebuilding, Clery's does not hold the record for Longest Time Trading as a Department Store. (Here's where we fly back up north.)

The Oldest, Longest-trading Department Store in Ireland is **Austin's in Derry**, which has stood on its original position in that city's centre since 1830. Austin's pre-dates Harrod's of London by fifteen years, Macy's of New York by twenty-five and the venerable Jenners of Edinburgh by five years. The business began nearly two centuries ago when Thomas Austin from Limavady opened a humble shop on the corner of the Diamond. The store is now a 2,322.5 sq m (25,000 sq ft), five-storey shrine to consumerism. It has a commanding view of the city and countryside of County Derry, the neighbouring county of Donegal and, possibly on a clear day, the Longest Main Street in Ireland in Letterkenny.

INTERESTING FACTS

- Despite being the biggest town in Donegal, Letterkenny is not the administrative centre. That honour goes to Lifford.

- Sackville Street's name was only changed to O'Connell Street in 1924, two years after the Treaty was signed. There are also O'Connell Streets in Limerick, Ennis, Clonmel, Sligo, North Adelaide and Melbourne. O'Connell, by the by, was a big fan of South American freedom fighter Simón El Libertador Bolívar, and his son, Morgan O'Connell, volunteered as an officer in his army in 1820.

- CS Parnell, one of the greatest politicians of the nineteenth century, almost won Home Rule with his Irish Parliamentary Party by deftly handling the balance of power between the Conservatives and Liberals in 1880s Westminster. He was a government-breaker and an electrifying orator. He also had a big, black, bushy beard. Clark Gable, on the other hand, did not. The Hollywood heart-throb was incredibly miscast as the patriot in the 1937 biopic, *Parnell*. The flick, which was loosely based around The Chief's life story, was a total stink bomb and the biggest flop of Gable's career. With screen goddess Myrna Loy playing his *femme fatale*, Kitty O'Shea (with whom Parnell had a notorious love affair), it was as if the entire studio had taken the day off and left the film's casting to a chimp with learning disabilities. Being from the ascendancy, Parnell probably didn't have a strong Irish accent. Neither did beardless Gable – he just didn't attempt one and instead used his Rhett Butler drawl to mercilessly horsewhip some of the most mangled dialogue ever written. Thus, when he tries to persuade Kitty of his love, he says: 'Have you never felt there might be someone, somewhere who, if you could meet them, was the person that you'd been always meant to meet? Have you never felt that?' Cue: sunset. Cue: silhouettes against the sky. Cue: pass the sick bag.

Longest Time Waiting To Fly At An Airport

There are two types of strikers that management at Dublin Airport really dread: baggage handlers, and birds. In the case of the former, disputes can mean long delays and general misery. Where the latter are concerned, strikes can sometimes mean permanent disruption.

The last thing a pilot wants to see heading for his windshield, propellers or jet engine as he is cruising across the sky is a flock of gormless birdies. Incredible as it may seem, 75% of all recorded bird strikes occur at airports and not in mid-air. The reason for this is because our feathered friends are attracted to the open, flat terrain at aerodromes where it is easy to spot predators, such as feral pussycats and the like. They particularly like runways and taxiways for this reason. The first fatal bird strike, for the record, happened in April of 1912, killing celebrated flier **Calbraith Rodgers** at an air show in the US (Calbraith was the first man to fly across America.).

Bearing in mind that birds have been flying considerably longer than man and it wouldn't be fair or feasible to shoot them all, a number of ways have been devised to deal with them. These include the use of human 'scarecrows' to monitor their presence and frighten them away, such as those employed at Dublin Airport. These highly-trained bird-spotters use recordings of the various species' distress calls to arouse the birds' curiosity (they wander over to investigate) and then let off a 'flash-bang' device that scares the crap (literally) out of the feather-brains who then bugger off at speed[5].

The **Dublin Airport Authority** (DAA) also operates a Long Grass Policy to deter birds. The airfield is surrounded by 303 hectares of meadow where the grass (a mixture of the Tall Fescue and Italian Rye varieties) is kept at a height of approximately 22.5 cm. Big birds such as gulls don't trust long grass, as any hungry pussycat will tell you.

Every bird strike at the airport is recorded and – we're absolutely not making this up – all birds involved in a collision are scooped up and kept in a freezer until they can be given an autopsy by a bird pathologist. After a

[5] The publisher would like to point out that no birds were harmed in the writing of this paragraph.

forensic examination to determine the species – sometimes DNA is used from the smallest scrap of remains – an ornithologist then advises the airport on what needs to be done to deter that type of bird in the future[6].

In one case, after a plane was struck crossing the Irish Sea, the ornithological team managed to identify the culprit as a migrating duck. They now know all about that species' holiday habits and how best to avoid it in the air.

The DAA also keeps an eye on building sites and hedgerows in the area as they can attract potentially hazardous animals and birds. It even micro-manages the ecosystems of the six streams that gurgle through the airport grounds. These people are about as obsessive as it gets when it comes to passenger safety and are definitely not 'for the birds' in any sense of the phrase. However, as with everything in life, there is always an exception to the rule. And, in Dublin Airport's case, his name is **Willie**.

By the end of 2007 Willie had set the record for Longest Time Waiting To Fly – ten years. He arrived at the north Dublin airfield in 1997 and, unable to get airborne, decided to take up residency. At time of writing, Willie can be seen strutting around the cargo area every day. By night he sleeps in a tree and every morning he rises at dawn to welcome the airport staff into work. Willie, you will have guessed by now, is a rooster. A big cock. Which is probably why he was called Willie and has nothing whatsoever to do with former Aer Lingus

---

[6] Think of the American TV show *CSI (Crime Scene Investigation)* with 'The Birdy Song' as its theme tune.

supremo, Willie Walsh. This strutting, puffed-up pecker (we're talking about the rooster here) is so beloved of the airport's workers that he has become their mascot and is considered a member of the team. He's also self-sufficient and manages to find his own food although his colleagues keep him well supplied with scraps.

Although nobody knows where he came from, flightless Willie probably wandered off from a local farm in search of some adventure. One theory suggests that he might be gay and ran away from his duties as barnyard stud. Then again, maybe he was hen-pecked. Perhaps he wanted to grow up to be a plane (roosters are not noted for their intelligence).

Whatever his provenance, Willie has led a charmed life and, miraculously, has managed to stay safe despite all the machinery and wheels and things one finds at airports. Even the bird flu scare of 2006 didn't ruffle his feathers as the staff – who were willing to cover any costs to ensure his welfare – made arrangements with a local vet to place him in isolation if anything happened.

Pet roosters have a lifespan of about fifteen years, so depending on when you are reading this Willie may have finally got his wings and gone to the Great Roost in the sky. If so, he'll always be remembered in Dublin Airport as the most grounded, down-to-earth member of staff ever.

He won't be replaced for, as they say in the cargo department, 'Cock-a-doodle-do, but not any cock will doodle-do, but our Willie'.

Longest Way To Go
For A Hamburger

'It's a long, long way from Clare to here.' So goes the classic Ralph McTell song. Well, it certainly is a long way, if the 'here' you're singing about is Iraq or Afghanistan and you're looking to order a burger and chips.

In April 2007, the *Limerick Leader* newspaper reported that 160 portions of fish and chips and hamburgers were transported, under Garda escort, from a County Clare takeaway to Shannon Airport to satisfy the hunger pangs of a plane full of US troops.

The American Trans Air flight had stopped in **Shannon** for technical reasons on its way back from the Middle East to discover that, apart from the in-flight meals which were delivered to the plane, no other hot food was available to feed the soldiers as they waited to take off. Due to cost-cutting measures, the Estuary restaurant had stopped serving grub at 3 p.m. and the twenty-four-hour bar in the departures area didn't do 'chow' (that's American for food). An army marches on its stomach, if the cliché is to be believed, so rather than have the Yanks invade County Clare in search of eats, an arrangement was made with the Gardaí to have the huge food order delivered from a takeaway in Shannon town.

It later emerged that this wasn't the first time that the Americans had organised a food drop from the same chipper and that on another occasion the Munster rugby team had sent out for pizza as they waited to depart for an away game.

While Munster may not be too long a distance to travel for fast food, Afghanistan certainly is. It is also the only recorded case of extraordinary rendition where the detainee was proved to have been battered in advance.

INTERESTING FACT

- If you're prepared to travel from Afghanistan to Clare for a Shannonside burger, then you probably won't consider it much of an effort to trot over to India for Mass. A newsagent in the Dublin town of Dalkey stocks funeral Mass cards signed by a Father Thomas – in the State of Kerala, India. Now *there's* outsourcing.

Shortest Fashion Week

The very first **Dublin Fashion Week** took place in October 2005 and was judged to be such a great success that it is now part of the, ahem, fabric of the capital's sartorial life.

The organisers describe it as an opportunity for buyers and the press to view the following season's collections. Unlike other weeks in the year, Dublin Fashion Week is unique in that it lasts for only three days. To add to this magnificent manipulation of the space/time continuum, it also takes place twice a year: once for Spring/Summer, once for Autumn/Winter.

With this Stephen Hawking-like ability to master the concepts of physics, surely delivering World Peace should be a piece of cake, girls.

Two weeks of three days duration each, adding up to six days, equals Dublin Fashion Week. With this Stephen Hawking-like ability to master the concepts of physics, surely delivering World Peace should be a piece of cake, girls.

Longest Occupied Castle

Killyleagh Castle in County Down has the distinction of being the oldest inhabited pile in the country and is a living link to the seventeenth century plantation of Ulster.

Originally founded in 1180 by the Norman Knight, John de Courcy, it was rebuilt in 1666 by the Earl of Clanbrassil and has been occupied by the Hamilton family since this period. Today, Gawn Rowan Hamilton is the king of this Disneyesque castle which was redesigned with turrets and all the bells and whistles associated with a Loire valley-style chateau.

During the War of Independence, the IRA attempted a little renovation of its own and Gawn Hamilton's great-great-uncle fought a 2 a.m. gun battle with the Volunteers from the battlements. Killyleagh was built to last, however, unlike the. . .

Shortest-Lived Castle

Question: what do Castlederg, County Tyrone and the Alamo have in common?

Answer 1: Davy Crockett and

Answer 2: They both fell during sieges.

Let's get **Colonel Davy Crockett** out of the way first. The King of The Wild Frontier (1786–1836) was an all-American hero. By turns soldier, politician and frontiersman, Crockett served in the House of Representatives representing Tennessee, fought in the Texas Revolution, and got his heavenly spurs at the battle of the Alamo. He was descended from a French Huguenot family, originally called De Crocketagne, who settled in Cork and eventually **Castlederg**. The raccoon cap-wearing hero's grandparents emigrated to the States in the eighteenth century and put their roots down in Tennessee where Davy was born.

The **Battle of the Alamo** was one of those disasters that reverberates through history. Crockett and his comrades at the fort were besieged by the Mexican forces of President Antonio Lopez de Santa Anna and were slaughtered after refusing to surrender. Only three people survived: an old woman, a slave and a young child. By anyone's standards this would be deemed to have been a bit of a cock-up by Crockett and the boys. However, they fought with such bravery that 'Remember the Alamo!' became one of the great American war cries. In fact, if you type the word 'alamo' into a Microsoft Word document, as the author did, it will autocorrect to Alamo with a capital A. That's how much the Yankees love their Davy Crockett.

Castlederg's Visitor Centre has a section devoted to Crockett and the exhibit includes a model of the Alamo where Davy and up to 250 Texans were killed by 1,600 Mexican soldiers.

Castlederg's own Alamo took place during the seventeenth century. Prior to this, the site of the present ruined castle was occupied by a round tower house which had been in the possession of both the O'Neill and O'Donnell clans (in 1479 Henry Óg O'Neill took Castlederg from the latter who regained it in 1505). The building was strategically important to both dynasties as it was located on a ford on the river Derg which flowed between their lands. It was also associated with St Patrick and the pilgrimage to his 'purgatory' on Station Island in Lough Derg. This is where the Saint is reputed to have seen visions of hell and has been a popular religious pilgrimage destination since the Middle Ages.

Ye Olde Hairdresser: Going anywhere nice on your holidays, love? *Snip, snip.*

Medieval client: Oh, nothing special, just taking the missus to hell for a fortnight.

After the Battle of Kinsale in 1601, Castlederg was acquired by a British lawyer, Sir John Davies (1569–1626), who brought sixteen Presbyterian families over from Scotland to colonise it. 'Planting', in case you didn't know, was a pretty way of saying 'ethnic cleansing'. It was the English Crown's policy to plant loyal,

Protestant subjects in Ulster after the Battle of Kinsale where the combined Irish and Spanish forces were beaten, marking the end of Gaelic Ireland.

The castle was built between 1609 and 1622, but didn't have the necessary planning permission from the local authorities (the O'Neills) and was subject to penalties and a demolition order. In 1641 Sir Phelim O'Neill of Caledon led a rebellion to drive out the newcomers (who all spoke with a whistle and wore bowler hats) and laid siege to Castlederg. He was driven off but had inflicted mortal wounds on the castle which was finished off by the locals who carried away the remains as building materials.

As Castlederg was only a castle for fifteen years it can proudly claim to be the Shortest-Lived Castle in Irish history, excluding the bouncy castle at Mary Harney's fortieth birthday party.

Longest Time Spent Trying To Get The Queen Out Of The Bog

On 24 April 1916 Pádraig Pearse and his boys and girls struck the first blow for Irish freedom when they declared our independence at the GPO. In December 1918 the people of our lovely little island gave this notion the thumbs up in the Westminster elections, electing a Sinn Féin majority (73 out of 106 candidates) who refused to enter the House of Commons. On 6 December 1922 Britain finally recognised that at least part of the island of Ireland should be ruled by the Irish alone and **Michael Collins, Arthur Griffith et al** signed the treaty that would eventually lead to the Irish Constitution (*Bunreacht na hÉireann*) of 29 December 1937. This in turn led to the Republic of Ireland Act of 1949 which finally, once and for all, absolutely declared that the Kings and Queens of England have no claim to the twenty-six counties of the Republic. Actually, make that twenty-four counties – we're forgetting Laois and Offaly.

Incredible as it may seem, these two diminutive midland counties were, up until April of 2007, still officially held in the name of the British Royal Family. Researchers working on the pre-1922 Statute Law Revision Bill were astounded to find that despite being part of a Republic, Laois and Offaly bore the titles Queen's County and King's County respectively and could, theoretically, be annexed by **Liz Windsor** and her Royal Court at the drop of a crown.

Ever since her namesake took the land from the native Irish chieftains during the 1500s, the monarchy had the right to seize any part of those counties it desired. Even Portarlington or Geeshill, God help us. This became enshrined in the statute books back in 1556 (Reference 3 and 4 Philip & Mary, Chapter 1 'An Act for the disposition of Leix and Offalie'). Prior to the bill being passed in 2007 land registry rules dictated that householders must register their homes as being in 'Queen's County, Laois'. The Queen must have been fairly fond of her little piece of Ireland to have held on to it for 450 years. It's all the more surprising then that she didn't kick up a fuss when she was finally banished from her own realm within a republic. No Britannic forces swept into Portlaoise and Birr to set up her new bogland kingdom, or Bogdom to give it its official title, in a sequel to the original conquest. (If someone had made a film about it the movie poster could have read 'Elizabeth II – and this time it's personal').

Liz II is a benign old queen and would have been far more preferable to another monarch found lurking in the law books when the Attorney General's office trawled through 25,000 old statutes in 2007 – **Henry VIII**.

In 1542, that model husband attempted to put the 'Irish question' beyond doubt by having the parliament on this island pass a law declaring him to be the King of Ireland and his descendants to be his successors to the throne. This law was not repealed until 1962. However, researchers working on the 2007 revisions discovered that a second law of 1542, which restated and expanded on the first had never been repealed, rendering Bertie Ahern, in legal terms, Queen Elizabeth II's Prime Minister in Ireland.

'We dub thee, Sir Bartholomew Ahern,' says Queenie.

'I know ma'am, de BBC dubs me because of me accent – easier dan sub-titlin' inannyway,' replies Bertie.

INTERESTING FACT

- Despite the 2007 abolition of 3,188 Acts which were passed by the English Crown from 1171 right up until the beginning of the 1920s, there are still 1,348 old laws that have not yet been repealed and may have some degree of modern relevance.

Shortest Route From Cork City To The End Of The World

This entry probably should have been 'Shortest Route From Dublin to the End of The World', but the whinging from certain quarters in Ireland's second city would have been almost too much to bear, even in anticipation. 'Arrooo, why is it always Dublin this and Dublin that, boy?' So, The Shortest Route from Cork City to the End of the World is 27 km or 17 miles.

Before we get around to explaining the above, let's take a trip to pretty **Kinsale**, the jewel of the south coast and the County of Cork. Apart from being regarded as Ireland's gourmet capital (an accolade it sometimes struggles to retain), it is one of the most history-rich places on the island. It was here that Hugh O'Neill's Ulster army was crushed by the English in 1601 and from here that the Wild Geese, the native aristocracy, set sail for

France in 1691. It was also here that the Norman inhabitants of Ye Olde Munster went to stock up on their Bordeaux.

Kinsale was one of sixteen wine ports licensed by the British in Ireland, and supplied ships for the Vintage Fleet – the forerunner of the Royal Navy – as long ago as 1412. Records show that in that year the fleet, which had approximately 160 ships journeying to and from Bordeaux, included five Irish boats, two from Dublin and three from Kinsale (go on Cork, give yourself a pat on the back). The town's connection with wine doesn't end there. The

> Here are a few names . . . Hennessy, MacCarthy, Lynch, O'Byrne, Dillon, Walsh, Barton, Spud Murphy and Wino MacMuckface. Okay, the last two are made up, but you've probably got rat-arsed on the fruit of at least one of these great men's vines. The author certainly has.

flight of the Wild Geese led to the emergence of the Wine Geese. Aside from distinguishing themselves in the various international brigades, many of the Irish emigrants became master winemakers. Here are a few names to wet your whistle: Hennessy, MacCarthy, Lynch, O'Byrne, Dillon, Walsh, Barton, Spud Murphy and Wino MacMuckface. Okay, the last two are made up, but you've probably got rat-arsed on the fruit of at least one of these great men's vines. The author certainly has.

These Wine Geese were mainly involved in French vineyards, but they also made their homes in Italy, Spain and Germany. Being pious tipplers they also brought with them the names of their favourite saints – St Patrick, St Fiacre, St Gall, St Fridolin (no, we never heard of him either), St Killian (who may have been named after a type of cheese), St Nessan and St Columbanus to roll-call a few. Their names can be found in various parts of France, Lombardy, Switzerland, Spain (particularly Jerez) and Germany.

Today the Wine Geese have their own International Museum of Wine in Desmond Castle which is also home to the Order of the Winegeese. This has members as far away as Australia and California.

Back in the twelfth century when the Normans were building the town and Kinsale sailors (or Kinsailors, if you prefer) were travelling to and from Bordeaux, nobody knew that the US of A existed as it hadn't been discovered. As a result, Kinsale in medieval eyes was the last 'civilised' port before you fell off the edge of the planet. This is why there is an area on Kinsale's waterfront called World's End, which is 27 km from Cork City . . .

INTERESTING FACT

- During America's War of Independence, dozens of Yankee ships and their sailors were imprisoned in Kinsale in rotten conditions. A Presbyterian Minister from Bandon, Reverend William Hazlett, and a Cork Quaker merchant named Reuben Harvey came to their rescue and saw to it that their conditions were improved. In 1783 the first President of the United States, George Washington, thanked Reuben Harvey for 'his exertions in relieving the distresses of such of our fellow citizens as were prisoners in Ireland'. Curiously, Hazlett (haslet) is a type of luncheon meat while a Reuben is a pastrami sandwich popular in New York. Both can be bought in delicatessens. Is this merely a coincidence?[5]

[5] Yes.

Highest and Lowest

Highest Mountain That's Really A Hill

Before we get stuck into this thorny issue, let's have a little geography lesson. Pay attention at the back and – you – stop dozing off. A mountain is defined as a natural elevation which rises to a summit at an altitude of greater than 610 m (2,000 ft). Anything smaller than this is a hill. Lesson over.

Although Ireland, by the by, is the third largest island in Europe and the twentieth largest in the world (sorry, slipping back into geography teacher mode), it is not particularly blessed with huge peaks. Kerry's Carrauntoohil is the **Highest Mountain** in the land at 1,041 m (3,414 ft) but compare this to Mount Everest at 8,848 m (29,029 ft) and you'll get an idea of how relatively flat the island is. As a result of this lack of truly towering mountains and our native aptitude for invention and pretension, a number of imposters have cropped up across the country in the 9,000 years that we have populated this island: hills that call themselves mountains. Here, for the first time, *Erindipity Rides Again* exposes the worst offenders.

As you probably know, *sliabh/slieve* is the Irish for mountain and *cnoc* is the Irish for hill. So, armed with this information, let's do a little rambling.

First we head to the black north of this island and take a trip to the Warrenpoint area of County Down where we can marvel at the imposing majesty of the loftily-named Black Mountain. But what's this? It's not actually black – and it's DEFINITELY not a mountain, rising as it does to a titchy 508 m (1,667 ft). Shame on you.

Heading west we come to a hill in Mayo that has all the grandeur of a **Padraig Flynn**, but none of the height (or neck for that matter). Slieve Fyagh, you are not what you claim to be at 335 m (1099 ft). You are, like the aforementioned politico, a 'slieveen' which can also be said of Killelan Mountain in Kerry (278 m or 912 ft).

We now get off the western seaboard and travel eastwards to County Cavan and Slieve na Calliagh which is not a slieve either at a miniscule 276 m (906 ft). But wait, there's another one over there – Slieve Glah is trying it on as well at 251 m (1047 ft). Legend has it that God offered the people of Cavan a real mountain but they

> Legend has it that God offered the people of Cavan a real mountain but they were too mean to buy it.

were too mean to buy it. Which reminds one of a seriously bad joke about Monaghan which doesn't deserve to appear in print. So here it is anyway: what do Monaghan and a pregnant heifer have in common? They're both near Cavan. Calving, get it?

Moving swiftly along and haughtily dispensing with Down, Mayo, Kerry and Cavan, we come to a truly spectacular non-mountain in County Louth. Miniscule is the only way to describe the gloriously pretentious Mount Oriel between Drogheda and Ardee, which measures only 251 m (823 ft) in height. They don't call it the Wee County for nothing.

Now, if you think the hills of Ireland are rising above their station, then spare a thought for our impossibly modest and self-effacing mountains.

Highest Mountain That Thinks Its A Hill

According to the guidebooks the Wicklow Mountains and the Dublin Mountains run in a north-south direction (how do they work these things out?) from south Dublin across Wicklow and on into Wexford. None of them are huge: Lugnaquilla is the highest at 926 m (3,039 ft), Mullaghcleevaun is second at 847 m (2,780 ft) and Kippure is the highest part of County Dublin at 757 m (2,484 ft). Croghan Mountain is the highest point on Wicklow's border with Wexford but, sadly, like those 'mountains' of the previous section it too is only a hill at 606 m (1,988 ft). Happily, there is another hill to take its place and stand head and shoulders with its mountainy siblings – the scarily named War Hill, which is not a hill at all rising as it does to 686 m (2,251 ft) east of Blessington. Neither is the even bigger Duff Hill to the south of it at 720 m (2,362 ft).

However, when it comes to getting geography spectacularly wrong, Kerry takes the top honours.

The county's Cnoc na gCapall is a horse of a hill at 639 m (2,096 ft) while Knocknadobar is cowering when it should be towering at 690 m (2,246 ft). These pale in comparison to Kerry's very own Highest Mountain That Thinks it's a Hill – **Cnoc na Péiste** which is a staggering 988 m (3,241 ft) tall – only 53 m shorter than Carrauntoohil mountain, which now that we look at it, appears to be harbouring part of a hill in its name.

INTERESTING FACT

- Nestling in the Wicklow Mountains (and hills) is Ireland's only pumped-storage hydroelectricity plant, Turlough Hill. Water is sucked up from a nearby corrie and kept in this enormous open-air tank to power turbines and do the kind of things hydroelectricity plants do. It was completed after six years' labour in 1974 for the ESB at a cost of IR£20million – which was a lot of spondooligs back then. Like the Shannon's hydroelectricity plant it was built by the Germans as they know loads about building big tanks and electrifying countries.

It's definitely a hill.

Highest Price Paid For Thin Air

If ever proof were needed (and it isn't) that Ireland is the world's largest open-air lunatic asylum then look no further than the property market. In July of 2007 it emerged that Dun Laoghaire-Rathdown County Council issued a warning over some home improvements taking place in affluent **Sandycove.** It appeared that a businessman had purchased a beautiful €5.3million Victorian dream home overlooking the sea – to demolish it. By the time the county inspector had checked in on work at the house, which was shrouded in plastic sheeting, most of it had been knocked down, contravening the planning permission which had allowed for only part of it to be demolished. This is not an isolated case. The purchasing of high-end homes to demolish them is not new on our fair isle. In 2006 there was a high profile case where a property developer agreed to rebuild a house he bought and almost demolished in upmarket Mount Merrion, County Dublin. In the same year a developer was halted as he prepared to raze a house in Palmerston Park, Dublin 6 he had bought for €7million. SEVEN MILLION! ARE YOU MAD????!!!!!

These gentlemen are in the ha'penny place, however, compared to the unnamed developer who made one of the most startling property purchases ever in the summer of 2007. As one house owner was happily chipping away at his new Sandycove home, a few yards away another was trousering €350,000 after selling a plot of . . . thin air.

This much sought-after, desirable, probably south-facing, tract of air runs between two houses on Summerhill Road, and came on the market courtesy of the owner of the access road underneath it. The owner made the perfectly reasonable decision to retain the road but sell the space above it – and someone bought it. The airspace could be successfully developed if planning permission was granted to build a 1,500 sq ft structure between the houses and above the road. The 'site's' owner had snapped up the access road for a mere €20,000 in 2005 and so made a nice profit.

Making money from thin air is something at which New Ireland excels. Take, as another example, the firm which claims to have designed a machine that creates energy out of air. No, it's not wind power we're talking about here, but real thin air. The **Steorn** company told the world's media in 2007 that its Orbo device uses the interaction of magnetic fields to generate a constant source of free and clean energy. If it's proved to be true, the technology would defy the laws of physics ('See, Scotty, you CAN change the laws of physics.'). At time of writing the miracle machine is being tested by twenty-two of the world's top eggheads, who are expected to report back in late 2008 on whether it's the real deal or just a load of hot[7] . . .

---

[7] Even by this book's standards that pun is too unbearable to finish.

Highest Amount Of Brass Made From Selling Muck

Some denizens of the great city of **Cork** have been known to grumble about Dublin's prominence in matters of national importance. Unfortunately for them, there is little that can be done about this as Dublin *is* the capital after all, and does have an awful lot of people living in it (40% of the Irish population live within 100 km of it and its citizens will top the 2.1 million mark by 2021, according to the Central Statistics Office). It's not that Cork's being overlooked, it's just overshadowed by big, bad, ould Dublin.

> Bit by bit Munster is being shipped off to the USA and soon (possibly sooner) there may be nothing left but a big hole where it once stood.

One clever company may now have inadvertently stumbled across a novel solution to the Leeside paradise's woes – by exporting their province. Bit by bit Munster is being shipped off to the USA and soon (possibly sooner) there may be nothing left but a big hole where it once stood. And away over the briney, a new Munster will rise up, bigger and better than anything those jackeens up in Dublin could ever build. New Cork, New Cork, so good they named it twice. Or something like that.

The Crookstown firm, **The Auld Sod Export Company**, is doing a roaring trade in shipping Irish muck to the US, where dreamy-eyed Irish-Americans are lining up to hold a little piece of the Emerald Isle in the palm of their hand. This is a touch ironic as their forebears probably headed to the States in the first place to get away from scrabbling in the mud. The company has patented a new process that makes it possible for them to comply with strict import laws and ship their 'Official Irish Dirt' stateside free, presumably, of any contaminants (insects, worms, leprechauns etc.). The soil comes in $15.00 340 gm ($^3/_4$ lb) polythene bags sealed for freshness. Well, you wouldn't want your muck to be 'off' when it plops through your letter box, would you?

According to the firm's website Hiberno-Yanks can now:
– Scatter muck all over the grave of a loved one.
– Admire overflowing bowls of shamrock on the dining room table.
– Plant a sapling in it to celebrate a birth in the family.
– Have oodles and oodles of lovely green shamrock to drown on Paddy's Day.

The website doesn't say it, but the Yanks can also:
– Scatter muck all over a living loved one.
– Collect as much muck as is needed to make a one-acre field and then start a feud with their neighbour over it.
– Grow opium plants in it.
– Make a muck igloo out of it.

Incredible as it may seem, the idea of buying Irish soil caught on rapidly in the Land of the Free. Within months of starting up business, one ex-pat from Galway – an eighty-seven-year-old Manhattan lawyer – snapped up

$100,000 worth of the dirt to fill in his future American grave. Another Corkonian spent $148,000 on nearly six and a half tonnes to spread under the house he was building in Massachusetts. And, according to *The New York Times*, a New York doctor with the very Irish name of Biegeleisen bought a bag the previous December after his (presumably Irish) mum-in-law died. He put it next to her ashes on a shelf in a touching display of affection. Hopefully, he'll never get the jars confused and walk in some evening to find the old lady sprouting shamrocks.

As of November 2007, the company was advertising what *Erindipity Rides Again* considers to be an excellent special offer: four bags of Official Irish Dirt, four bags of Shamrock Seeds and free shipping – FOR ONLY $20.

And to prove the old adage is correct about the co-location of soil and significant amounts of a copper/zinc alloy, the firm posted a bumper turnover from November 2006 to March 2007. The Highest Amount of Brass Made From Selling Muck is . . . €2million in five months.

INTERESTING FACT

- At www.BuyIreland.com, the discerning Hibernophile can purchase a square foot of a field in 'rural Ireland' for $49.99, which is ideal for those dreaming of owning a small farm. An ant farm, for example.

Lowest Morals Of Any Irish County

The Province of Munster may be home to some of the most innovative business people on this island, but it also harbours one dirty, shameful, seedy little secret – it is the County with the Lowest Morals in Ireland.

In 1937, as the new constitution was being unveiled, one judge was displaying a weak constitution of his own, declaring his difficulty in stomaching the antics of the go-boys and girls of a certain place in west Munster. **Judge McElligott** regretted that his court would go down in history as the filthiest ever due to the alarming number of cases (seven out of eleven) before him of sexual assault on girls under the age of seventeen. One other case was against a woman for concealing the birth of her 'illegitimate' baby.

Displaying a curious brand of moral loftiness combined with an offhand racism, the judge told the court that the Irish missions were sending people to China and the 'nigger countries' but the youth of Ireland needed to 'take stock of themselves' and their own 'moral relations'. He didn't say 'take themselves in hand' as this was still a sin back then. After one man was found guilty of a serious offence against a girl under seventeen, the jury recommended that he be shown mercy 'owing to the immoral state of the country'.

After commenting that he was shocked to be asked to go leniently with the guilty party just because everybody else in that part of the country was at it, the judge sentenced him to five months, minus hard labour.

Interestingly, the county in question witnessed a fictional (and doomed) moral crusade in 1995's third episode of *Father Ted*. 'The Passion of St Tibulus' sees the clerics attempt to disrupt the showing of the eponymous blasphemous, sexually explicit movie at Craggy Island's cinema.

Craggy Island doesn't exist, of course, but Father Ted's parochial home, as seen in the opening credits, does. However, it is not on any island, fictional or factual, but can be found outside of . . . Lisdoonvarna.

Down with that sort of thing, County Clare, as Ted might say.

Highest Cliffs

County Clare may have the Lowest Morals in Ireland, but it also has the **Highest Cliffs in Munster**. They are not the Highest Cliffs in Ireland, however. That honour goes to **The Back of Beyond**.

The highest cliffs in Munster are the Cliffs of Moher at 214 m. They may not be the highest in the land but they are the most popular tourist spot, with one million people visiting them in 2006. They are also a great place to go if you like to get devoured by midges while listening to a hairy busker playing the tin whistle in a force five gale. Sadly, over the years countless people have been blown off the cliffs and into the Atlantic after straying too close to the edge.

Ronan Keating once shot a music video there,

shhlurring and warbling away at the sheagullsh, but, ash the shaying goesh, 'not even the tide would take him out' and he'sh shtill with ush. Thank God. Actually, that wash Weshtlife, but let'sh move on, regardlessh, ash thish ish getting on our nervsh.

The second highest cliffs in the land can be found in Donegal at Slieve League (the non-mountain), which has a drop of 601 m into the sea. To put this in context, that's almost the height of two Eiffel towers.

Cue drum roll please, as we announce that the Highest Cliffs in Ireland are on the north side of **Achill Island** at Annagh. This beauty spot nestles under Croaghaun mountain, which provides the 668 m of sea cliffs that keep it hidden away from the world. Surrounded by cliffs on three sides and looking out onto Blacksod Bay, Annagh can also lay claim to having the ...

Lowest Lake

Or to be more specific, the **Lowest Corrie Lake in Ireland.** Freshwater Lough Nakeeroge, only 16 m above sea level, was made by a retreating glacier (as all corries are). At one time it supported a thriving community as there is evidence of habitation, with one beehive-shaped stone building still remaining. Annagh is known locally as The Back of Beyond after an article of the same name which appeared in the 1973 *Capuchin Annual*. It's steeped in local lore and is said to very, very haunted. 'Wooooooooooooo, woooooooooooooo' (That was for atmosphere.).

Achill is Ireland's largest island, at 20 km from east to west and 18 km north to south. It's joined to the mainland by a bridge at Achill Sound and has been a tourist attraction since the first hotel opened there in 1830. It's entirely possible that Ronan Keating has paid the island a visit at one time, maybe shortly after falling out with former manager Louis Walsh. The latter was once reported as saying that he reckoned Ronan could be the 'new Cliff Richard'. If that is correct, then Ronan would be the Newest Cliff near the Highest Cliffs in Ireland.

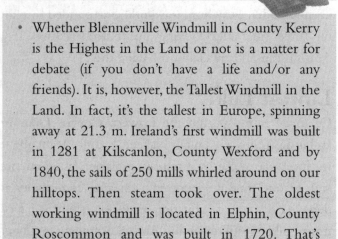

INTERESTING FACT

- Whether Blennerville Windmill in County Kerry is the Highest in the Land or not is a matter for debate (if you don't have a life and/or any friends). It is, however, the Tallest Windmill in the Land. In fact, it's the tallest in Europe, spinning away at 21.3 m. Ireland's first windmill was built in 1281 at Kilscanlon, County Wexford and by 1840, the sails of 250 mills whirled around on our hilltops. Then steam took over. The oldest working windmill is located in Elphin, County Roscommon and was built in 1720. That's enough about windmills.

Highest Hotel Room

In pursuit of this entry the reader will not be required to scale mountains, hills or even large mounds of rubble. There are countless hotels in Ireland boasting panoramic aerial views of the surrounding countryside, but they are just fortunate to be located on elevated terrain. Where's the skill in that? They are merely piggybacking on Mother Nature and are, quite frankly, cheating. A sky-high hotel room must be man-made and measured from the lobby up, not up from sea level. Wicklow and Kerry both have a disproportionate amount of these so-called 'High Hotels', with their fancy ways and their haughty bedrooms pretending to be what they can only dream of aspiring to. For a night spent resting one's head in the lap of the gods, head west across the Shannon and trudge wearily into **Limerick**. Lovely, lovely, lovely Limerick.

The Treaty City, renowned for its hospitality, is home to **Ireland's Tallest Hotel**, the Clarion, on Steamboat Quay. This 158-room inn is seventeen storeys high and the discerning guest on the top floor can rest soundly in the knowledge that he or she is 56 m above street level.

Limerick people have a great head for heights (perhaps it's a desire to get away from the feuding gangs) and are also the proud custodians of the **Tallest Spired Church**, St John's Cathedral which is 93.8 m tall.

Other highpoints on this verdant isle are: **Tallest . . .**

Bridge:	The Boyne River Bridge (95 m);
Obelisk:	Monument to Duke of Wellington, Phoenix Park (63 m, tallest in Europe);

Standing stone: Punchestown (6.5 m);

Stadium: Croke Park (40 m);

High cross: Muiredach's, Monasterboice (6.45 m);

Crane: Samson, Harland and Wolff in Belfast (106 m);

Lighthouse: Fastnet Rock (44.5 m);

Round Tower: Kilmacduagh Monastery (34 m);

Power Station Chimney: Moneypoint, (218 m);

Radio Mast: RTÉ 1 Medium Wave mast, Tullamore (290 m).

At time of writing, the **Tallest Buildings In The Republic And The North** are Cork County Hall (67 m) and Windsor House, Belfast (80 m) respectively. Depending on when you are reading this, these two structures may have been overshadowed by the Heuston Gate in Dublin (134 m, 117 m without the spire). You may even be reading this as you sip a cocktail in Ireland's **Highest City Bar**, atop the 120 m Point Village Watch Tower which is due for completion in 2009 (NB: The skangers down below can see your knickers.).

The Point's not the only man-made point in Dublin that's 120 m above the city – the tip of the Spire (Ireland's tallest sculpture) also shares the same airspace. If a person was sitting on top of the Spire he would have a bird's eye view of the Daniel O'Connell monument, while receiving a novel cure for piles. By a remarkable coincidence, if he was perched on top of the spire of St John's Cathedral in Limerick he would have the same view. This is because this county's main thoroughfare is also named O'Connell Street, which also bears a statue of O'Connell. Furthermore, it is right around the corner from . . . the country's Highest Hotel Room.

INTERESTING FACT

- Superstitious American hotel owners generally omit the thirteenth floor in their numbering, and the lifts either go directly from twelve to fourteen, or the floor may be given another name, such as 'Not The Thirteenth Floor'. This has never been a serious issue in Ireland as most hotels are still below ten storeys high. In China, because the word 'four' sounds like 'death' in Chinese, it's often skipped in their hospitals. So imagine if a doctor there is referring to a patient in Room No. 4, this is the likely dialogue: 'Ahhhh so, Matron, make sure Mister Wong gets plenty of sleep . . . in Death'. It's certainly one way of dealing with overcrowding.

Smallest and Biggest

Smallest Amount Of Romans Needed To Invade Ireland

Everybody knows that **the Romans** never invaded Ireland. They knew they were no match for the ancient Paddies and stayed well away, hiding in Wales. They even had to build a wall to contain the Scots and, as that word is derived from the Latin *Scotii* which means Irish, you can safely say that they soiled themselves at the mere mention of our name.

Hmmm . . .

The popular belief that the Romans never came to Hibernia has been challenged in recent years with new archaeological evidence indicating that this was not the case. They were certainly aware of us with two first century AD geographers, **Strabo and Pomponius Mela**, portraying Ireland as a wintry island populated by monstrous natives who ate the flesh of their dead fathers and committed incest with their mothers and sisters (treble YUCK). They also noted that the vegetation was so lush and yummy that the cattle would explode if allowed to graze for too long.

Exploding cows aside, the second-century geographer **Ptolemy** drew a surprisingly detailed map of Hibernia, giving the names of fifty-five tribes, settlements, headlands and rivers. These coordinates could have come either from Irish traders or, more tantalisingly, Roman expeditions to these shores.

In the early years of the Roman occupation of Britain, the Irish tribes were regularly raiding Wales, England and even Gaul for slaves and may have posed a threat to the stability of the new colony. There is evidence that the Latins contemplated invading Ireland and even fortified Britain's western seaboard against attacks from the marauding Irish. Historian Tacitus wrote that his father-in-law **Gnaeus Julius Agricola**, who governed Britain during the 80s AD, had 'lined the side of Britain that faces Ireland with his forces'.

However, he claimed that this wasn't to keep the Paddies out: 'This was more from hope than fear,' he continued, explaining that Ireland, 'lying between Britain and Spain' and accessible by sea from Gaul, could prove to be a

> . . . First century AD geographers, Strabo and Pomponius Mela . . . noted that the vegetation [in Ireland] was so lush and yummy that the cattle would explode if allowed to graze for too long.

valuable link between the Roman provinces. He then outlined how in its climate, soil and people Ireland 'is much like Britain' adding that Agricola believed the country could be conquered with one legion and a few auxiliaries.

> Agricola had given shelter to a prince of Ireland who had been driven out by a rebellion at home and under the guise of friendship retained him to be used as opportunity offered. I often heard my father-in-law say that with one legion and a small force of auxiliaries [Ireland] could be overpowered and that it would be easier to hold Britain if it was surrounded by Roman armies, with liberty banished from view.[8]

This prince is believed to be **Tuathal Teachtmhar**, the first proper High King of Ireland. In Irish mythology a story tells how Tuathal's father, High King Fiacha Finnfolaidh, was killed by the revolting King of Ulster (pun intended) around AD 60. Tuathal's mum hightailed it to Britain with her son and twenty years later he returned to defeat his enemies and occupy the throne at Tara. From here he passed laws and took land from all four provinces to create the new fifth province of Míde. Could he have returned with Roman technology and a few military advisers?

A few years after Agricola's boast, Juvenal wrote that the Romans had 'indeed advanced our arms beyond the shores of Hibernia and the recently captured Orcades [Orkneys]'.

Juvenal was a bit of a joker and his claims were written off until recent archaeological discoveries reignited the debate about whether the Romans had actually landed here.

[78] The *Agricola* (*De vita et moribus Iulii Agricola*), Chapter 24

Roman finds in Ireland are rare and no roads or large settlements have been positively identified. This paucity of discoveries isn't of any major significance in itself – everyone knows Julius Caesar briefly invaded Britain in 55 BC, but his army left no physical trace of their presence.

However, Romanesque cemeteries and large quantities of artefacts have been dug up in the east of Ireland. In 1927 on Lambay Island, off the coast of Dublin, archaeologists discovered a group of first century AD Roman-style burials containing brooches and metal ware of a kind that has also been found in England. Exciting as this may be, it isn't proof of an invasion and the graves may have been dug by British refugees fleeing the bloody aftermath of **Queen Boudica**'s failed revolt of AD 74.

Elsewhere, Tara, Newgrange, the hillfort of Clogher and Cashel have all produced early and late Roman material. Again, this doesn't prove that the Romans came here in any great numbers but might represent plunder, trade or the presence of more displaced Romanised Celts. Refugees had been arriving in Ireland since the 40s BC when the Romans first took an interest in Britain. Ptolemy's map of the southwest of Ireland reveals tribal names identical to those of clans in Britain and Gaul, which suggests settlement here by the Brigantes and Belgae.

One of the most intriguing finds to date may provide the answer to the question of whether the Romans ever attempted an invasion. Trial explorations at **Drumanagh**, near Rush in north Dublin, have hinted at the presence of a possible Roman coastal fort. The site covers 200,000 m^2 and is 'defended' on three sides by cliffs and on the fourth by a series of earthen ramparts and ditches. Coins found there are said to date to the period in which Tacitus and Juvenal were making their claims about invading Ireland. If it is a fort it could have accommodated hundreds of soldiers. One problem with this theory is that no weapons have been found on the site, which has been designated a national monument. This may be because large-scale excavation has been on hold for years due to a legal dispute between the government and the owner of the site. Until the case is resolved it's not possible to say whether Drumanagh was a Roman fort, trading post or a native settlement.

However, if it is proved to be a fort, Drumanagh may well have been a beachhead for an invasion by Agricola's 'legion and a small force of auxiliaries'.

During this period the largest of Rome's auxiliary units were 1,000-men strong. These outfits, should it come up in a pub quiz, were made up of non-Roman citizens and comprised archers, cavalry, slingers, skirmishers and the like. If Agricola reckoned he needed only a small amount of these chaps then let's put that figure at 500, half the size of the biggest auxiliary unit.

As a legion numbered 5,500 during the Imperial age of the Roman Empire (4,200 in the Republican age), the Smallest Number of Romans Needed To Invade Ireland is 6,000.

Ireland, as everybody knows, was never conquered or subdued by the Romans. So if Agricola did stage an invasion from Drumanagh, then 6,000 is also the **Smallest Number of Romans To Get Their Arses Kicked By The Paddies**.

INTERESTING FACT

- The name Hibernia is long believed to derive from the Latin term *hibernus* meaning wintry. However, there is another school of thought that claims Hibernia comes from *Ivernia*, which is the Latinised name Ierne. This was the monicker given to Ireland by the fourth century BC Greek merchant/ explorer, Pytheas of Massilia. Ierne may actually derive from the name of the Celtic patron goddess Erin, or Eriu, which gives us the modern name for Ireland: Eire/Eriu-land/Ireland. Eriu's sisters Banba and Fodhla (the Celts liked to spread the work around) are also patron goddesses. So if you're Irish, Folish or Banbish, come into the parlour. If you're Roman, bugger off.

Biggest Landowner

If Agricola (mentioned above, if you've just joined us) had managed, or even bothered, to conquer us then his boss in Rome would have been the First Biggest Landowner in Ireland. Now if you think that's a smart-bottomed way of revealing that the Catholic church is the Biggest Landowner here, think again. It's not.

It is, however, the **Biggest Institutional Landowner**. In Ireland there are currently 1,368 parishes with 2,643 churches in twenty-six dioceses and archdioceses. There are also approximately 2,940 priests on 'active service', but that's just a bit of bonus information for you. The last major estimate of how much all these parish lands were worth was published in 1998 by a leading property magazine, which floated a figure of €3.8billion. Considering inflation, other variables and life being too short etc., *Erindipity* isn't going to attempt to work out what that equates to on today's market, but if you consider that the average house price outside Dublin was IR£145,700 in 1998 and €257,945 today, then you're talking a lot of noughts. Noughts and holy crosses, even.

The Biggest Landowner in the State is – wait for it – **Coillte, the Irish Forestry Service**, with more than 442,000 hectares of Irish soil to its name. Sorry if you're disappointed.

It's consoling to know that in this age of land-hungry builders and crooked politicians, the Biggest Landowner in the country will never get planning permission to build housing estates on its holdings. For this reason Coillte is also the **Least Successful Property Developer**.

While we're on the subject of builders, you might be interested to know that two of them made . . .

Biggest Tax Settlement Ever

In June 2006 the Revenue's quarterly list of tax defaulters revealed 150 named individuals who had coughed up €55.5million to the exchequer. It was a very nice sum of money indeed, but even more remarkable because the lion's share of it had been paid by one company – **Bovale Developments**. Owners Michael and Tom Bailey, you may recall, were co-stars in the Flood and Mahon Tribunal investigations into payments for planning favours. They had originally owed €12.4million in PAYE, PRSI, corporation and income tax, but with interest and penalties this soared to a grand total of €22million.

The average house price in Dublin at the close of 2006 was €427,300, so that figure could, theoretically, have bought fifty-one new houses – an entire road, if space with planning permission was available.

INTERESTING FACT

- The Biggest Landowner On Earth owns a huge swathe of this island. All of Northern Ireland to be precise. Liz Windsor owns about one sixth of the planet's land, a total of 2,671 m hectares. Bet she's never cycled around it.

Smallest Museum

A trawl through the 'B' section of *Erindipity Rides Again*'s dictionary (*Erinictionary*) reveals the following definition of the word 'barnacle': 'a small invertebrate animal that lives in a cone-shaped shell attached to rocks, ships' keels or other hard places'.

Another entry reads: 'A device used to pinch a horse's nose for the purpose of restraining him'. As we don't condone the theft of horse's noses, and this definition is entirely irrelevant, we will ignore it and concentrate on the words 'small, hard and place' in the opening sentence instead.

For the sake of their sanity, one can only hope that the Barnacle family of No 8, The Bowling Green, Galway City were extremely small people. Their nineteenth century house was the smallest in the street, consisting of two rooms and a miniscule back yard. The ground floor room was, by turns, the kitchen, dining room and bedroom.

The family cooked their food over an open fire and during the summer months the back yard may have served as an extended kitchen area. Water had to be drawn from a pump out in the street until No 8 received its own supply in the 1940s. The upper room was the communal bedroom for this family of nine.

This was, indeed, a hard place to live, but no more so than many other small dwellings occupied by large families across Ireland at the time. What made this astonishingly modest house special (as if you haven't twigged it yet) was that it was home to one of the most famous women in literary history – **Nora Barnacle, wife of James Joyce**.

The author of *Ulysses* first met his mother-in-law Annie Barnacle in the kitchen (they weren't spoiled for choice of venue) of No 8 when he and his son Giorgio visited in 1909. In 1912 the Joyces (James, Nora, Giorgio and Lucia) visited Galway *en famille* for three weeks and spent most of their time at the house. Talk about the twin elements of the ideal holiday:

1. Galway in the rain, and
2. Nowhere to escape it except in either of two rooms already stuffed with eleven people.

Imagine the whang of wet socks.

Annie Barnacle lived in the house until her death in 1940 and in 1987 it was bought by Mary and Sheila Gallagher who restored it and opened it to the public. Since then Annie and Nora's kitchen has been visited by a president, scores of literary luvvies and has the singular distinction of being The Smallest Museum in Ireland.

As Nora Barnacle left the house for Dublin in 1904 and met Joyce soon afterwards on 10 June, you could say it didn't take her long to come out of her shell.

INTERESTING FACT

- Galway may have the smallest museum but in 2005 Cork became the Smallest Place In Europe With The Most Amount Of Culture. As European Capital of Culture, the Leeside metropolis was the smallest city ever to host the year-long festivities.

Biggest Kerry Joke About A Whale

Question: When is the right whale the wrong whale?
Answer: When **Kerry's** involved.

In early 2007 a showpiece TV advertisement urging Irish people to hump off to Kerry and go humpback whale-watching was revealed to contain a rather large error – the whale featured wasn't a humpback whale.

So what, says you: a whale's a whale. They're big, slippery and tend to hog the bathtub if you let them. That attitude would not have been appreciated by **Mr Jim Wilson of the Irish Whale and Dolphin Group** who pronounced himself flabbergasted (or even blubbergasted) to see the Fáilte Ireland advert claim a 'right whale' was a humpback. The right whale, he pointed out, was an endangered species that had been almost hunted to extinction in the north Atlantic. If that wasn't bad enough, Mr Wilson said he didn't believe the footage of a whale frolicking off the Kerry coast had even been filmed in Ireland. The marine expert told the *Mooney Goes Wild* show on RTÉ 1 that the advert looked like it had probably been filmed off the South African, Western Australian or Argentinian coasts and then edited to give the impression it was shot in Ireland.

What? Wrong right whales posing as Kerry natives? Can this outrage be true, you might ask?

What? Wrong right whales posing as Kerry natives? Can this outrage be true, you might ask?

The man responsible for the ad would have been the last man to ask with regards to this maritime blunder. The Fáilte Ireland Director of Regional Development admitted he hadn't known that the wrong whale had been used in the advert. He also admitted that the footage of people in a boat had been shot off the Kerry coast but he didn't know where the whale featured had been filmed.

To be fair, the Fáilte man wasn't an expert on whales and already had his work cut out for him as the ad was part of a €5million campaign to encourage people to take activity breaks at home – a near-impossible task during the drenched, dreary summer of 2007.

Besides, it wasn't the first time that whale 'personation' had taken place in Munster. In 1954 film director John Huston turned Youghal, County Cork into New Bedford, Massachusetts in a movie about the most famous whale of all time.

If the role of Moby Dick was played by an Irish whale, then it's only fair that a non-national should get to pose as a Kerry native.

Speaking of dicks, humps and blowholes, Kerry has another claim to infamy: it's the . . .

Biggest County For Slappers

For almost fifty years Kerry has been synonymous with all things wholesome and nice, from Kerrygold butter to the Rose of Tralee festival[9]. While Marlon Brando introduced the world to an entirely novel and depraved

[9] The former brand name was launched in 1961, while the Rose-fest first jigged its way into our consciousness in 1959.

way of using dairy products in *Last Tango in Paris* (1972), the Rose festival always kept the Kerry flag flying for clean, sexless entertainment. However, starched knickers and knitted knee socks may not be enough to preserve the county's reputation as the world's moral epicentre.

In January 2007 **Kerry** exposed itself as the 'sex kingdom of Ireland' to a largely uninterested nation. Actually, no one noticed or if anyone did they chose to ignore it and that's why you're reading about it on these pages. Kerry – brace yourself Julia – has the liveliest sex trade in the country. The number of prostitutes and sex agencies operating in that county is rising at a frenzied pace and the shameless hussies are touting openly for business in all of Kerry's main towns.

According to *The Kerryman* newspaper the sex business quadrupled in the twelve months from 2006 and internet advertising is driving it through the roof. Escort agencies employing foreign girls are now operating in Tralee and in the capital of Paddywhackery, **Killarney**. It's now so bad there that the American tourists are advised not to ask the locals for a ride in their jaunting cars for fear of causing offence. Certain Kerry hotels are unwittingly being used as bonk-houses and the menfolk of the county are being corrupted.

And that's not the worst of it. According to the *Irish Independent* these agencies are in addition to 'independent escorts' (presumably not from the paper) who tour the countryside to promote their arrival in advance. One of them, Marian (28), is a bisexual Portuguese girl who announced her decision to descend upon Tralee on 11

February 2007, and charge clients €270 for a one-hour *séisiún*. In her bumph she described herself as a 'sophisticated companion fluent in three languages'. Business-smart, bisexual and a mistress of many tongues? Could she be described as a 'cunning linguist'? Prostitutes from Malaysia and Thailand are also operating in the area.

So what can be done about this Kerry sex epidemic? One idea might be to deport all the exotic ladies and set up a Rose of Tralee escort service instead. If that doesn't kill off the sex trade, nothing will.

Alternatively, let the shady ladies stay – Kerry's always been famous for cute hoors.

Smallest Kite

The smallest kite in the world was built and designed by Nobuhiko Yoshizumi of Kyoto, Japan and was unveiled at the Drachen Foundation's Great Miniature Kite Contest in 1999. It measures just 0.4 cm x 0.6 cm and can actually fly. Nobuhiko (Nobby to his chums?) is a bit of a wizard kite maker and won the competition for three consecutive years. Would you like to know some more about kites? Good.

–   The largest number of kites flown on a single line is 11,284.
–   Kite flying was banned in China during Chairman Mao's Cultural Revolution. Anyone found kiting was sent to jail for up to three years.
–   There are seventy-eight rules in kite fighting in Thailand.

– In 1826 there was a coach service between London and Bristol using kites instead of horses.

The ancient Chinese believed that looking at kites floating high in the sky maintains good eyesight. They also believed that when you tilt your head back to look at a flying kite your gob opens just enough to let some body heat escape. This maintains yin-yang balance – and you wouldn't want any imbalance there.

So, essentially, to lead a healthy life all you need to do is stand around gawking at the sky with your mouth open and a piece of string in your hand. Sounds attractive, doesn't it?

Perhaps the natives of **County Sligo** think so. Ballymote, a sparkler in that tiara of a county[10], is a veritable hub of kite innovation, being the hometown of www.kitecompany.com. This splendid business produces a flyer that would put the eyesight of even the most seasoned Chinese kitewatcher to the test – the 'WORLD Smallest KITE' (That's how they spell it.). This piece of kite measures approximately 115 mm x 80 mm (4.5 in x 3 in) and is guaranteed to provide hours of (yawn) endless (YAWWWWN) enjoym . . . zzzzzzzzzzzzzzzz.

While it is not the smallest kite ever built, it may be the **Smallest Commercial Kite In The World**. It's the smallest in Ballymote at any rate.

If you're ever over that way, don't be surprised to see the streets and fields full of slack-jawed, squinting folk staring into space.

And people flying kites too.[11]

---

[10] The author's mother is from Sligo. Hello Auntie Patsy, Uncle Tommy and Aunty Maeve if you're reading this.
[11] Only joking, cousins.

INTERESTING FACT

- On 12 December 1901 Guglielmo Marconi used a 122 m kite-supported antenna to broadcast the first transatlantic radio signal. Marconi qualifies to make a guest appearance on this page for two reasons: (1) Because he was half Irish. His mother was Annie Jameson, granddaughter of the founder of the Jameson Whiskey distillery. (2) He married an Irishwoman, Beatrice O'Brien, daughter of the fourteenth Baron Inchiquin. Is that Irish enough for you?

Best and Worst

Best Place To Avoid Getting Bombed By The Jerries

Germany.

Next Best Place To Avoid Getting Bombed By The Jerries

A German embassy.

Best Place To Avoid Getting Your Knickers Bombed By The Jerries

Ballsbridge, Dublin 4.

   During the Second World War the best way to avoid getting bombed by the Bosch was to either get a job in the German Embassy in Ballsbridge or become a laundry van driver.

While the first piece of advice is obvious, the second will surprise most Irish people below the age of forty.

For over fifty years the residents of leafy Dublin 4 lived happily under the shadow of the biggest swastika to be found outside of Nazi Germany. Even more horrible than this was the fact that it was painted on something that Herr Hitler would have approved of – a chimney stack.

From 1912 right into the mid-1960s there existed a cleaning company known as the **Swastika Laundry** on the Shelbourne Road in Ballsbridge. Their fleet of electric delivery vans which were painted red with a black swastika and stuffed with knickers and sock were a common sight on the city's streets.

One tale tells how the exiled physicist **Erwin Schrödinger**, who had fled the fascist regime, was almost killed by one of the vans as he crossed the road and believed he had been the victim of a Nazi assassination plot.

What Dr Schrödinger didn't know was that, ironically, the swastika used by the laundry was an ancient Indian symbol for good luck which comes from the Sanskrit word 'svastika'. Even after the horrors of the Third Reich were fully revealed the company still clung to its 'good luck' name and logo until it was absorbed into the Spring Grove company.

Perhaps it was this positive symbol that caused Ballsbridge to remain unscathed during the war while Dun Laoghaire and the North Strand were both bombed.

INTERESTING FACTS

- On the night of 30 May 1941, Dublin's North Strand was hit by Nazi bombs, with the loss of thirty-eight civilian lives and seventy houses. The Germans claimed afterwards the raid was a mistake and blamed high winds for throwing the pilots off course. Recently, it has been claimed that the Germans were sending out a warning to the Government not to help the Allies after the Dublin fire brigade went to Belfast to put out incendiary bomb fires in the shipbuilding city.

- During the war, Irish military intelligence held clandestine meetings with the British to discuss the possibility of a Jerry invasion of Ireland as a means of attacking Britain. The Germans had such a plan, code-named 'Operation Emerald'. Imagine if they had invaded and, on entering Dublin had encountered one of the Swastika Laundry vans. 'Mein Gott Fritz, zat driver is whistling, "We'll Hang Out The Washing On The Siegfried Line!"'

- Contrary to popular belief, Eamon de Valera did not go to the German embassy in 1945 to give his condolences on the fuhrer's death. He went to the Ambassador's residence instead. Either way, it was an incredibly insensitive thing to do.

Worst Place For Understanding Dolphins If You're A Dubliner

If man's best friend wasn't a dog, it would probably be a dolphin. Granted, they're difficult to cuddle, and they couldn't drag you out of a burning house or rescue you from under an avalanche, but go for a swim with one and they'll chat happily with you for hours and whistle at you if you say something witty. They'll even keep sharks away if you fall overboard during a sea battle and you can strap a bomb onto them if you run out of torpedoes. Catch Rover being that useful.

The flip side of Flipper, however, is that he's a desperate gossip. At the start of 2007 scientists discovered that, just like humans, dolphins have their own names they use when talking to each other, they eavesdrop on each other's conversations and have been heard gossiping about one another.

While studying 130 bottlenose dolphins in the River Shannon near **Carrigaholt, County Clare**, Dr Simon Berrow and his colleagues at the **Shannon Dolphin and Wildlife Foundation** found that they have their own unique language. What's more, they have their own distinctive west of Ireland accent, making them official culchie dolphins.

These loveable creatures use two types of sound to communicate – clicks and whistles. The former are to navigate and fish, and the latter to chat with each other. Each has their own unique signature whistle to identify themselves ('whistle, whistle, hup ye boy ye, it's Mickey

Each [dolphin] has their own unique signature whistle to identify themselves ('whistle, whistle, hup ye boy ye, it's Mickey Joe here, whistle, whistle').

Joe here, whistle, whistle'). Using a hydrophone underwater system to record the Shannon dolphins, Dr Berrow's team discovered eight new, unidentified whistles.

On the other side of the Irish Sea, a biologist working in conjunction with Dr Berrow's team discovered that bottlenose dolphins in Cardigan Bay, Wales were using a different dialect to their cousins living off the Irish coast. Dr Berrow is now compiling a dolphin dictionary from the 1,800 whistles he has recorded so far. Presumably it will be waterproof.

Whatever about understanding County Clare culchie dolphins, the average Dubliner would have serious difficulty making sense of Ireland's most famous sea mammal, the heavily Kerry-accented Fungi.

The playful bottle-nosed beastie first arrived in Dingle, County Kerry back in 1983 and is worth approximately €4million a year to the local tourist industry. He's believed to be about fifty years old. The only way to find out the exact age of a dolphin is to section one of their teeth, but as Fungi is unlikely to allow this to happen, the townsfolk can only surmise and hope that he will be around for a few more years to come.

The obvious thing would be to ask him, and scientists are currently trying to decipher that strange, gargling, unearthly dialect so that the question can be posed. Then, when they've finished with the locals, they'll start to work on the dolphin.

Best Place for Tarzan Impressions

A trip to Maynooth Castle in the County of Kildare will reward the visitor with a view of the FitzGerald family's coat of arms. This is carved in stone over the gateway and – bear with us here – is technically described in heraldic gobbledygook as: Arms: Argent a saltire gules. Crest: A monkey statant proper environed about the middle with a plain collar and chained. Supporters: Two monkeys, environed and chained as in the crest.

If you happen to know what a 'saltire gules' is, please send it on a postcard to:

> We Don't Care,
> You Need To Get Out More Road,
> Loserville, Co Tosspot.

It's the monkeys we're interested in.

Legend has it that when **John FitzThomas FitzGerald**, the First Earl of Kildare, was a baby, a fire broke out at his home in Woodstock Castle near Athy. As the servants raced around trying to douse the flames they forgot to rescue little John and when they finally got around to looking for him, they found his bedroom in ruins.

It was brown trouser time.

As they were figuring out what to say to his dad, a strange noise rang out from one of the towers – and no, it wasn't a baby crying. The forgetful servants looked up and saw the castle's pet monkey, which had managed to escape from its chains, cradling the infant in its arms[12].

When John was made an earl in 1316 he adopted monkeys for his crest, out of gratitude for his salvation. The family also added another motto: *Non immemor beneficii* (Not forgetful of favours).

To this day many residents of County Kildare drag their knuckles along the ground or beat their breasts while yodelling, 'AGGGGGGHHHHHH-UHHHHHHHH-AGGGGGHHHHHHH-UHHHHHHHHHHHH-GGGGHHHHHHHHHHHUGGGHHHHHHHHHH-AGGGHHHHHHHHHHHH!!!!!!!!!' in memory of the occasion.

Curiously, alcohol seems to enhance these people's memories rather than impair it.

Best Place For Well-Informed Pigs

Dromcummer, County Cork.

New Year's Day normally marks the end of the festive season with all its bells and whistles and partying and eating etc and so forth. For many, the prospect of

---

[12] *Location: Kildare*
Scene: *A medieval castle ablaze . . .*
Servant One: Library saved?
Servant Two: Check.
Servant One: Banqueting hall saved?
Servant Two: Check.
Servant One: Arsenal saved?
Servant Two: Check.
Servant One: His Lord and Ladyship saved?
Servant Two: Check.
Servant One: Aren't we forgetting something? Small, makes a lot of noise, pees and poos a lot?
Servant Two: The monkey! The monkey!! We forgot the monkey!!

returning to work is actually attractive after the three-month-long Christmas celebrations enjoyed/endured on this soggy little island of ours. Keeping up the pretence of jollity while your liver is atrophying, your bowels have quit in disgust at your gluttony and your short term memory is what were we just talking about? Well, it all gets a bit boring.

New Year's Day 2003 was celebrated by more than just the fed-up workforce – Ireland's pigs also oinked and wagged their squiggly tails in delight as the clocks struck midnight.

This was because new EU directives on keeping pigs happy came into force that year. Pig boredom is a serious issue for farmers as they are intelligent animals and need distraction and entertainment or else they can get aggressive and surly (that's the pigs we're talking about, not the farmers). Pigs need to chew and root and the new rules named specific rooting materials including hay, compost and wood to keep the piggies occupied. They also love to toss things around and it was decided that footballs and novelty items should be used to keep them amused. The rules further state that pigs 'should be kept in groups with as little mixing as possible' and should have 'adequate opportunities to escape and hide from other pigs'. To show they meant business the Eurocrats threw in a fine of up to €2,000 for non-compliance.

In February of that year one Munster farming family revealed that they had the happiest and most erudite pigs in Ireland. In their endeavours to banish boredom, farm owners **Dermot and Margaret Lehane** ruled out balls and old boots as they realised they would end up blocking the slurry pipes. Instead, they employed fertiliser bags hanging from hooks and ropes dangling from the ceiling as toys for their pigs.

However, the key to the Lehane pigs' state of preternatural happiness lay not in these playthings alone. The family went a step further and introduced an intellectual element that transformed the lives of their smart and frolicksome animals – *The Corkman* newspaper.

The paper itself reported that the family discovered the pigs loved nothing better than to get stuck into a copy of that fine organ every morning and this was the secret to keeping them content. It even published a picture of four young pigs browsing the front page of the weekly paper and, unbelievable as this may seem, they really did look like they were reading it. Three of them did, at any rate . . . one of them may have been probing some poo with his snout.

'Consistency', the paper said, was the main reason for choosing *The Corkman* over certain other publications. The pigs would have turned their snouts up at the vacuous *VIP* magazine as, according to Margaret, mags just aren't absorbent enough. *The Corkman* is now such a hit with the Lehane piggy-wiggies that their neighbours bring it up to the farm by the carload.

The progressive Lehanes are well known and respected in the farming community and Margaret regularly hosts school trips to the farm to educate children about where their food comes from. *Erindipity Rides Again* wishes them and their pigs all the very best.

As for *The Corkman*, while it's a fine newspaper, it's

responsible for proving that there's nothing but crap in the papers these days.

INTERESTING FACT

- There are 1.7 million pigs and 5 million sheep in Ireland which seems a sizeable population if you're not aware that cows are the most plentiful farm animals in the country. Two million calves are born every year and join the ranks of the 7 m cows consuming 70 kg of Irish grass every day. 70 kg of grass per day means an awful lot of poo. Two of Ireland's most famous businessmen breed cows: Michael O'Leary (Charolais and Aberdeen-Anguses) and . . . *Irish Independent* owner Tony O'Reilly (Charolais). Note to Anto: new market possibility? Moospapers??

Worst Place To Get Stuck Behind A Tractor

County Louth.

You know how it is: you've spent two weeks squeezed into a caravan in Wexford, listening to the rain drumming on the roof and the screeching of three bored children, with a partner who's either going to divorce you or put a pillow over your head when you're sleeping . . . and now you're on the road home, stuck behind the **World's Slowest Tractor** listening to the rain drumming on the roof and the screeching of . . . etc., etc., etc.

If this sounds familiar, then *Erindipity* advises avoiding Cooley, County Louth on the first Sunday of every August. In the late summer of 2007 the roads of the Wee County were clogged with thousands of tractors of all styles and hues when it hosted a most unusual and eye-catching record attempt – for the **Biggest Number of Vintage Tractors Working Together**. This farming benchmark was first set in Cooley back in 1995 when 322 machines took to the field, tilling and sowing and generally mucking up the place and was broken by Australia in 1998 with a new standard of 798 tractors. Cooley's riposte came in 2002 when the tractor men of Ireland regained the record with a staggering 1,832 oldsmobiles. Their proud achievement stood for four years until the British topped it with 2,141 in 2006.

The farmers of Ireland are as closely bonded with their tractors as they are to the land. It was, after all, an Irishman – Harry Ferguson (see page 7) – who invented the modern tractor. Determined not to be bettered by our British cousins or the expat Paddies of Oz, they organised an attempt to put the record beyond the grasp of any would-be challenger.

On 5 August 2007, what was described by one competitor as a 'tsunami of tractors' crashed into County Louth from all over Ireland. The vehicles were vintage models, which means they were over thirty years old, but many dated back to the early 1900s.

Old they may have been but they were still as eager to work as their owners. As the steam whistle blew to signal the start of the attempt, 4,758 farmers climbed up on their beloved tractors and set to labouring on the field. The final whistle sounded after a quarter of an hour to mark the setting of the new record, but the happy farmers kept driving together for another hour, just for the fun of it.

As the 4,758 record is almost twice that set in Britain it's unlikely that it will be broken for a long time to come – if ever.

As they wended their way home that evening at 8 kph the farmers were unaware that they were also inadvertently setting another world record: **Highest Number of Road Rage Cases Ever**.

Best Place To Survive Gout, Heart Disease And Definitely Diabetes

Mrs Delany's dining room, Glasnevin, Dublin.

Mary Delany was an upper class English aristocrat who married Jonathan Swift's best friend Patrick Delany, and was on close terms with George III and his missus Queen Charlotte. She was a good landscape artist and a competent musician. However, it's not for these qualities or her high-faluting friends that she is remembered, but for her biography – in six volumes – and her correspondences. She was one of Dublin's first celebrities in the modern sense of the word and was highly popular within her social circle and outside of it in the merchant classes of her adopted city. The latter was because Mrs Delany knew how to host the most sumptuous dinners and her tables groaned under the weight of the best of everything to be bought in Dublin.

If you're one of those people concerned about obesity and the amount of fast food we twenty-first-century Irishers consume, take a look at what Mrs Delany and her contemporaries used to fill their faces with 250 years ago: For a woman besotted with food Mary Delany started her day off with a modest cup of warm whey (the watery remains of milk after the curds had been removed) flavoured with sugar or rosewater. She would then set to writing the day's menu. This would vary daily, depending on the amount and rank of guests for dinner, which began at 2 p.m. and continued for up to three hours. When everything had been arranged with the housekeeper she would then have her breakfast, another apparently modest affair of bread and butter with tea, coffee or chocolate. This was, in fact, the height of luxury as those drinks were prohibitively expensive in Mrs Delany's day. A half pound of her favourite tea cost three shillings and threepence in 1758 – approximately €28 at today's prices.

Dinner, in one instance, consisted of 'turkeys endove [endive], boyled neck of mutton, greens, soup, plum pudding, roast loin of veal and venison pasty'. And that was just the FIRST course. For the second she served 'partridge, sweetbreads [thymus glands of veal, young beef, lamb or pork], collared pig [a boned, rolled affair which was stuffed and pickled], creamed apple tart, followed by crabs [now there's a taste sensation], fricassee of eggs and pigeons'. There were also side dishes of biscuits and pickles, sloshed down with buckets of wine.

There was no dessert.

Mrs Delany may have been popular with her guests, but her kitchen staff must have dreaded the sight of her. The cook's job of turning out fourteen dishes and keeping food warm before serving was a nightmare. There were no gas stoves or microwaves in the Delany kitchen; everything was done before an open fire using small cranes. Not that Mrs D seemed to give a fig about the poor woman. She wrote to a friend that she was burdened with a very 'indifferent cook, not worth transporting'.

The courses were brought through the regularly freezing house by the Delanys' footmen whose strutting peacock performances were integral to the guests' enjoyment.

Mistress Delany, who referred to her kitchen staff as 'Cinderellas', nicknamed one of her footmen 'Fatty John'. What a joker she was.

The dining experience at Mrs Delany's was typical of its day – excessive, delicious (if you like crabs with your apple tart) and designed to reinforce the social order, that is, natives in the kitchen, ascendancy at the dinner table. Even here though, there were social conventions: the eighteenth-century code of hospitality meant

Mrs Delany had to bring her guests into the conversation according to their rank in society, sex and age. The conversation was genteel and non-controversial, as befitted the studied manners of that age. After dinner, when the ladies left the room, polite conventions were set aside and the men chatted, presumably in earthier tones, and then relieved themselves on a communal commode in the corner, which was emptied by one of the footmen. The ladies, in an adjacent room, struggled to use gravy-boat-shaped potties called voideurs. Thankfully for them, curry was seldom on the menu in Georgian Dublin[13]. Feeling peckish?

Next up was tea in the drawing room and a stroll around the garden before supper a few hours later. This meal generally consisted of leftovers from lunch and pre-prepared dishes from the pantry. Here's an example of the grub you could expect to find on a typical Georgian supper table according to the contemporary *Modern Cook*: 'Jellied calf's head [yum, yum], ham, Dutch or hung beef [dried meat, grated or cut into thin slices], collared [pickled and stuffed] beef, mutton, pigmeat, veal, pork, potted [preserved] beef, pigeons, hare, venison, eel, char [a type of fish], lampreys [a type of eel], trouts, etc.'

Mrs D describes one such supper in January 1733 in one of her many letters:

Yesterday we spent at home, had a petite assembly,

[13] Curry rapidly became popular in Britain in the eighteenth century. In 1747 Hannah Glasse wrote the first known recipe for curry in *Glasse's Art of Cookery* and by 1773 the London Coffee House had curry on its menu. In 1780 the first commercial curry powder was launched and in 1791 Stephana Malcom included a curry recipe – Chicken Topperfield plus Currypowder, Chutnies and Mulligatawny soup – in *In The Laird's Kitchen, Three Hundred Years of Food in Scotland*. Rest assured Mrs Delany would have been aware of curry – and of its side effects.

which we among ourselves call a ridotto, because at ten o'clock we have a very pretty tray brought in with chocolate, mulled wine, cakes, sweetmeats [candied fruits], and comfits [sugared nuts or fruits], cold partridge, chicken, lamb, ham, tongue – all set out prettily and ready to pick at.

Shortly after this Mrs Delany's husband would head off to bed with a cup of 'caudle' – gruel flavoured with eggs, wine, spices and sugar. If the lavish nosh he had consumed earlier didn't give him Gout, Heart Disease and Definitely Diabetes, then surely this nightcap would. You'd presume so, at any rate.

Incredible as it may seem, despite years of over-indulgence that would have left a weaker person with the above afflictions, Dean Patrick Delany died in 1767 in his eighty-third year – a remarkably old age in the eighteenth century. As for his beloved wife, she passed away in 1788 at the great age of eighty-eight.

On the strength of this longevity, the Delanys' house in Glasnevin was surely the Best Place To Survive Gout, Heart Disease and Definitely Diabetes.

Worst Way To Take Your Time (If You're Irish)

You've got to love the Brits. Not content with 'civilising' the planet in the nineteenth century they also decided that a town in England should be the centre of time and space.

A little bit of history:

In 1880 Westminster passed an Act to adopt Greenwich

Mean Time across the island of Britain and four years later the International Meridian Convention at Washington announced that GMT would be the standard by which all world time was set.

The convention was organised by US President, Grover Cleveland, and attended by forty-one delegates from twenty-five nations. Its aim was to adopt a single world meridian to replace the numerous ones in existence at the time. This would be the 'initial meridian' at zero degrees and all longitude would be calculated east and west from it up to 180 degrees. International time would then be based on the moment the sun is at its highest and passing over it (that is, at noon). Delegates voted 22–1 to place this meridian at the **Royal Observatory in Greenwich, London**. There were two abstentions: France and Brazil, while San Domingo voted against the motion placing it there (They were always a troublesome bunch, those San Domingans.).

So, as a result of this agreement Greenwich became the 'centre of the world' – the base coordinate for travellers wishing to know where they were. And, with a dastardly twiddle of its waxed moustache, England now controlled the world's clocks based on the one kept at the Royal Observatory. It might interest you to know that it's not accurate.

A little bit of astrophysics: Noon Greenwich Time isn't necessarily the moment when the sun passes across the Greenwich meridian. This is because the Earth is rotating at an uneven speed and its orbit of the sun is elliptical (not circular) and it's also tilted on its axis. In other words, the world's a bit bockety. It tends to stagger along, which it's entitled to do – it's getting on a bit, after all. Noon at Greenwich may be up to sixteen minutes away from actual noon time. Not even Queen Victoria's astronomers could control this and that's why the word 'mean' was added: GMT is the annual average of the sun's motion through the Greenwich meridian.

So, in order to colonise the world the British developed a standard time that they then had to batter about and knock lumps out of to make work – which is pretty much what they were doing with the Paddies at the time. The other countries that adopted GMT had the luxury of doing so voluntarily. Typically, Ireland did not.

Nowadays we children of the Republic use Irish Standard Time (*Am Caighdeánach na hÉireann*) to tell us when to get up or go to bed. Prior to 1916 our forefathers used Dublin Mean Time. This was introduced in 1880 by the same Act of Parliament that brought GMT to Britain. Due to Ireland's westerly location Dublin Mean Time was twenty-five minutes behind London time – that is, the sun passes over Greenwich at noon, twenty-five minutes before it passes over Dublin at noon. So far, so (relatively) uncomplicated.

In 1916 Westminster decided to introduce British Summer Time by adding an hour on to the end of the day. This was to apply for the duration of the Great War and could be dispensed with after it was won (they didn't contemplate defeat). The rationale behind this was that longer daytime hours would help the war effort and reduce the need for lighting fuel in the evenings. This new, more cost-effective summer period for 1916 was to run from Sunday 21 May to Sunday 1 October.

Dublin during that time was still seething after the last of the Easter Rising executions on 12 May and the island was under martial law. The extra hour of daylight may have benefited those involved in the post-Rising clean-up but it confused the country's bovine population who were used to being milked at dawn, which now came an hour later. Eventually, everyone – including Daisy the cow – got used to the new arrangement which was still based on Dublin Mean Time.

However, what London gives, London can take away and in August of that year, Westminster decided that the rebellious Paddies needed to be brought further into line. It decided that a novel way to achieve this would be to take away our local Dublin Mean Time and replace it with GMT when official summer ended in October. To achieve this, all clocks in Paddyland would be set to the same time as the clock in the Royal Observatory at Greenwich. As Dublin is twenty-five minutes behind London this meant that on 1 October 1916 night-time arrived twenty-five minutes earlier than usual.

Despite it being a slap on the wrist for the Rising, we actually liked it. So much so that that Irish Standard Time is still based on London time despite the twenty-five-minute discrepancy.

Erindipity Rides Again would like to believe that our laid-back forefathers welcomed this shortening of their daytime as it meant they could knock off work and head to the pub a bit earlier. The British, on the other hand, probably didn't see any irony in taking the time of a race renowned for taking its time. Could this also be the **Most Popular Case of Daylight Robbery** the world has ever seen?

INTERESTING FACT

- The Longest Summer in Ireland's history was six years in duration. In 1940 Britain decided to extend British Summer Time for the duration of the Second World War. Ireland followed suit with the result that our clocks went forward an hour in 1940 and weren't turned back until 1946. The second longest summer lasted three years after the Standard Time Act of 1968 extended official Irish Summer Time to the entire year. The experimental act wasn't popular and the clocks were turned back again in 1971.

Best Place To See
Drew Barrymore In The Nip

In 2001 Hollywood actress Drew Barrymore told an interviewer about one of her favourite hobbies – running naked through Irish fields. *Charlie's Angels'* (2000 and '03) star Drew revealed to US magazine, *Parade*, that she's a free spirit who likes nothing better than to go driving in Ireland, park her car, leg it out into the nearest field, rip her clothes off and run through the wheat. Note here that

Whatever about her trampling the stalks underfoot, one imagines that [Drew Barrymore's] ponderous boobies would make some interesting crop circles.

she specifically mentioned wheat – not cabbages, turnips or carrots. Pretty painful to fall on a carrot when you're running in the nude. Or a parsnip for that matter.

While she didn't name any specific field, one presumes that she's never done it during the National Ploughing Championships. She also didn't say whether she keeps her shoes and socks on while she interferes with the farmer's livelihood. Whatever about her trampling the stalks underfoot, one imagines that her ponderous boobies would make some interesting crop circles.

When the story was picked up by an Irish newspaper it made for at least one intriguing pub conversation:

Drinker One *(reading Daily Star):*

It says here: 'Barrymore Runs Naked Through Wheatfield'.

Drinker Two *(splutters into pint)*:

What? Michael Barrymore?!!

Drinker One: No, *Drew* Barrymore.

Drinker Two *(snorts)*: Those bloody prisoners get the best of everything.

Best Place To Get A Free Computer

September 1997 marked the beginning of Ireland's evolution as one of the world's leading cyberpowers. The Information Age had landed on our shores – and promptly headed for the small town of **Ennis**. The County Clare metropolis was promised hundreds of software jobs over a five-year period when Telecom Eireann named it as Ireland's first Information Age Town. As one reporter put it, the €19million investment was designed to 'fast-track it into the twenty-first century', and Ennis was to spearhead the country's entry into the cyberworld and become one of the most advanced towns on the planet.

As the *Irish Independent* reported, the town of 15,000 would be a role model for the rest of the country where surfing the net[14] and the internet café would be as much a part of life as the local pub and the grocer. The paper announced that:

– Every home would have a phone with a 'sophisticated' digital mailbox.

– Businesses in the town would get ISDN connections (remember ISDN?) and high-speed access to the internet.

– Most homes (82%) would have a personal computer – partly financed by Telecom Eireann.

– Smart card technology would come into operation as Ennis strode into the 'cashless society'.

Shopping from home, electronic banking and ordering

[14] Isn't it strange how dated the phrase 'surfing' has become? People 'go online' these days. The former sounded much more fun in a sun-bleached hair, beach boy kind of way.

meals on wheels online would be commonplace, and the town's alarm systems would be linked directly to the Gardaí. The paper went on: the locals could even monitor their air conditioning by remote computer. It's hard to believe this was only ten years ago.

In August 2007 Ennis was still the Captain James T Kirk of Irish towns, boldly going where . . . blah, blah, blah. Wrong. In the late summer of 2007 the Central Statistics Office released figures that revealed that not only did Cybertown have one of the lowest broadband penetrations in the country, but that the amount of houses with a computer had actually dropped significantly.

Broadband usage in Ennis was just 21% and nearly half of its homes had no internet access at all. Just over 59% of households owned a PC – a drop of 23% from 1997. Compare that with computer ownership in Swords, County Dublin and Naas in Kildare – both at 67%. Incidentally, the highest penetration of ownership was found in Malahide, at 78%. The northside and Kildare? Have you no pride, Ennis?

The drop in Information Age values in the Clare town isn't down to lack of interest or a 'return to nature'. Ennis people are still highly computer-literate. It's because of the housing boom. The rules applied by the town's Information Age Taskforce stated that only houses built between 1991 and 1998 should qualify for a free PC. Over the past ten years the population and size of Ennis have increased, whereas the number of cyber-nerd homes has remained the same.

In the last decade of the twentieth century, Ennis was the Best Place To Get A Free Computer. Today it's the **Best Place To Open A Shop Selling Computers.**

Worst Place For Blocked Toilets

You're standing in it. The place that is, not something nasty and unmentionable.

Not only are the Irish flushed with the success of the so-called Celtic Tiger, they are also flushing more toilet paper down the loo than almost any other country in Europe. Maybe the two are connected – more money, more consumption, more trips to the bog. It makes sense.

In February 2007 the **European Tissue Symposium**, or ETS (it really does exist), revealed that Ireland and the UK use the most toilet tissue in Europe, with the average person in both countries going through 110 toilet rolls each year. Compare this with the Ukraine, which has the lowest usage of toilet paper in Europe – four rolls per person per year.

According to the symposium, the combination of softness and strength (and the introduction in some cases of aloe vera), have made toilet rolls on these islands the very best in the world – the top of the bottom charts if you will. We actually enjoy using it – so much so that Seosamh Public goes through an average of 17.6 kg per year, while the Yanks use only 15.7 kg and the western European average is 12.4 kg. US bog roll, apparently, has not been a hit on the European market because, say the experts, it's too soft and falls apart too easily. Unlike German loo paper, which is so hard they patch up tanks with it. Russian rolls 'are like newspaper: grey and crepey', of very poor quality and extremely cheap. So cheap that the Russians spend only €2 a head per year on it.

The average Irish person, meanwhile, spends €14 a year, while the UK public spends €17, and France, Germany and Spain €12 a year. The Poles average annual bog roll expenditure is €5 a year.

The ETS said overall consumption rose by 40% from 1997 to 2007 and the trend is set to continue. Hopefully, this had more to do with the accession of extra member states and the subsequent population growth. Otherwise, one shudders to imagine what that 40% of us Europeans had used instead of toilet tissue. Leaves? Grass?? The *Sunday Independent*???

So be proud the next time you're blocking the toilet with that four-ply, double thick, ultra absorbent, Preparation H–impregnated bog tissue. When it comes to having a squeaky-clean bum the Irish have wiped the rest of Europe's eye.

Best Place To Go To The Loo In Public

In August of 2002 the VHI (Voluntary Health Board) hosted a singular beauty contest – to find Ireland's **Top Ten Public Toilets**. At the announcement of details of the Lovely Loo competition the board stated that the provision of good, clean public toilet facilities was essential for every Irish town, noting that bladder control problems are a common medical condition. Indeed, no one likes to get caught short for want of a nearby, non-manky, bog.

All of Ireland's public loos were eligible and the prize on offer was a cheque for €2,000 towards enhancement of the winning town's 'facilities', with four regional runners-up scooping a Top Toilet plaque. All the entrants had to do was to submit a colour photograph of their town toilet's interior and exterior.

We'll stop here for a moment to reflect on the bravery of the photographers who stood outside and inside their public loos taking photographs ('no really, officer, it's for the Top Ten toilets competition'). Many of them lived to submit their pictures.

For the record, the top toilet snapper lives in the Cork town of **Gougane Barra**. So if you're ever in the area please feel free to drop into the Best Public Loos in the country to spend a penny.

Just try and be sparing with the loo roll. As they say in Cork: 'Paper doesn't grow on trees, you know'.

Just try and be sparing with the loo roll. As they say in Cork: 'Paper doesn't grow on trees, you know'.

INTERESTING FACT

- An Irish pub in the US made headlines here in early 2007 after 12,000 people signed a petition protesting against the removal of its confusing toilet signs. Leading American politicians were among those who signed up to support McGuire's Irish pub in Florida, after the State Department of Business and Professional Regulation issued an order for the signs to be removed. This was all down to a complaint from a teenage girl who found the signs misleading – which was the whole point of them. 'Ladies' was the most prominent word on the door for the gents' toilet, with the words, 'Don't go in here' in much, much smaller type. Vice versa with the ladies' loo. The pub eventually won the battle to have the signs put back up in a landmark case of toilet humour winning over political correctness.

Best Place To Walk Into
A Black Hole

Picture yourself on a bog (peat, not ceramic) in Donegal. The year is 1868, it is evening time, a storm is brewing and you're heading home for tea. Suddenly, out of the corner of your eye, you see a flash of light. You swing around to face it and before you is . . . E.T. stepping out of a Black Hole.

Sorry, wrong fantasy. It's not too far off the mark though.

In that year a ball of fire ripped up a 100-m trench on a Donegal bog and created an enduring mystery that has baffled eggheads for a century and a half. The event was witnessed by local engineer, **Michael Fitzgerald**, who reported that he saw a 'globe of fire in the air, floating leisurely along' the bog. He wrote that he found a hole 'about 20 ft square [6 m] where it first touched the land with the peat turned . . . as if it had been cut out with a huge knife'. The eerie fireball covered over a mile (1.6 km) for 'more than twenty minutes', he said. 'It appeared at first to be a bright red globular ball of fire, about 2 ft [0.6 m] in diameter, but its bulk became rapidly less, particularly after each dip in the soil, so that it appeared not more than three inches [3.6 cm] in diameter when it finally disappeared.'

In January 2007 a leading American scientist came out from behind his Bunsen burner to offer the world an explanation for the phenomenon – the fireball, said **Pace VanDevender**, was a mini black hole. 'A mini black hole?' says you. 'A gravitational field so strong that nothing can escape its pull, created in the Big Bang at the birth of the universe fourteen billion years ago? Surely this is unfeasible? They're in outer space – how could one crash into Donegal?'

Eminent physicist VanDevender has visited the Glendowan mountains six times to examine the still-visible trench and damage caused by the fireball to the bank of a stream. He has carbon dated the soil, done various experiments, and estimates that Fitzgerald's ball lightning displaced more than 100 tonnes of turf. After working his way through all the options he believes the only explanation not dismissed by science is that the fireball was a massive condensed object, which could only be a mini black hole.

We'll take a little break at this point in the narrative. You don't really want to know how he reached this conclusion, do you? It involves quantum mechanics, plasma and something called the 'gravitational equivalent of an atom'. Didn't think so. Back to the narrative.

VanDevender's theory is that about 10,000 mini black holes hit the Earth each year, most of them going into the ocean or absorbed by dry land. He contends that they behave differently when they strike bogs – like the one in Donegal. VanDeMan is hedging his bets, however, claiming to be sceptical about his own theory until more facts are known. He puts the odds of mini black holes existing at one in ten and the odds of finding one at least at one in 1000.

Whatever about these space oddities, fireballs are relatively common. There are currently 10,000 reports from around the world of the phenomenon's weird behaviour and meteorologist **Peter Van Doorn** has reported several incidents of what appear to be ball lightning in Ireland.

In 1697 the residents of Athlone witnessed a 'great round body of fire' falling from a 'fiery cloud'. The subsequent explosion destroyed the town's bastion (a stronghold where citizens sheltered during a battle) and killed seven people.

Also, according to Van Doorn – who discovered Fitzgerald's account in the archives – in 1895 a boy saw a bright, round object near his house on the Inishowen peninsula. Some of the fireball broke off and hit him, resulting in injuries that necessitated the amputation of two fingers and part of his thumb.

These are two extreme cases, but the kind of damage inflicted on the Glendowan bog is unprecedented, which is why there is so much scientific interest in it. VanDevender's black hole explanation cuts no ice with many of his fellow scientists, some of whom believe that if one had hit Donegal it would have sucked up everything in its path in far less time than ten minutes. Others believe that it would have eaten the entire island of Ireland, possibly even the planet. These things are supposed to be all-consuming after all. 'You cannae change the laws of physics,' as Scotty might whinge, adding in this instance, 'for peat's sake, Cap'n'.

Until someone comes up with a better idea, the Glendowan bog in Donegal is still the Best Place To Walk Into A Black Hole.

As all good scientific theories have to have a name, and this one concerns turf, let's label it 'Sod's Law'.

Best Place For 4,000-Year-Old Organ Music

Archaeologists monitoring the building of a residential development in Wicklow in 2004 discovered what could be the oldest wooden musical instrument in the world.

The find consisted of six loose, graded pipes, five of which lay side by side at the bottom of a wood-lined cooking pit or *fulacht fiadh* in **Charlesland, Greystones**. The largest of them was over 50 cm long and experts believe they may have originally been joined together. A wooden peg used in the construction of the trough lining has been carbon dated to between 2120 BC and 2085 BC, indicating that the instrument may be 4,000 years old – nearly as old as Twink.

The lovingly-crafted pipes, which are made of yew wood, don't have finger holes like a flute or whistle, but appear to be part of a set and were attached to something that has rotted away over the millennia. They're a one-of-a-kind find, unparalleled anywhere, and archaeologists believe they may have been a multi-flute instrument or pipe organ.

Much older Neolithic bone flutes have been discovered in the past, but they are nowhere near as sophisticated as this set. The pipes are not the only prehistoric wooden instruments to have been found in Ireland – there is also a set of four curved pipes from Killyfadda, Co. Tyrone (400 BC); County Mayo's Bekan Horn (AD 700); and a conical wooden horn found in the River Erne in Co. Fermanagh (AD 700). There are also some beautiful examples of Bronze and Iron Age cast horns in the National Museum. There might be something Freudian in this horn stuff. Feel free to speculate.

Initial experiments on the pipes showed that they generated the notes E flat, A flat and F natural. Interestingly, D natural – a mere semitone down from E flat – is the most popular key for playing modern traditional Irish music on the Uileann pipes. However, it's unlikely that this was part of a bagpipe as it doesn't have a blowpipe (called a chanter) and the pipes were laid out in a way to suggest that this was not the case. Some think the Wicklow find may be a pan-pipe but most veer towards the belief that it is the oldest wooden organ in the world.

Erindipity Rides Again is with the majority on this and as far as we're concerned Greystones is the Best Place For 4,000-Year-Old Organ Music in the world.

Let's finish here with the following thought: if rock was all the rage in the Stone Age, then Bronze Age man was heavily into Metal. Except for our Wicklow organist, who was into Piped Music.

INTERESTING FACT

• The second-best place for musical old fossils is Ballsbridge in Dublin 4. Jury's cabaret jigged and reeled for approximately 3,000 years before the site on which it stood was sold for a record-breaking €260million in 2005. Many legends surround this venerable old place where captured tourists were tortured by grey-haired old men in tuxedos singing lyrics like 'Tahhh a nyellow ribbannn nround de ole oak treeeeeeee' while washing an imaginary window.

Best Place To Get Stoned

Earlier in this book, the morals of the people of County Clare were called into question and impugned – possibly unfairly, possibly not. People in glasshouses shouldn't throw stones etc. and so forth – certainly not if they live in the aforementioned county.

The residents of Corofin in North Clare are the greatest stoners on the planet, hosting as they do, the annual **World Stone Throwing Championships**. Every May the tranquillity of the Burren is shattered by the sound of smashing glass as the locals hurl rocks at (empty) bottles behind the Inchiquin Inn.

The event was dreamed up in 2000 by publican **John Campbell** and veteran journalist **Cormac MacConnell** after downing a few pints. The former schoolmates decided it would make a good fund-raiser for RTÉ's *Telethon*, and MacConnell now occupies the exalted role of President of the Stone-Throwing Association of Ireland.

There are ladies' and gents' events. Competitors each pay €5 for five stones and fling them from twelve yards at a bottle, upside down on a pole. The bottles, not the competitors, are stuck on the pole, lest there be any confusion – although with the amount of gargling and good-natured mayhem it's not inconceivable that someone could be left 'up the pole' after the event.

Once an entrant has broken the bottle, they progress to the next round and so on to the final. The stones are not hewn from the Burren, should you be concerned about conservation issues, but are brought from the beach, appropriately, in a barrel. Netting behind the target stops them going 'thither and yon', as they say in Clare.

Despite the sport being little more than a fledgling one it has attracted participants from Glasgow, Chicago, Germany and London, and hundreds of spectators throng the back of the pub to witness this unique charitable event.

There are no breathalysers or doping tests to ruin the competitors' flow and, according to publican Campbell, 'as long as they are able to stand up, we let them participate'. Most, though, take the sport quite seriously and prefer to play in a relatively sober state.

If you ever wish to watch dozens of men, deep in concentration, fingering their rocks behind a pub, then Corofin is the place for you.

Worst Place For Snubbing Bono

Let's put one thing on the record here: *Erindipity Rides Again* is an unashamedly Bono-friendly zone. His music is top-notch, he does great work for the poor and he's an all-round decent skin.

Not that that matters to **Canadian Prime Minister, Stephen Harper**. The self-proclaimed U2 fan refused to meet the singer at the G8 summit in June 2007, saying he was too busy to discuss the African AIDS crisis with him. 'Meeting celebrities isn't my shtick,' he told the press. 'That was the shtick of the previous guy.' Harper's comments inadvertently helped Bono's cause as the snub generated far more column inches than a meeting would ever have done.

Another snub that probably bothered his Bononess a lot less was delivered earlier in the year and led to a little confusion concerning a legendary singing duo. In February, politicians in North Dakota, USA rejected a resolution to honour the Killiney resident for his fight for debt relief for impoverished nations. The move had been sponsored by State Representative Scot Kelsh who said the issue was something that mattered to the 'citizens of North Dakota, the United States, and the world at large'. Despite these fine pronouncements the motion was defeated 58–35.

Of the ninety-three lawmakers who voted, one proved that politicians can't, by their nature, ever be 'cool' no matter how much they claim to be 'in touch' or 'down with the kids'. Republican Gil Herbert admitted he originally thought the resolution was to honour an older, hippier, 60s-style Bono – **Cher's** former husband and singing partner, Sonny Bono.

Gil hadn't considered the fact that Sonny would find it difficult to personally accept the award as he is now Sonny Bono RIP.

Talk about getting the wrong end of the shtick.

Most and Least

Most Electrifying Night With A Little Pussy

The cheetahs of County Cork may be fast and dangerous, but they're no match for the moggies of Louth when it comes to making lightning-fast moves.

In 2007 **Fota Island Wildlife Park** in the Rebel County introduced a novel scheme to rouse their lazy cheetahs and put a little zip back into their step. In the wild these graceful animals reach speeds of up to 100 kph for about twenty seconds while they're hunting, so the staff decided to make a 'cheetah run' and get them working for their dinner. They now tie dead rabbits and chickens to a rope suspended from an overhead cable in the cats' pen and the cheetahs have to chase and catch their supper as it flies back and forth. They don't hit the 100 kph mark, but they get a good workout nonetheless and can boast that they are the only creatures in Ireland eating fast food that actually makes them lose weight. Or at least they would say that if they could. They're cats after all, and cats aren't renowned for their sense of humour. Although they sometimes look as if they're smiling, or grinning (like the Chesire cat). Maybe they are smiling. Who knows? All of this has nothing whatsoever to do with the Most Electrifying Night With A Little Pussy other than to highlight the fact that Cork's big cats are better able to cope with overhead cables than their distant cousins in Louth.

In January 2007, 20,000 homes in Louth and Meath were plunged into darkness after an explosion at the **Drybridge** substation in **Drogheda**. The unprecedented event was seen 16 kilometres away and caused a blackout which took two hours to repair.

The ESB launched an enquiry amid fears that vandals had been behind the blast, but the culprit turned out to be a tom cat who had evidently believed he was on life number seven when he decided to take a look inside the substation. Felix probably sat down and gave his balls a good, celebratory lick after he managed to evade the plant's tight security. It's possible even that, drunk on this considerable achievement, he decided to do a tightrope-walk on a high-voltage cable to

> It's possible even that, drunk on this considerable achievement, Felix decided to do a tightrope-walk on a high-voltage cable to impress some lady friend . . . It was to prove, quite literally, an electrifying performance.

impress some lady friend watching from outside the compound. It was to prove, quite literally, an electrifying performance.

Later, his friends would say power went to Felix's head. It also went to his legs, ears, whiskers and, most definitely, up his hole. When the ESB researchers examined his remains they concluded that he had been, at 4 kg, a fat cat, which is curiously appropriate for one who had so much power at his toe tips.

There may be a lesson to be learned in all of this: if you give a cat an overhead cable in Cork you'll get a dinner date, but give one to a cat in Louth and you'll wind up with some hot pussy at the end of the evening.

Or maybe not.

Most Popular Place To Get A Brazilian

To carry on the *Carry On* tone of the previous entry, it might interest you to know that The Most Popular Place To Get A Brazilian is **Gort, Co Galway**. According to Census 2006, the population of that bustling burgh on the western seaboard is 2,646 and one third of it is Brazilian. Per capita, Gort is the Brazilian capital of Ireland. The soccer-mad, samba-dancing South Americans make up the vast majority of the percentage of the town that is non-national – 40.7%. That figure makes it the Most Cosmopolitan Small Town In Ireland, beating by a couple of points Ballyhaunis in County Mayo, whose population of 1,632 is 36.6% foreign.

Signs in Gort's shops are written in both English and Portuguese, and the Portuguese language has been put on the curriculum of the local school.

Since 2003 the town has hosted its own Brazilian carnival for the traditional festival of Quadrilha and every year the streets team with gyrating bodies, bumping and grinding. Think mart day on Viagra.

The South Americans originally came over to work in Sean Duffy's meat plant after he travelled to Brazil and brought back a handful of skilled people. In time the population grew as the Brazilians brought over their families and extended families and these spread out to work in other parts of the town. Money wiring company, Western Union, has even set up a branch in Gort because the immigrant workers send a large amount of euros back home each week.

Roscommon County is also a Hiberno-Brazilian utopia, with an estimated 10% of its 58,770 population coming from the Central Brazilian State of Goias. The total Brazilian population in the Republic of Ireland is 4,388.

Apart from a beef trade responsible for the deforestation of the Amazon, Brazil is famous for its passionate love affair with soccer and bestowing upon the world the magnificent Edson Arantes do Nascimento, otherwise known as Pelé. It's only a matter of time before a Brazilian togs out for the Roscommon football team. If he does, he can call himself 'Cluiche Pelé'.

INTERESTING FACT

- Gort is also the name of the robot in the 1951 science fiction classic movie *The Day the Earth Stood Still*, played by 2.34 m (7 ft 7 in) tall actor Lock Martin. Film geeks love to greet each other with the film's most famous line: 'Gort! Klaatu barada nikto!' which may translate as 'Gort? What the hell are we doing in Gort?? I said Milky Way, not bleeding *Gal*way'.

- Roscommon may love Brazil's meat workers, but in August 2007 it declared war on its beef. The Chairperson of Roscommon Irish Farmers Association Livestock Committee and local Fine Gael Deputy Denis Naughton, criticised the government after it was revealed that Brazilian beef was used in Irish Army ration packs. Why, asked Deputy Naughton, was beef from a country with traceability problems good enough for Irish soldiers, but not acceptable to the armies of the US, Japan, New Zealand and Australia? Clearly, he wasn't mincing his words.

Most Provocative Name

First, here's a selection from Dublin: Stillorgan, Lad Lane, Tonlegee Road (say it with a French accent), Glasthule (gentle with that, Maisie), Bushy Park, Diddywank

Avenue, Mount Street and Butt Bridge. The rest of the country: Termonfeckin (Louth), Effin (Limerick), Hackballscross (Louth), Nobber (Meath), Furry Glen (Wicklow), Cocktown (Wexford), Bastardstown (Wexford), Muff (Donegal) and let's not forget the river Suck (Roscommon). Alright, there's no such place as Diddywank Avenue but Dublin did once have a Gropecunt Lane, right up to the Victorian era. It was near the Savoy cinema and before you fling this book away in disgust, this was quite a common place name in the Middle Ages and could be found in most English-speaking towns in Britain and Ireland. The name was given to an area where prostitutes plied their trade. London's Gropecunt Lane was near the present-day site of the city's Barbican Centre and was renamed Grub Street in the eighteenth century. Oxford's became Grope Lane and then Grove Lane.

As vulgarity is in the eye of the beholder *Erindipity Rides Again* can only suggest that the following is Ireland's Most Provocative Place Name – Blue Ball in the county of Offaly. Remarkably, this painfully-named hamlet is only a stone's throw away from another singularly named location – Geeshill. Perhaps the person who named Blue Ball did so after straining himself while racing up the hill. Whether he caught any geese is a matter purely for conjecture.

Least Arousing/Most Generous Place Names

Kilcock (County Kildare) and Shercock (County Cavan).

Most Threatened Slimeball

One hundred and fifty of Ireland's native species have been placed on the 'Facing Extinction' list because of the pace and scale at which the countryside is changing. Property developers, road builders, farmers and foresters have all been targeted by the government as we attempt to come into line with the UN convention on sustaining biodiversity by 2010. Seeing as how property developers and farmers are generally to be found snuggled up to Fianna Fáil – which as the senior government party is also responsible for roads and forests – cynics might be excused for snorting 'hypocrisy' at these 'get tough' plans.

Building and bad farming practices (pesticides, pollution etc.) are damaging enough, but environmentalists have warned that the massive forestation of the non-native Sitka spruce tree is also destroying wildlife and bogland. In 2007 it was pointed out to the Government that for Sitka spruce planting to be economically viable, it requires huge blocks of 'clearfell'. Clearfelling means cutting down almost all the existing trees, bulldozing and burning the undergrowth and replanting an even-aged crop of a selected species (for example, Sitka spruce). This is disastrous news for the resident flora and fauna. In the case of Irish bogs, according to the European Environmental Agency (EEA)

84% of forest plantation between 1990–2000 was on peatland.

Among the best-known creatures that are most at risk from all this chopping and changing are:
- The otter, which is now rare in mainland Europe.
- Native red squirrels, which are being bumped off by grey squirrels and deforestation/reforestation.
- The barn owl and . . .
- the Kerry spotted slug.

So threatened is the **Kerry spotted slug** that in 2007 a major bypass was re-routed by Environment Minister **John Gormley** to save a woodland directly in its path containing the little slimers. Cascade Woods would have been destroyed had the bypass of **Ballyvourney** in County Cork (part of the Macroom bypass) been built along the selected route. It was a bold move by the Green Party minister who had been unable to save the Tara Skryne valley from the National Roads Authority. This may yet prove to be too little too late as the slug is still officially endangered and may soon vanish from our fields and woods. Imagine generations of Irish children not knowing what the Kerry spotted slug looked like? (Spotted, sluggish.) It's all very well for the cuddly, wuddly otters, the wise-old owls and big-eyed, look-at-me-I'm-soooooooooooo-cute squirrels of this island. They've had films and books made about them (*Ring of Bright Water* (1969), *Squirrel Nutkin*, *The Legend of Barney The Owl* to name but three), but who is going to champion the Kerry spotted slug? Who will lull little kiddies to sleep with tales of its woodland adventures?

Who will fill their Christmas stockings with stuffed Kerry Spotted Slug toys? Every year countless numbers of these little crawlers wind up Slugtoxed in the gardens of Kerry. It's time now for a proper, national campaign (newspaper editors please note) to keep this unique Munster slug from disappearing from the landscape. Public awareness must be raised, slug pellets should be banned and cabbage patches thrown open to these oily little marvels, which are normally only found in the north of Spain and Portugal. Could it be that some ancient, migrating Celt-Iberian landed in Kerry thousands of years ago with a pair of pet slugs in his pocket? Could they have mated and had loads of baby slugs? Could the Kerry spotted slug be The Most Celtic Of Irish Slugs? Whatever about that, *Geomalacus maculosus* (to give it its Latin name) has another claim to fame: it's the only slug in the world capable of rolling itself into a ball and sticking its head up its backside. For this reason alone Ireland's Most Threatened Slimeball should be rescued from the brink of extinction.

Other beasties at risk of vanishing are nine species of our bats, including the tiny pipistrelle which weighs no more than 6 g, the yellowhammer bird, the black-necked grebe, the red-necked phalarope (a real bogger of a bird), the nightjar (sounds like a Victorian commode), the quail, the corncrake and the curlew. Another reason for our native fliers being at risk can be found in the following section . . .

Least Money Needed To Pick Up A Bird

€20 is all it takes to get your hands on a pair of tits (at a tenner each) down one Dublin market.

Let's stop here for just a moment.

Erindipity Rides Again would like to apologise for causing any offence with the opening sentence of this piece. It was silly, juvenile, vulgar and obvious. In mitigation, it was a poor attempt at lightening the mood as the next few paragraphs aren't very uplifting. Bear with them though, as there's a happy ending. Now please continue reading (at your leisure, of course) . . .

A bullfinch will set you back €25, while redpolls, chaffinches and siskins are making up to €15 in the capital's trade in wild songbirds. Thousands of these creatures are captured each year during the months of September and April to feed (not literally) a huge demand both here and abroad, particularly in Belgium and Spain. Trappers use cages or nets to catch their warbling prey, which, in the main, die of shock once they have been made captive. One method used to stop the caged creatures flapping around and injuring themselves is to glue their claws to the perch while they feed. Despite this callous trade being illegal, one *Sunday Times* writer reported seeing hawkers selling them openly at Bride Street Market in Dublin's Liberties in the opening months of 2007. A year earlier the son of a prominent Dublin businessman was fined €800 after wildlife rangers swooped on his home and found dozens of songbirds, caged or trapped in netting.

While loss of habitat is absolutely responsible for the decline in the numbers of wild songbirds – bullfinches have seen their population fall by more than half in the past thirty years – poachers can shoulder the blame as well.

Happily, one noisy bird who was taken from his habitat by a birdnapper lived to tell the tale. **Cheeky the parrot** – or Green Conure to be precise – is the only bird on record to have been abducted and subsequently talk its way to freedom.

The thirteen-year-old bird disappeared from his home in the St Mary's Park area of Limerick and for almost a week Gardaí sought high and low for him (more high rather than low – he is a bird after all) to no avail. Evidently unhappy with being separated from his family for so long, Cheeky – who was being held only a kilometre away – decided to take matters into his own claws. Spotting a passer-by from the window of the house where he was being held captive, he began squawking out his owner's name and generally roaring his head off. The pedestrian, who was a local person, twigged who he was and called the Gardaí who sped to Cheeky's rescue. As five burly officers stormed the house Cheeky's nerve went and he flew the coop screeching 'Mary! Mary!' and intermittently telling the pursuing Gardaí to 'f*** off' (one of his favourite expressions). The plucky parrot was eventually caught and brought home where he immediately began calling out for his beloved mistress again. It was all very heartwarming indeed.

His owner later said that Cheeky, who has sixty phrases, is like his name suggests and that the fearless parrot would 'say anything'. Some of the phrases he most frequently employs are 'I love you', 'Get away' and the aforementioned 'F*** off' – although not necessarily all at the same time. He also says 'Hello' and 'Cheeky wants a cracker'.

We will now round off this piece about birds and thieves with a reference to one of the strangest things ever to be found in a prison raid. While officers at **Portlaoise** were searching cells during a clampdown on contraband in May 2007, they uncovered drugs, home-made alcohol, mobile phones . . . and a budgie.

The authorities were relieved to find that bird had not been smuggled in secreted in somebody's posterior – the normal route for contraband into jail.

In that case they would have been dealing with a stool pigeon.

INTERESTING FACT

- The Kerry spotted slug isn't the only Hiberno/Spanish item on the extinction list. The rare strawberry tree, which grows on the fringes of woodland in Killarney is also under threat. It hails from the Atlantic side of the Iberian peninsula and is the only Irish tree that's not also a native of Britain. Ironically, one of the tree's main predators is the . . . Kerry spotted slug.

145

Most Irish Of Caribbean Islands

The island of **Montserrat** is known as The Emerald Isle of the Caribbean, has a shamrock carved above the door of the governor's home, places called Kinsale and Cork and people named O'Garra and Riley. It's flag and crest bear the symbol of Erin holding a harp and a passion cross and your passport will be stamped with a green shamrock on arrival there. It even hosts a Paddy's Day parade. On top of this, the non-stop sunshine and sunny demeanour of its inhabitants definitely make it the Most Irish of Caribbean Islands. (That's sarcasm, by the way.)

This sunny Paradise of Paddywhackery was settled in the 1600s by Irishers from the nearby islands of St Kitts and Nevis. They said they were escaping from anti-Catholic sectarianism but the other St Kitts dwellers claimed they booted them out after growing tired of their incessant groaning about the weather and non-stop Irish dancing. This was a gross calumny of course, but nonetheless the very Irish tradition of going on and on and on about the weather persists on Montserrat to this day.

The truth is that the Irish, who were badly-treated indentured servants, became

> **This sunny Paradise . . . was settled in the 1600s by Irishers from the nearby islands of St Kitts and Nevis . . . the other dwellers claimed they booted them out after growing tired of their incessant groaning about the weather and non-stop Irish dancing.**

unwelcome on St Kitts and Nevis because they shared the same religion as the Spanish and the French – Protestant England's enemies. In 1632 a British chap called Thomas Warner left those twin islands for Montserrat with Irish – and English – Catholics and their new home became renowned as a safe haven for Papists from North America as well as the rest of the colonies. By 1648, there were one thousand Irish families on the island. The following year **Oliver Cromwell** did his bit to boost the population by sending over prisoners captured after his massacre at Drogheda to be slaves in the plantations.

Anti-Irishness and outright cruelty continued for years and the servants still living in St Kitt's revolted in 1666 with the Montserrat Paddies following suit in 1667. The French took the island twice – in 1644 and 1782 – but ceded it for good to England in 1783.

The Irish hung in there over the centuries, surviving tropical storms such as the 1989 monster, Hurricane Hugo, and the 1997 eruption of the Soufrière Hills volcano which devastated the island and forced the evacuation of 90% of the population.

The first decade of the Noughties has seen Montserrat getting slowly back on its feet as a tourist destination, where many come to witness a St Patrick's Day parade of particularly powerful significance.

Montserrat is the only country besides Ireland to have Paddy's Day as its national holiday. It is also the only Caribbean country with an Irish heritage. However, the festivities commemorate more than the island's Irishness.

For the majority of Monserratians they mark a tragic defeat – that of the African slaves who died there in an abortive rebellion on St Patrick's Day, 1768. Three-quarters of Montserrat's 4,000 population are descended from these Africans and their descendants who were forced to work (like Cromwell's Irish) in the island's sugar fields. The first of these slaves landed in 1651.

They had been bought by an Irishman.

INTERESTING FACT

- Apart from slavery and shamrocks, two other lasting aspects of Montserrat's Irish legacy are a dance (called bam-chick-lay) and the national dish. The latter is goat water, which is a meat dish flavoured with herbs and 'chibble' (thyme and scallions). Apparently it's a bit like Irish stew.

Most Lawless Island

Inis Óirr is the smallest of the three Aran islands, the other two being Inis Mór and Inis Meáin. There's not much to do there except build stone walls, talk about fish, shelter from the rain, talk about fish, knit an Aran jumper and talk about fish. This lack of anything better to do is probably why, in 1975, the island suffered a complete breakdown in public order and became the Most Lawless Irish Island. According to the State Papers for that year, locals petitioned their TDs and the Minister for Justice to provide more Gardaí to stamp out late night drinking and antisocial behaviour during the peak tourist season. At the time 275 people resided on the island, but this figure swelled in the summer months creating monstrous problems, they said.

The Gardaí at Cill Rónáin on Inis Mór also wrote to the commissioner about their difficulties in solving crimes committed on this veritable Van Diemen's Land of the western seaboard. What was to be done? The place was going to hell on a Honda 50.

Absolutely nothing, came the reply from the chief of police, who said the island didn't need a Garda station. This was because official records show that the amount of crimes reported for the first half of 1975 was ... one. And that was for looking lewdly at a herring.

The story doesn't end there, however. The state of affairs on Inis Óirr preyed on the minds of Inis Mór's diligent crime-busters to such an extent that twenty-one years later they carried out the most unusual undercover operation ever staged on the island. In 1996 the Seanad was told of this operation, which sounded like a scene straight out of Father Ted. Senator Billy Kelleher told his incredulous colleagues that a Garda had recently got on the ferry to the island disguised as a backpacker. After setting up his tent and his groundsheet for the evening, Deep Cover Cop donned his uniform and strode into town where he raided three pubs for late night drinking. Presumably, he then returned to his tent for the rest of the night, which would have taken some courage as tents may provide ample protection from the rain, but where speeding tractors are concerned, they aren't much help.

Senator Kelleher added that 'nobody condones people staying in pubs all night, but the vast majority of people would suggest, as would Gardaí if the matter was left to their discretion, that raiding a pub on the Aran Islands is not a priority'.

Nor for that matter would be raiding Inis Rath island on Lough Erne, which happens to be Ireland's . . .

Least Dangerous Island

Even during the Troubles in the mid–1980s this little corner of **County Fermanagh** was a haven of peace and tranquillity. Its inhabitants don't drink or smoke, are strictly vegetarian and have strange haircuts. They spend their day in prayer or tending to the organic vegetables that are grown on the 6.8-hectare island. Yes, they're monks – but not of the Christian variety. **Inis Rath** island is the spiritual centre for Ireland's 350-strong Hare Krishna community. Only six people live on it, along with a dog (Kali das), some moggies, a clatter of peacocks and any amount of wild deer and hare (the luckiest and safest creatures in the country), but during daytime this number swells as pilgrims are ferried over from the mainland to attend religious services at the temple.

Hare Krishnas started appearing on Dublin's streets back in the 1970s where their saffron coloured robes and chanting of the Harinam raised a few eyebrows. Their number has remained constant and, as Ireland has changed, they're no longer regarded as tambourine-waving nutters but are generally respected for their peace-loving brand of Hinduism.

The **Hare Krishnas** bought a 12-hectare site, which included the island, back in the 1980s for €200,000 – a knockdown price courtesy of the Troubles. Most devotees live on the mainland part of the area.

The daily routine revolves around services and the worship room has statues of Rada and Govinda. These are treated as if they were the gods themselves and, accordingly, there are rules to be obeyed about how the worshippers interact with them. It's frowned upon to have one's back turned to them and it's forbidden to touch them unless you've just had a bath.

The first of seven of the day's services takes place at 4.30 a.m. These are called 'aarti' and last for a couple of hours, so when one is complete, it's nearly time to start the next. When the 6.30 p.m. service is finished, the mainland Hare Krishnas are ferried home and the inhabitants eat their evening meal and go to bed after the 8.30 p.m. service.

Unsurprisingly, the island has never been raided for after-hours drinking.

INTERESTING FACT

- In 1990 Boy George, whose parents hail from Tipperary, cited Hare Krishna as one of the factors that helped him overcome heroin addiction.

Most Clamped Street

Nowhere on the planet does officialdom enjoy torturing motorists more than in Ireland's capital city. Take, for example, the Rock Road in **Booterstown**, County Dublin. In 2006, traffic on this main artery to Dublin's southside was brought to a virtual standstill for the best part of a year during the construction of a new bus corridor and cycle lane. Every morning frustrated drivers were treated to the sight of breakfast rolls and builders' cracks as they sat in their stationary cars. When the corridor was finally opened at the end of July 2007, the same frustrated drivers passed the time in their stationary cars counting the number of cyclists and buses using it – on one hand. This scenario didn't last for long though. Soon after, those motorists were passing the time in their stationary cars counting the number of cyclists and buses on one hand and enjoying once more the sight of breakfast rolls and builders' cracks as work commenced on a new road-widening scheme to alleviate the traffic jams caused by the new bus corridor and cycle lane.

When Dublin drivers aren't being confined to their cars for hours or being forced out of the bus lane by a taxi driver[15] after making a dash for freedom, they're being taxed, fined and tolled into submission. At the start of 2006, **Pay and Display** began creeping out through the suburbs and has now become a handy way of extracting money from, say, a son or a daughter visiting their parents in net-curtain land. These P & D meters earned the council €26.9million in 2006, €1.5million more than the previous year.

Is there some evil genius at work here?

Of all the instruments of torture officialdom employs, none is more horrible than the clamp. The nationwide practice of disabling a person's car and making them pay for the privilege of freeing it was abolished in Galway in 2006 after a series of public relations nightmares. In one incident, a clamper actually refused to remove a clamp from a car outside a doctor's surgery so that a father could take a sick child to hospital.

Evidently, western officials are pussycats compared to their counterparts in Dublin, who thrive on clamping, which they first introduced in 1998. In the same year, 57,390 vehicles were clamped in the capital netting fines worth €4.5million. Overall, the number of vehicles clamped in 2006 had increased by 14% compared to the figure for 2005 (50,118). This raises two questions: had the message not got through to Dublin drivers about illegal parking or had the Nazi-like clampers become

---

[15] Why should taxi men be allowed to use the city's Quality Bus Corridors? After all, they're private enterprise making money out of a public traffic system. The drivers stuck in traffic are also attempting to make a living by getting in to work on time, which means leaving home earlier and working later to avoid the snarl-ups.

more enthusiastic about their job?

The latter appears to be the case for the ones operating on North Great George's Street. At time of publishing, that stretch of thoroughfare was the Most Clamped Street In The Capital according to the council's own figures, released under the Freedom of Information Act (it was also top of the charts back in 2003).

In June of 2006 the street's most colourful resident, **Senator David Norris** (the scholar and gay rights activist) told the Seanad during a debate on a road traffic bill that, on two occasions, his neighbours were clamped although they had a visible, valid ticket and were within their time limit. (That's his neighbours' car, not the neighbours themselves.) Although the clampers had taken a picture of the car they refused to show it to the driver, saying they had no right to see it. The driver then pointed out that the ticket was in the car and inside the time, but was then told the ticket could have been bought at any other time and just placed there. This is, of course, a steaming pile of goat's poo, as parking tickets are printed with the time of purchase. On the two occasions the car owner had no choice but to pay up.

At this point you probably expect some cheap gag about Senator Norris not being a happy camper or a reference to some fictitious Pinewood comedy called *Carry On Clamping*. *Erindipity Rides Again* is pleased to announce that no such jokes were contemplated in the composing of this piece.

Should you be thinking of driving in Dublin and don't wish to be tempted to use a clamp on a clamper's privates, then here are the Top Ten Most Clamped Streets:

1. North Great George's Street
2. D'Olier Street
3. Burgh Quay
4. Clarendon Street
5. Hume Street
6. Noel Purcell Walk
7. Synge Street
8. Dawson Street
9. Smithfield
10. South Circular Road

INTERESTING FACT

- The official handbook of Dublin's clampers is titled *Mein Clampf*.

Most Struck Railway Bridge

It is probably fair to say that one doesn't need to be a rocket scientist to become a lorry driver. Grab yourself a licence, a country and western CD, a Yorkie bar and a GPS and away you go. The other good thing about being a lorry driver is that you can call yourself Tex or Chuck or Deke and affect an American accent and nobody will bat an eyelid. This is because many people automatically presume that lorry drivers are selfish, road-hogging, delusional gobdaws. This is unfair as the majority are not.

Those who are, however, are ineluctably attracted to the nation's bridges.

> The IRA may have attacked and damaged the Customs House during the War of Independence, but they were mere amateurs when compared to the gallant truckers who regularly bombard the Dart bridge across the road from it.

Incredible as it may seem 743 oversized lorries ploughed, scraped and sheared their way into, through and under the country's railway bridges between May 2001 and May 2007.

Most of these strikes occurred in Dublin city with the **East Wall Bridge** being a favourite target of these dozy truckers. It was hit 104 times over eighteen years until its height was increased from 4.6 m to 5.3 m in 2003.

The IRA may have attacked and damaged the Customs House during the War of Independence, but they were mere amateurs when compared to the gallant truckers who regularly bombard the Dart bridge across the road from it. The Loop Line, as it is known, has been struck approximately eighty times in the past decade. The council have even considered renaming it Loopers' Line bridge after the morons who keep bashing into it.

In 2006 it was hit sixteen times and there were thirty-six other strikes on the rest of the Dart line.

The top four rail bridges that suffered the most in Dublin over a ten-year period from 1998 to 2007 were:

1. Custom House Quay
2. Sandwith Street (between Pearse and Grand Canal Dock)
3. South Lotts Road (between GCD and Lansdowne)
4. Erne St (between Pearse and GCD)

Dublin may be the city with the Most Struck Railway Bridges in the country, but the county with the Most Struck Railway Bridge (singular) for 2007 is Laois. On Thursday 17 September a truck carrying large rolls of paper completely demolished the bridge over the **Mountrath Road in Portlaoise**. The genius at the wheel somehow didn't seem to notice some of his paper rolls and the sides of his oversized vehicle being ripped off as it continued through the archway, like the motorised equivalent of a giant Andrex puppy. This was the bridge's sixteenth strike of the year, but its torment wasn't going to end there.

The following Tuesday, as surveyors were scratching their head in bewilderment at the monumental (with the emphasis on mental) stupidity of the lorry driver, the bridge (or rather what remained of it) was struck again.

It's a rare talent to be able to crash into a bridge that isn't even there any more.

The top three reasons for crashing into railway bridges are:

1. Altitude sickness from sitting perched in a lofty cab.
2. Penis envy (tunnels, ramming etc.).
3. CB radio distraction.

There are those who believe that these bridge strikes are part of a low level al-Qaida campaign to disrupt

Ireland's transport system and ultimately its infrastructure.

If this is the case then it's in vain. Ireland has a long history of coping with rogue drivers and railway strikes.

Remember **Brendan Ogle and ILDA**, anyone? Ogle led the Irish Locomotive Drivers Association during an unsuccessful – and highly unpopular – ten-week strike for recognition in the summer of 2000. Some said the union's motives were, indeed, loco.

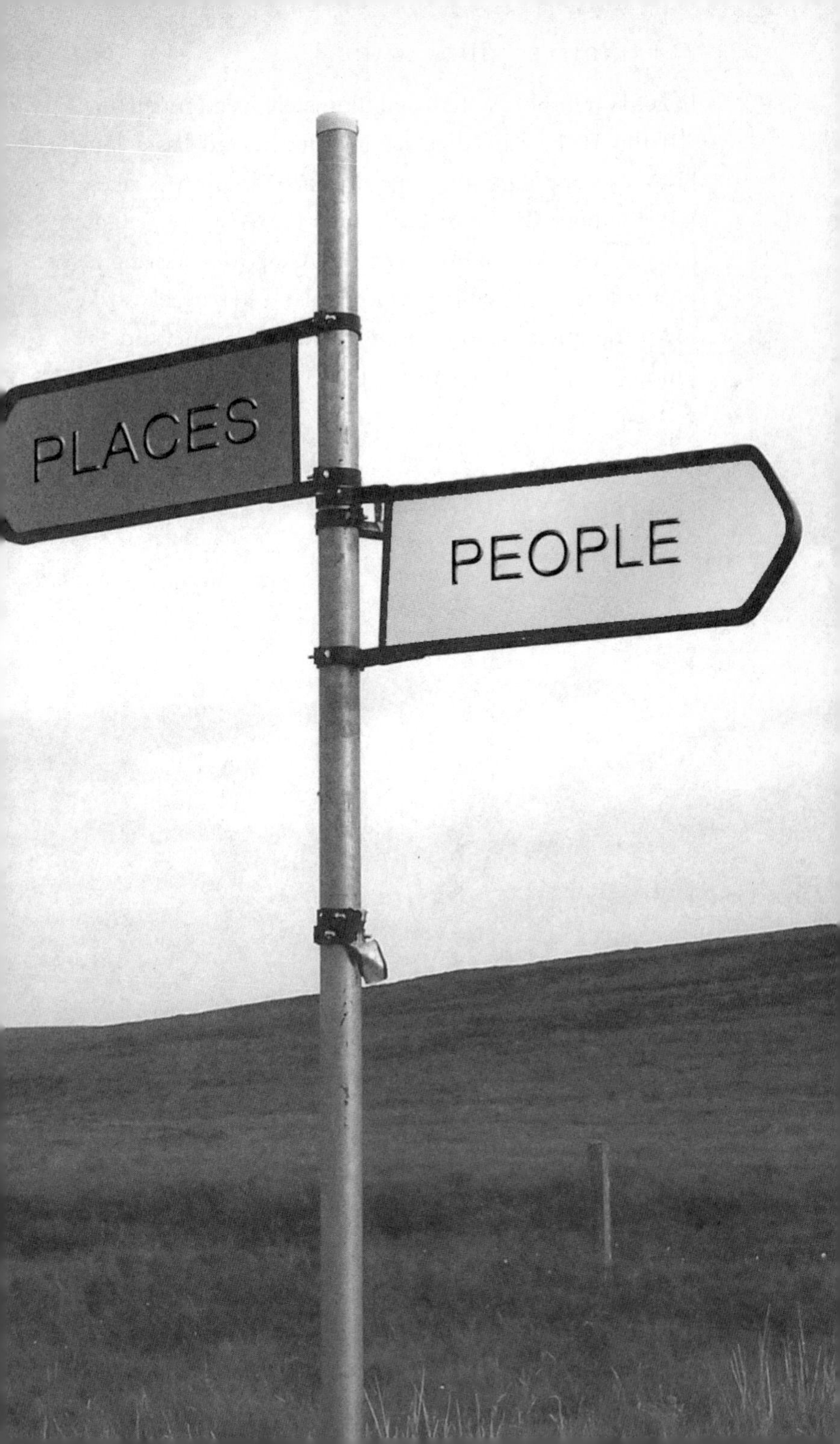
PLACES
PEOPLE

Best and Worst

Best Proverbs For Confusing People

For those of you employing the linear approach to reading this book (a straight run from start to finish) we say 'welcome to the People section'. To those of you who are Erindipping in and out, we say 'welcome back'.

If you have ever read any Sommerville and Ross novels (which you haven't, so stop lying) about the adventures of an Irish Resident Magistrate, then you will be aware that the Victorian Irish were great hoors for the fine proverb. Characters named Slipper and Flurry were forever coming out with fine phrases to sum up comic situations. The RM, played with aplomb by actor Peter Bowles in the enjoyable TV adaptations, wore a constantly confused/irritated expression as **Niall Toibin** or **Brian Murray** blathered and conspired to get one over on him. The following are some of the most confusing Irish proverbs that Sommerville and Ross may or may not have encountered. They're translated from the Irish and are genuine enough to be printed on tea towels, novelty aprons and mugs and sold at airports.

Wisha, put a little money away for a rainy day.
Why? What's so special about spending money on a rainy day compared to a sunny one? Besides, it rains every other day in some parts of Ireland, so you wouldn't have much money to spend if you were only saving on the few dry days of the year.

A change of work is as good as a rest.
Not if you're a civil servant starting a job as anything else, it isn't.

Idleness is a fool's desire.
May we refer you to the above civil servant?

One may live without one's friends, but not without one's pipe.
Sound advice for plumbers with sociopath tendencies, perhaps.

It's not a delay to stop and sharpen the scythe.
The grim reaper has, indeed, all the time in the world.

The dog that's always on the go will listen to the sound of the river and get a trout.
???

The day will come when the cow will have use for her tail.
As will the dog with the trout.

A spender gets the property of the hoarder.
Again we say: ?????

An ounce of breeding is worth a pound of feeding.
To be sure, to be sure.

It's a long way from penny apples . . .
Actually that's not a proverb, but it sounds like it should
be. It's the 2002 title of businessman Bill Cullen's
autobiography. Bill entered the Guinness Book of
Records for the **Largest Ever Book Signing** in 2005
when he signed 1,849 copies of his subsequent book
Golden Apples in Eason's of O'Connell Street, Dublin. He
beat the previous record by thirty-two books.

Worst Irish Customs

This section was originally intended to be a Top Ten of
our worst customs, but as this would be subjective, we
have decided to give you, the reader, the opportunity to
make up your own ascending/descending chart of
offenders. To achieve this aim the publisher has agreed to
an ingenious innovation which crosses new frontiers in
literary interactivity – the placing of a box beside each
entry into which you may place a number. For example,
if frog sucking is middling worst in your opinion, then
place the numeral 5 within the aforementioned box etc.
and so forth.

Spitting on babies
This charming custom still persists in parts of Galway and

Kerry. One writer describes how, thirty years ago, he observed an old woman being handed a newborn baby in the West and spitting on it for luck. The same applies to fair days when men of sound mind spit on coins – or luck money – after sealing a deal. Spitting on one's palms before shaking someone's hand is also considered the height of good manners in parts of rural Ireland.

Bilberry Sunday

This has almost completely died out, as most people have never heard of a bilberry. It was a special time of year when young women and their gentlemen admirers would go out into the countryside and pick bilberries. The couple that spent the longest time in the bushes searching for them and returned with the least amount would be married within nine months, the tradition went.

Llama wrestling (naked and/or clothed)

A very popular tradition practised on Midsummer's Eve, llama wrestling is believed to have originated in the 1920s especially in the Courtown area of the South East. Sometimes oil or raspberry jam is applied to the (human) wrestler's torso to make life more difficult for the llama.

Frog sucking

'Suck a frog before you break your fast, and your hangover will not last', the old County Fermanagh saying goes. It is unclear where this advice originated from, but many old men north of the border still believe that sucking a frog (toads are not as powerful) first thing in the morning will cure a sore head. This may have some sound scientific basis as placing a reptile in one's mouth is sure to have an immediate emetic effect. The subsequent bout of honking purges the sucker of the remnants of the previous night's boozing. Eminently preferable to the traditional medieval cure where the overhung person was buried up to their neck in badgers.

Cursing cakes ☐

St Columcille is credited with many things: promoting the spread of learning throughout these islands, being holy and cursing cakes – or rather, their bakers. Anyone who completely baked one side of a cake before the other side had a turn was in for some stick from the Saint. It's said that Columcille arrived at a house tired and hungry and asked for a slice of the bread that was baking before the fire. The woman of the house told him she couldn't give him any as only one side was baked, so he placed a curse on anyone who baked a cake in this manner. The unfortunate woman promised to regularly turn her loaves in future. Columcille knew what he was about as a flat loaf – or bannock – would end up misshapen and unevenly baked if it was not alternated. And while we're on the subject of half-baked, who came up with the custom of . . .

Leaving booze and mince pies out for Santa on Christmas Eve ☐

It's dangerous to encourage an old man to drink and fly. And the mince pies play havoc with his cholesterol. So stop it, you bad children.

Trick or treating for 'candy' ☐

The Irish exported the game of rounders to the

Americans over a century ago and they kept it, gave it some more rules, added some awful organ music and it became baseball. They tried to export the new version back to us and we said 'no thanks, we'll stick with the hurling'. We did the same with Hallowe'en, which the Yankees also loved and successfully exported back to us with a few tweaks. The original Hallowe'en was based on the old Celtic New Year's festival where the spirits would mingle with the living on the feast of Samhain. As they would regularly make off with the neighbourhood's children, parents deemed it necessary to dress their little girls up as boys and vice versa to confuse the ghosties. To make things even more confusing the children would then call at each other's hut asking for muesli for the Hallowe'en otter. 'Any apples or nuts? Any apples or nuts?' they would inquire in a spooky sing-song voice, before setting fire to their sacrificial 'Hallowe'en napkins'.

The Americans didn't like the fires and the breakfast cereal aspect of the festivities and so introduced pumpkins with candles in them and replaced 'any apples or nuts' with 'trick or treat'. Irish children just loved it and the custom persists to this day.

Dolores Keening

This is where a group of middle-aged women gather together to wail and screech about the disgraceful lack of treatment centres for women with low blood pressure. 'My heart-rate is low', they mournfully sing, 'as only a woman's heart-rate could be'. They then go on tour and make a lot of money.

Doing the Wren

This is a custom – which still makes the RTÉ TV news every Christmas – where grown men stuff straw down each others Y-fronts and wander around Dingle dressed as birds with a wren (made out of socks) on the end of a pole. These rugged cross-dressers are preceded by a belly dancer wearing the traditional ear muffs and wellies of the seancháí as they call at each house demanding money. If it is not forthcoming, they threaten to stick the pole 'up the hole' of the miser, who must then make them beans on toast. Sometimes the Wren Boys are confused with . .

The Straw Boys

One of the strangest customs of all can still be witnessed at winter weddings in the West of Ireland from time to time. This is the unannounced arrival of the Straw Boys during the festivities. These chaps appear wearing long straw hats that cover their faces and grab the bride up to dance before legging it back out the door. Nobody knows why they do this, as nobody has ever managed to catch one (drunk wedding guest versus young bloke wearing a straw wig? No contest. Unless he runs into a wall). One theory goes that the original Straw Boys were castle rustlers who stole bricks from stately homes after dark. When the bricks were hidden away (normally in another castle), they'd avoid capture by disguising themselves and sneaking into a wedding. There they would drink with the bride but never utter a word and disappear off into the night.

INTERESTING FACTS

- Handfasting is another Celtic custom that no longer exists. It was practiced in Ireland and Scotland up to relatively recently and was where a bride and groom's wrists were literally tied together at the start of the wedding ceremony. This is where the phrase 'tying the knot' comes from.

- Milkmaids in Monaghan and Donegal were taught to milk the first few squirts out of each teat on to the ground for the fairies to drink. If she didn't there would be reprisals (or at least an embarrassing scene involving raging fairies). This was good advice as there are many thousand times more microbes in the first yield than in the remaining milk. There was a similar custom where any food that fell to the floor during a meal should not be eaten. This was because a hungry fairy had plucked it from your hand. Again this was sound advice as eating off the average farmhouse floor was a bit like bobbing for apples in a septic tank. However, during lean times, if a large portion fell on the floor the country folk compromised by breaking off a small bit which was thrown away and the rest eaten. Hunger is good sauce, as your granny used to say.

Best Printer In A Rising

Erindipity Rides Again is delighted to introduce a very special man few of you may have heard of – **Matthew Walker.** This fine old gentleman was descended from the Walker family of Carlow/Kilkenny. These were planted landowners with ties to the Kilkenny militia, who fought on the winning side during the 1798 rebellion. As far as we can ascertain his father, Francis, broke with his family and set up business in Carlow town as a printer. One night as he was working late a fire broke out in the nearby convent of an enclosed order of nuns. He saved a young novice, breaking various rules about silence, which meant that she couldn't return to her order. Being a decent old skin he did the right thing by her – and put aside his Protestant faith to marry her. Thus started the Catholic branch of the Walker family, from which sprang Matthew and his rebellious brood.

Matthew was a member of the IRB (the Irish Republican Brotherhood, also known as the Fenians) who went along with the 'New Departure' of 1878, where the physical force revolutionaries agreed to support constitutional initiatives to secure Irish freedom. He became a friend of **Charles Stuart Parnell** and continued to support him after his long-term love affair with Kitty O'Shea, a married woman, became public and the people turned against him. He also set up the *Carlow Vindicator* newspaper to rally support for his leader. This greatly angered the local parish priest, who 'read' him from the pulpit. The venture ended in financial catastrophe and Matthew, who was the first Linotype operator in Ireland, and his family moved to Dublin where he continued to publish seditious Republican material in his new venture, *The Gaelic Press*. By the time of the Rising he had retired and passed *The Gaelic Press* on to his son-in-law, Joseph Stanley (remember this bit, it's important later on).

The apple doesn't fall far from the tree and the Walker children became active in the independence movement. The most famous of his offspring was Mary Walker, known better as **Máire nic Shiubhlaigh.** She was the first leading lady in the **Abbey Theatre** and led Cumann na mBan under Thomas MacDonagh in Jacobs during the Rising. In fact, on the day the Abbey opened, Máire played Cathleen ní Houlihan, her brother Frank played the young man in 'On Baile's Strand', her two sisters Anne and Patricia sold programmes in the auditorium and their mother Margaret was the wardrobe mistress. Maire later led a breakaway group from the Abbey and went on to form the Theatre of Ireland with the Pearse brothers, **Countess Marciewicz** and the main players of 1916, leaving the Abbey floundering for many years. Her portraits by **John Butler Yeats** hang in the bar of the current Abbey Theatre and in the National Gallery.

On Easter Monday morning 1916 Matthew and Máire received a telegram from **Eamonn Ceannt's** sister-in-law, Lily O'Brennan to 'Come at once'. The Rising they had been waiting for was taking place. Máire had spent the previous day with Lily at the Ceannts' and recalled how strained Eamonn looked as he bade her farewell for what would prove to be the final time. She put on her uniform and caught a tram to Dublin city. Then she retrieved her bicycle from South Richmond Street and headed off to where the action was. As she sped past Wellington Barracks a car skidded out of a side street and hit her, sending her flying. She was helped up by the driver, a young British soldier. When she refused his help (making vsure her coat was well fastened over her uniform) he followed her, pleading with her to let him take her to a doctor. Eventually he gave up, which was good luck for him because if he had continued to follow Máire to her final destination, which was the Jacob's garrison, he would have been in need of a doctor himself.

> . . . if he had continued to follow Máire to her final destination, which was the Jacob's garrison, he would have been in need of a doctor himself.

While all this was going on, Máire's little sister Patricia was racing around the city trying to get into one of the Republican strongholds. She didn't succeed but did spend the rest of the week carrying despatches.

Neither sister knew that their father was preparing to join the action himself . . .

It is at this point, dear reader, that we must take a little break from the narrative to point out that there are two schools of thought about what happened next. According to the 2005 book, *Joe Stanley – Printer to the Rising*, the eponymous hero made all the running in the following events. On the other hand, the Walker family tradition places Matthew at the helm of one of Ireland's most impressive printing jobs. *Erindipity Rides Again* is standing by the latter. Now let us resume . . .

After sending Máire off into Dublin to fight, Matthew now aged sixty–nine, walked all the way into town from Glasthule as the trams had stopped running. He demanded to be let through the cordons and made his way to the GPO. Once inside he told **Pádraig Pearse** that he wished to 'do his bit'. Pearse thanked him but asked him to go home on the grounds that he was too old to fight. Matthew insisted that he be given something to do as a fellow IRB man. Pearse grabbed a sheaf of typing paper and scribbled the following historic message:

Irish War News
The Irish Republic
Vol. 1, No. 1, Dublin, Tuesday April 25th, 1916.
Price One Penny.

Stop Press!
The Irish Republic

(Irish) War News is published today because a momentous thing has happened. The Irish Republic has been proclaimed in Dublin, and a Provisional Government has been appointed to administer its affairs. The following has been named as the Provisional Government: Thomas J. Clarke, Sean MacDiarmada, P. H. Pearse, James Connolly, Thomas MacDonagh, Eamonn Ceannt, Joseph Plunkett.

The Irish Republic was proclaimed by poster which was prominently displayed in Dublin. At 9.30 this morning the following statement was made by Commandant-General P. H. Pearse:

The Irish Republic was proclaimed in Dublin on Easter Monday, April 24, at 12 noon. Simultaneously with the issue of the proclamation of the Provisional Government the Dublin Division of the Army of the Republic, including the Irish Volunteers, the Citizen Army, Hibernian Rifles, and other bodies occupied dominating positions in the city. The GPO was seized at 12 noon, the Castle attacked at the same moment, and shortly afterwards the Four Courts were occupied. The Irish troops hold the City Hall and dominate the Castle. Attacks were immediately commenced by the British forces, and everywhere [they] were repulsed At the moment of writing this report (9.30 a.m., Tuesday) the Republican forces hold their positions and the British forces have nowhere broken through. There has been heavy and continuous fighting for nearly 24 hours, [and] the casualties of the enemy have been much more numerous than those on the Republican side. The Republican forces everywhere are fighting with splendid gallantry. The populace of Dublin are plainly with the Republic, and the officers and men are everywhere cheered as they march through the city. The whole centre of the city is in the hands of the Republic, whose flag flies from the GPO.

Commandant-General P. H. Pearse is Commandant in Chief of the Army of the Republic and is President of the Provisional Government. Commandant-General James Connolly is commanding Dublin districts.

Communication with the country is largely cut, but reports to hand show that the country is rising. Bodies of men from Kildare and Fingal have already reported in Dublin.

'Mr Walker,' Pearse said, 'You're a printer – so print this for me.' Matthew left the GPO, and with his son Charlie, son-in-law Joe Stanley and two others – James O'Sullivan and Thomas Ryan – they persuaded O'Keeffe's printers on Halston Street to lend them their premises. And so 12,000 copies of the single-sheet *Irish War News* rolled off the presses and onto Dublin's streets. Matthew's little garrison made two more forays into the GPO to collect Pearse's material for what are now known as the *Irish War News Bulletins*. These are so rare that in July 2007 a copy of the first issue fetched a record €26,000 at auction.

Matthew died in 1925. He appears to have been a much-loved, modest man who devoted his life to his family and country. He was, we hope you'll agree, the Best Printer In A Rising Ireland has ever known.

Great-grandad, if you're reading this book beyond the Pearly Gates, please forgive any typos.

Worst Man For Standing His Round

Éamon de Valera was many things to many people: a statesman who helped Ireland achieve its independence, an isolationist who kept her out of the Second World War, a long streel of misery, a man with a keen intellect … etc. and so forth. He is also remembered as a tight-wad when it came to standing his round, at least in the County Clare town of Parteen.

While canvassing there more than sixty years ago, the Chief and some of his supporters popped in to Browne's bar to slake their thirst. According to pub historian Austin O'Donovan the owner, Jack Browne, entered the unpaid booze in the accounts book after Dev left without

PEOPLE / BEST AND WORST

paying. Jack's grandson Billy now runs the bar and claims that **Síle de Valera** had offered to pay his father when she heard of the story a number of years ago. However, Billy Browne says his father checked the shop books and noted that another customer had stood the drinks to Dev and his chums. Not so, says O'Donovan, who counter-claimed that he had it on good authority that the Long Fellow's crowd had left without paying for their round. To further confuse the issue, there was a local man living in Parteen at the time who also went by the nickname of Dev and the entry in the book might actually refer to a purchase made by him in the shop attached to the bar.

O'Donovan was sticking to his guns when the story was made public in early 2006 and insisted that all the gargle drunk that night was entered in the accounts book (or put on a tab) in Dev's name. The politician had necked a few and tottered off to leave the longest outstanding bar slate in the history of the State.

And how much was the bill for? A presidential one shilling and four old pence.

INTERESTING FACT

- While the folk down Parteen way may not be too enamoured of Dev's closed wallet, the people of India have rewarded his generosity by giving him a place of honour in their capital. At the start of

2006, when the Parteen row erupted, the Indian government inaugurated 'Eamon de Valera Street' in New Delhi. Dev is regarded as a great friend of the movement for Indian freedom and is remembered for donating 20 million rupees in 1943 to aid famine relief in Calcutta. When he addressed the Friends of Freedom for India in New York in 1920, he made it clear that he saw India and Ireland as having a common cause. His 1937 Constitution so impressed the Indian leadership that Pandit Nehru studied it as a model for the framework of his new State. This is why so many Indians are called 'Dev', including the one in *Coronation Street* who keeps getting photographed locked in Lancashire nightclubs.

Best Céilí Dance For Winning A World War

In the first *Erindipity* we mentioned the extraordinary work of Kerry priest, father Cornelius Neil Horan. As this is not a pathetic attempt to whet your appetite in the hope that you will rush off and buy that book, we will gladly tell you that the section was called Longest Period Spent Dancing for World Peace and that the period was twenty years. If you want to know any more about this man and his twinkle toes, you know where the nearest bookshop is . . .

Whereas Dancing for Peace is a laudable pastime, Dancing for your Enemy's Complete and Utter Annihilation could be regarded as non-PC depending on whose side you're on.

Colonel John Coldwell-Horsfall was on the right side in the Second World War. He is described in his obituary as a tall, aloof man, with an exceptional presence who led with exemplary courage. It was said he would stroll around, seemingly unconcerned, under fire wearing only his soft peaked cap (and clothes, of course), encouraging his Royal Irish Fusiliers and getting personally stuck into the business of killing the Bosch.

'John Henry Coldwell-Horsfall' isn't as Irish a name as 'Neil Horan', but the Putney-born hero did as much to introduce the use of Irish dancing as a means to ending lives as the Kingdom priest has done to save them. A crack shot, in 1935 he was commissioned into the Royal Irish Fusiliers – known as the 'Faughs' from their battle cry 'Faugh-a-Ballagh!' ('Get out of the Way You Bollix or We'll Burst You!') – and made an immediate impact, raising the unit's level of marksmanship. In November 1942 the Faughs took part in Operation Torch, the Allied invasion of North Africa, following a period of intensive training in Scotland. This included some unusual fitness exercises to keep them in peak condition on the long journey by battleship.

Decrying squat jumps and press-ups as being only for cissies, Colonel Coldwell-Horsfall brought his men on deck and ordered the regimental pipers to strike up the Irish dance favourite, 'The Walls of Limerick'. Soon the battleships carrying the cream of the British forces to fight Rommel were swinging and whooping in the biggest céilí the high seas had ever seen. They repeated this every day and it was deemed to be a most efficient way to maintain good health and morale.

> **The Colonel and his men went on to distinguish themselves on the field of combat where they would do a couple of jigs and reels . . . [They] would then finish [the enemy] off with some brilliantly executed hornpipes and a special, secret, Polka code-named The Secret Polka.**

The Colonel and his men went on to distinguish themselves on the field of combat where they would do a couple of jigs and reels in sight of the enemy before engaging him. This was designed to enrage Fritz, who, thinking they were taking the mickey out of the Nazi Goosestep, would throw caution to the wind and rush headlong into battle. The Irish would then finish him off with some brilliantly executed hornpipes and a special, secret Polka code-named The Secret Polka.

According to *The Daily Telegraph* obituary, Colonel Coldwell-Horsfall was injured during an attack on Casa Tamagnin in Italy in December 1944 and was subsequently sent home. He had been shot in both legs. Happily he recovered and enjoyed a full life to the age of ninety-one. Whether he kept up an interest in céilí dancing after the war is unclear. What is known, however, is that he absolutely never became a dance instructor, which is a shame, as he was well before his time in terms of 'Dance-ercise'. After the doughty old warrior's passing in January 2007, one newspaper – the *Daily Mail* – set out to discover how effective his ship dancing was. Significantly, it appears that an hour spent dancing 'The Walls of Limerick' burns off approximately 600 calories – almost twice as much as aerobics, which is only 350.

It's just as well: one imagines that a flotilla of spandex-leotard, headband-wearing British soldiers going 'step–2–3–4, kick–2–3–4' to the 1940s' equivalent of the Village People might not have been quite so effective.

INTERESTING FACTS

- Ireland was the first country to broadcast dancing on the radio. Do not adjust your set – you really did read the words 'Dancing', 'On', 'The' and 'Radio'. In 1953 the State radio station began transmitting 'Take the Floor', with host Din Joe, to regular audiences of over a million listeners. It featured an hour of dancing to the Garda Céilí Band, complete with stamping feet and cries of 'hupyeboysye' and continued to 1965. It was succeeded by Céilí House, which still airs today. It wasn't the daftest idea the radio station ever had: that would be the 1978 one-hour special performance by mime artist Marcel Marceau. The second was to extend the *News For The Deaf* to radio in 1984.

• During the 1920s and 1930s the concerned clergy of Ireland agitated to have Crossroads Dances controlled. This was because they were deemed to be lewd and to lead to immoral behaviour. In 1935 they finally had their way and the Public Dance Halls Act was passed in the Dáil. This required all these halls to be licensed and effectively put an end to crossroad dances. If Irish people wanted to shake their legs at each other then they would have to do it under the glare of the parish priest. It wasn't all bad news – road fatalities dropped.

Best Dressed Aeronaut

Richard Crosbie was the first Irishman to get as high as a kite. On 19 January 1785 the popular scientist and showman from Wicklow took to the air in a brightly-coloured balloon from Ranelagh Gardens in Dublin and came back down to earth on the northside near Clontarf. His achievement was on a par with a modern moon landing and came just fourteen months after the Montgolfier brothers had recorded the first manned balloon flight in the Bois de Boulogne in Paris.

Crosbie was a mechanical genius. After reading newspaper reports about the Montgolfiers' pioneering work he embarked upon a series of experiments of his own. The main difference between his contraption and the French boys' was his use of hydrogen as a propellant. This cut out the risks involved in carrying and stoking a furnace with straw, wool and other sparking materials which could set fire to the balloon. His plan was to become the first aeronaut to fly over the Irish Sea. First he needed to raise some cash, and he did this by displaying his patented Aeronautic Chariot, which was to carry his equipment and ballast, to the public for a small fee. He also gave a pay-per-view daily aeronautical display at **Ranelagh Gardens** where he would launch some unfortunate animal skywards in a 3.6 m balloon which was tethered to the ground. In a final act of showmanship before his own flight, he cut loose the balloon with a pet moggie on board. The petrified pussy screeched off into the north east and was observed passing over the coast of Scotland that very same day. On the following day the wind changed and Mogs ditched into the sea off the Isle of Man, to be rescued by a passing ship.

Crosbie's preparations for his date with history included crowd control, as a great multitude was expected to turn up to see him perform his feat of derring-do. And so a traffic plan was announced which requested the gentry to park their carriages in an orderly manner behind Ranelagh House. Stationary coaches weren't allowed to block the road between Cold Blow Lane and Northumberland Street and their drivers were told to drive on and park in Milltown after setting down their passengers. Transgressors would have their horses clamped.

Proving that Dublin has always had a disproportionate amount of skangers, it was soon discovered that forged tickets to the event were doing the rounds, which meant that genuine passes had to be recalled and new tickets issued. The stress of all this began to take its toll on Crosbie, who came down with a bad bout of biliousness. His friends implored him in vain to postpone the launch. Fortunately, bad weather prevailed and prevented an attempt on 4 January. A fortnight later Richard Crosbie finally made his flight with a fair wind behind him (that would have been due to the biliousness). At 2.30 p.m. he stepped into the Aeronautical Chariot attached to his balloon, which was gaily painted with images of Mercury, the messenger of the Gods, carrying the Arms of Ireland and of the Roman goddess of wisdom, Minerva. Thirteen minutes later he gave the order for the ropes to be cut. *Faulkner's Dublin Journal* described the scene:

> Mr. Crosbie's experiment yesterday proves his genius as great as his intrepidity . . . [at] about half past two o'clock he took his aerial flight, amidst the concourse of at least 20,000 spectators – [one cannot imagine] anything more aweful and magnificent than his rise; he ascended almost perpendicular and when at a great height seemed stationary, he was but three and a half minutes in view when he was obscured by a cloud. It was agreed upon by his particular friends as the wind was to the SE and being late in the day that when he cleared the city he should descend as soon as possible, accordingly, by means of his valve he [should] let himself down near Clontarf.

His dream to cross the Irish Sea hadn't been realised – and never would be – but he had become the first Irishman to become airborne. However, it's not for this that he's remembered in these pages. Richard Crosbie was famous for his flamboyant style and he was universally acknowledged as the Best Dressed Aeronaut of his day. His carefully chosen flying gear was the talk of Dublin a long time after the initial excitement of his flight had died down. Looking somewhat like a Georgian hip-hop artist, he wore a long robe of oiled silk, which was lined with white fur, a waistcoat and breeches of white quilted satin, spit-polished Morocco boots and a Mantero cap of the finest leopard skin.

Bling Crosbie, indeed.

INTERESTING FACT

- The Best Dressed Rebel In Irish History was Thomas FitzGerald, the 10th Earl of Kildare, who led the 1534 rebellion against the forces of Henry VIII. Thomas, who was renowned for his 'gorgeous trappings', rode into Dublin on 11 June with 140 horsemen who wore silk fringes on their helmets. He thus earned himself the nickname Silken Thomas. Unfortunately, he wasn't the best rebel in Irish history and was betrayed and executed three years later.

Worst Aeronaut For Losing His Way . . .?

Douglas Groce Corrigan checked the fuel gauge of his modified Curtiss Robin high wing monoplane and counted his rations: two chocolate bars, two boxes of fig bars and a quart of water. He then ran a last-minute eye over his map of the US and the route he had marked out. The Irish-American had spent three years trying to get permission to fly from the Big Apple to Dublin. Every time he applied he was turned down on the grounds that it was a very, very dangerous thing to do.

A compromise was eventually reached and he secured a long-distance licence to fly non-stop from New York to California instead. And so, on 17 July 1938 Corrigan found himself in Brooklyn's Floyd Bennett Field, preparing to fly to the west coast of the USA as opposed to the west coast of Ireland. Observers recall that it was a particularly foggy morning as he took off and disappeared. Twenty-eight hours later, 'Wrong Way' Corrigan landed in Dublin and became an international hero.

Soon after he took off, Corrigan's plane, *Sunshine*, had developed a gas leak, but the determined thirty-one-year-old decided he wasn't going to waste time mending it. When he took off at 4 a.m. the aircraft was so laden with fuel that it struggled to become airborne. Ten hours later he noticed his feet were very cold – the leak had got worse and fuel was sloshing around the cabin. He was doomed. DOOMED!!! What was he to do? He had a choice: either risk a blaze on board or ditch the excess fuel and say a prayer that he would make it to his destination.

He could die frying, or die trying flying.

Reaching below his seat he pulled out a screwdriver

and punched a hole in the fuselage on the opposite side to the exhaust pipe. He then put his foot to the floor (or whatever they do on planes) and hoped for the best. Several agonising hours later he saw a fishing boat and flew low to examine it. He knew then he couldn't be that far from land as the boat was too small to wander very far from shore. He celebrated by munching on a pack of fig rolls and half a chocolate bar. Soon he noticed some nice green hills and was on the home straight to Baldonnel Aerodrome.

He had become the first airman to fly solo across the Atlantic to Ireland, but he was up to his oxters in the brown stuff after breaking the rules. The first person to greet him as he stepped out of the plane was an army officer. Corrigan introduced himself and uttered the words that were going to make him an aviation legend: 'I left New York yesterday morning headed for California. I got mixed up in the clouds, and I must have flown the wrong way.'

To his surprise, the officer replied; 'Yes, we know,' adding with heroic understatement, 'There was a small piece in the paper saying someone might be flying over this way.'

During his interview with an official from the American Embassy, Wrong Way Corrigan doggedly stuck to the story that later appeared in his autobiography. He said he was so weighed down with fuel that *Sunshine* wouldn't climb fast enough, so he flew east for a few miles to burn some off before turning around and heading west. His main compass was broken and he had

had to use a backup one. Which was, evidently, crap.

'Couldn't you see anything below you?' asked the official.

'It was just too foggy,' replied Corrigan, who explained that there had been one break in the clouds and he had seen a city he took to be Baltimore which would have meant he was on course for California. The city, it turned out, was Boston. When the clouds finally parted twenty-six hours later, he was over an ocean. Well fancy that, he mused, I can't have come to the Pacific yet, can I? Looking down at his compass he saw – now it was brighter – that he had been following the wrong end of the magnetic needle for the whole flight. He had headed east instead of west, the silly man.

Even the normally glum-looking Dev had to laugh when Wrong Way repeated the story to him the following morning.

Corrigan and *Sunshine* were later sent back on an ocean liner to the US where he received a hero's welcome, despite the threat of serious charges hanging over him. His punishment was to have his licence suspended until 4 August, the day his ship docked in New York. In the following year, 1939, he played himself in the movie *The Flying Irishman*. Although there were some unconfirmed reports in the 1980s that he finally owned up to deliberately making his 'mistake', Wrong Way Corrigan officially stuck to his story for the remaining fifty-seven years of his life.

INTERESTING FACT

- Wrong Way is not the only exotic creature to get lost and wind up on these shores. In February 2007 a giant Japanese tiger prawn was found in the nets of a West Cork fishing boat, the appropriately named *Coral Strand*. The shellfish is normally found in the Indian and Pacific Oceans and its presence off the south coast prompted fears of an invasion, which so far hasn't materialised. A spokesperson for the Department of the Marine told the press they believed the wayward prawn star (as *The Irish Times* called it) was not right in the head and simply decided to go 'swimabout'. 'The prawn's crackers,' the official said.

Worst Name For A Restaurant

Some readers may feel that this entry should be included in the Places section, dealing ostensibly as it does with a place to eat. They have a point. However, *Erindipity Rides Again* believes that it's the people behind a restaurant that make it, not necessarily the location. Take, for example, the superb **Chapter One**, which is a Michelin-starred success story on Dublin's Parnell Square, which – with respect – is in an area better known for chips, kebabs and African shops selling dried beef and wigs.

2007 was a slow news year for the *Sunday Independent*.

Between squeezing Bertie Ahern's unmentionables over the reform of Stamp Duty before the election, and stroking them after he agreed to abolish it for first-time buyers, they had little else to write about. Apart, of course, from the high jinks at the highly controversial *Charity You're a Star* (zzzzzzzzzz) and insightful opinion pieces by various wannabe models and part-time waitresses from the coffee shops of Blackrock about Sinn Féin ('very, very bad people') and Sir Anthony O'Reilly and the rest of the *Sunday Independent* family ('very, very good people'). Then it broke The Story of the Century. This concerned an annoyingly persistent, self-publicising model and her restaurateur fiancé who had had a spat in front of a *Sunday Independent* snapper who was doing his best to photograph her in her knickers on a table in the former's eaterie. Raised voices were heard, recriminating texts were sent (and dissected in the *Sindo*) and the engagement was off. THE ENGAGEMENT IS OFF!!! THE ENGAGEMENT IS OFF!!! the *Sindo* trumpeted. WHO THE HELL CARES??? WHO THE HELL CARES??? the public replied.

It should be pointed out here that the names of the protagonists in this cringeworthy episode are not going to be published in these pages. This is not to protect their privacy, which would be a touch ironic. They're just not getting into this book. They're not 'on the list'. They're barred. In their defence, this pair are only a symptom of the *nouveau riche* malaise our Tigerland is suffering from. The rise in our prosperity has been matched by the rise in the amount of magazines and newspaper diary columns gliding off the presses, like well-oiled socialites, to cater for the country's self-regarding models, PR girls and clothes shop owners.

For the record, there are three types of social event in the main urban areas (Dublin, Cork, Limerick etc.). They are: A): The 'Bottle Launch', where crazeeee twenty-year-old skater dudes and dudettes lark about in woolly hats sipping the latest vodka / fruit juice / Lucozade / lemonade / tea / concoction by the neck. These drinks are generally named 'Gr8', 'Vom 69' or 'Shag' by some cool marketing executive who's hip to what the kids are at. B): The 'Never Mind The Botox' launch favoured by the classier, mid-twenty to mid-thirty-year-old socialites.

> For 'classy', read overdressed by being underdressed, that is, think lurid azure/fuchsia cocktail dresses pared back to reveal marmalade-coloured shoulders and décolletage in which you could park the front wheel of a Harley Davidson.

For 'classy', read overdressed by being underdressed, that is, think lurid azure/fuchsia cocktail dresses pared back to reveal marmalade-coloured shoulders and décolletage in which you could park the front wheel of a Harley Davidson. These parties are to publicise new face creams with scientific names designed to confuse the less intelligent, for example: 'Midnight Shower Repair Creme (now with added Hydrochloraminoacidethyloxide Magic Mini Moisture Capsulettes'). The highpoint at the end of these affairs is a goody bag and a consultation with a plucked, scrubbed, eighty-year-old male make-up artist, who's made a comfortable living from pretending to be gay ('You're a greasy T-shape, dahling. Less pancake on the forehead and nose will sort out that disgusting oil slick – we don't want to look like someone who works in a chipper, now do we?').

C): The 'Arty Party' where middle class, middle-aged retired socialites stand around sipping warm white wine and nibbling on deep-fried prawns, discussing the merits of the latest happening artist. As retired socialites tend not to travel into the metropolitan area for fear of not being able to get home (this used to be the case in the 1980s when all public transport ended at 8 p.m.), these events are held in the suburbs of Malahide, Dalkey, Moyross and that place where Roy Keane comes from. The artists have nicknames like Sausages, Eggy and Whiskers and enjoy painting gollywogs and cans of beans. The attendees, whose saggy backsides are clad in the finest designer denim and crêpe de chine, queue to fawn over the young genius and then leave without buying anything. Eventually the painter dies in penury, in a garret after surviving for years on Cup A Soup (with croutons) and cornflakes. The attendees then cluck-cluck over their newspapers and chide themselves for not having bought one of their works, which must be worth a 'fooortttune' now that Eggy's popped his clogs.

All the effort spent scrambling to reach the apex of society can very often do the climber more harm than good and may result in the ridicule of their peers – an unthinkably horrible fate. Too much time spent gracing the 'society' pages can often do more harm than good. In the case of our model's brightly-tanned fiancé, the time spent publicising his new venture might have been better spent discussing its name.

The sign above Number 10, South William Street Dublin 2, reads '*il pomo d'oro*'[16] with a natty red tomato separating the words '*pomo*' and '*d'oro*'. The Tomato is a nice name for an Italian diner, given that it's an integral part of so many dishes. So what's the problem? The problem is that the Italian for 'the tomato' is '*il pomodoro*' and not '*il pomo d'oro*,' according to the *Oxford Italian Dictionary* and various translation sites, including Google and Alta Vista. If you have a smattering of French, then you are probably thinking *pomo* = *pomme* = apple. You're also thinking '*d'oro*' means 'golden'. The Golden Apple is also a nice name for a pasta palace. This, however, translates into Italian as *la mela d'oro* and not *il pomo d'oro*.

So what does *il pomo d'oro* stand for in Italiano?

The owner may, or may not, have blushed through his perma-tan, when he discovered that he had called his new restaurant . . . The Golden Knob.

'Fancy having a bite at The Golden Knob?' is probably not something you're going to want to ask on a first date.

If the owner thought he had it bad, then he should have spared a thought for *Erindipity Rides Again's* favourite Celtic Roots and Trad band, Kila. This collective made up their name purely because it sounded nice. Among its many translations (in Swahili it means 'everyone'), the Croatian stands out – if you'll pardon the expression – meaning, as it does, 'Swollen Scrotum'.

---

[16] The restaurant's name is spelt lower case on the sign.

INTERESTING FACT

- The most appropriately-named flooring showroom in Ireland is located beside the best-named kebab emporium. Treat yourself to a day out at Lino Ritchie's in Finglas followed by din dins at Kebabylon. Alternatively, head out to Dundrum and get a Chinese take-away at the Great Wall. It's right across the road from the Central Mental Hospital.

Best Royal Graffiti Artist

Teenage whims are cyclical. Take fashion: when the author was growing up in the early 1980s, the early 1960s were all the rage. Skinny jeans, fishtail parkas, tight-fitting jackets, pork pie hats and crew-cut hairstyles were the height of fashion. Before this, at the close of the 1970s, older sisters were jiving and twisting to the sounds of the 1950s, wearing twin sets and bobby socks inspired by the movie *Grease* (1978). Then in the 1990s the early 1970s were back, tripping over their flares in a clash of deliberately mismatched colours. In this part of the 2000s the 1980s have already made a comeback. *Erindipity Rides Again* has a theory about this called, imaginatively, The *Erindipity* Twenty Year Cycle Theory. Teenage sons and daughters who are terrified of winding up dressing like their parents wind up dressing like their parents did, when *they* were terrified of dressing like *their* parents did. Confused?

Recall being a young person (which shouldn't be too hard given that you're only a spring chicken. You're looking well, by the way.). Now stare across the flock-carpeted floor of your memory and observe your dad. Normally you fight like two ould ones at the bargain counter during Frawleys' closing down sale, but this evening you are quietly watching the telly. He is wearing a chunky knit cardigan of an indeterminate colour, grey parallel slacks and a pair of shoes that scream, 'Don't look at me!!! Don't look at me!! We were made to be ignored!!'

'I'm not ending up looking like that,' you vow, not realising that he had said the same thing himself when he was a youngster. Two days later your younger sister is rooting around in his wardrobe looking for his chunky cardigan to wear with her boot runners and rolled-up jeans (she's a student) and she finds a pair of winkle-picker shoes.

'Hey Spotty,' she shouts down the stairs, 'Come see what I've found.' After the initial disappointment has dissipated that it's not a stash of girly mags, you try on the shoes. They fit. And they'd look good with that ancient herringbone sports jacket. And that old knitted tie. Next thing you're in your bedroom mixing and matching button-down collar shirts and drainpipe trousers thinking you look like Napoleon Solo in *The Man From Uncle* (the 1960s TV series) or George Segal in *The Quiller*

Memorandum (1966). The girls at the Bective rugby club dance will be fighting over you on Friday night.

'You look just like me when I was your age,' a voice behind you says, and Napoleon holsters his gun and Quiller kicks off his winkle pickers in disgust.

You've become your dad.

This rambling discourse is intended to highlight the fact that there is no such thing as an original teenage thought. Each generation makes the same mistakes, rebels against the same 'enemies' and follows the same silly trends. Like their parents who bemoan 'the youth of today', they are entirely predictable.

That is why Dublin's suburbs are currently suffering from one of these periodic trends – stupid graffiti.

For a good many years, Dublin has been a comparatively graffiti-free city, in comparison with other cities in Europe. It seemed with the advent of the Celtic Tiger, Fran and Anto finally married Jackie and Linda and were no longer daubing their undying love notes on the sides of bus shelters. The only piece of obvious graffiti in the city's 'burbs over the last few years was written on the Rock Road in Blackrock. It was political in nature: 'Free Nicky Kelly', someone had painted. 'With every packet of cornflakes' someone else had added.

Now a new group of teenagers, bored of their Xboxes and Playstations have taken to the streets with their spray cans. They don't do politics because they can't understand them and they can't do colourful Los Angeles-style murals because they're not clever enough. We are talking moronic, semi-legible scrawls written everywhere from alleyways to the gables of peoples' houses. 'Dalkey bom cru' and 'D4 massive' are but two examples. 'Boomshak' and 'Spreehorga Mingzat' are two others.

A dog peeing against a wall after drinking a pot of Dulux could produce more interesting graffiti.

It's the parents *Erindipity Rides Again* blames. Or at very least a noble Victorian mathematician and an exotic, high-born beauty.

On 16 October 1843, **Sir William Rowan Hamilton** – one of the greatest mathematicians of all time – discovered magical numbers called quaternions. We won't pretend to understand what they are. Say 'something to do with multiplying points in three dimensions', or some other gobbledegook if someone asks you. Hamilton had been trying to find a solution to a mathematical problem for several years and it finally came to him as he was walking with his wife by the Royal Canal in Cabra. Not having his laptop to hand he carved his now famous formula into the bridge on which he was standing:

$$i^2 = j^2 = k^2 = ijk = -1$$

This is probably the most baffling piece of graffiti ever written, but it made Broom Bridge a national monument. The figures are no longer visible but a plaque, unveiled by Taoiseach Eamon de Valera in 1958 commemorates Hamilton's Eureka moment.

Remarkable as this is, it could never match the glamour of our **Best Royal Graffiti In A Pizza Restaurant**. In May 2007, as *Erindipity Rides Again* was enjoying a cup of tea in Dan Finnegan's fine Dalkey establishment, a most peculiar scene was unfolding around the corner in what is locally known as 'Little Italy'. This section of the Mean Streets of Dalkey is so named due to the presence of **Mr Fabio Perrozzi's** two famous Italian restaurants, Ragazzi and Wine Not on either side of the narrow strip of road. Fabulous Fabio is the undisputed Pizza King of Dalkey (it's just as well he doesn't sell burgers) and his eateries have entertained some of the biggest names in that business they call show. REM, Bono, Sinéad O'Connor, Neil Jordan, The Corrs, scores of models, Hollywood actors and directors have all stuffed their faces with pizza capricciosa in Ragazzi and then signed the stairwell wall in gratitude.

On the aforementioned evening in May, two large black people carriers (the carriers were large and black, not the people if you get what we mean), screeched to a halt at the end of Convent Road. Two large armed men (they were armed with guns, not that they had large arms, please stop confusing us) jumped out, earpieces crackling, and sealed off the road. It was fairly dramatic stuff for a village where a broken Fendi strap or a dented Ferrari fender will fuel pub talk for weeks. There was general consternation among the passersby and, just as it looked like this book would be including a section titled Largest Hold-Up Of Pizzas Ever, a well-dressed couple stepped out onto the pavement.

Inside, they were ushered to a quiet corner with their party and soon were enjoying Fabio's fine fare. The woman was dazzlingly beautiful and, despite being a mere slip of a thing, ate an entire wagon wheel of a pizza, preceded by a salad.

Once replete, the lady was asked to do the restaurant the honour of signing its wall. She graciously agreed and wrote her name and the date, within a heart shape, at the top of the stairs. It's beside **Rosanna Davison's** should you ever be tempted to go looking for it.

Unlike Rosanna's Miss World crown, this lady's crown is for keeps. Only after she glided away in her blacked-out car did Fabio examine the signature. It's the only graffiti of its type in Ireland. Possibly the world.

There had never been any suggestion that her dinner partner, **Bono**, would have to sing for his supper. Who would have thought that **Queen Rania Al–Abdullah of Jordan** would have to sign for hers?

INTERESTING FACT

- Bono has a bit of a reputation for being a bad influence on today's youth. A glance at the graffiti-splattered remains of the walls of Windmill Lane studios will testify to this. Fans from all over the world travelled to Dublin over the years to get 'write on' with the U2 frontman. Could this have been because of an incident on 11 November 1987 at a free U2 gig at Justin Herman Plaza, San Francisco? During the performance, Bono spray-painted 'Rock 'n' roll stops the traffic' on the Vaillancourt fountain. This resulted in an official rebuke from the then San Francisco mayor Diane

Feinstein. 'I am disappointed that a rock star who is supposed to be a role model for young people chose to vandalise the work of another artist,' she snorted. Bono later pointed out that he too was an artist and put the incident down to 'tour madness' during a very amusing press conference. 'I left my art . . . in San Franciscooooooo,' he crooned. Or if didn't, he should have.

Best TV Show For Giving You A Heart Attack

RTÉ has an outstanding history of producing quaint, but rubbish, shows. Things are much better now, but back in the 1970s the national broadcaster scaled new heights of unintentional comedy. The legendary *Leave It To Mrs O'Brien* is always the one that TV critics hold up as the finest example of RTÉ's lack of a funny bone. It concerned the antics of two priests and their housekeeper. While that may sound like the perfect formula for a money-spinning niche website, in RTÉ's hands it produced nothing but a half hour of good, clean broadcasting. What it didn't produce were any laughs.

Actually, if you're amused by the sight of an ageing priest being chased around his kitchen table by a middle-aged woman (without hot sex on her mind) then there was one laugh. It's unfunniness was probably due to RTÉ's decision not to hire a professional scribe to write the script. Instead it enlisted the formidable talents of a real-life housewife to give it an 'authentic' feel. This was not as mad as it sounds. Ireland at the time was still living in the Age of the Housewife where the mammy would cook meals, bake cakes, iron, hoover, have babies, go to Mass, make sandwiches, do the week's shopping for 10p, go to Mass again, do more hoovering, go to confession, have another baby, darn underpants and knit sixteen bawneen jumpers all before daddy came home for his tea. Ireland bred Super Housewives and loved them so much that they even had their own annual TV show – the *Calor Kosangas Housewife of the Year*. This featured **Gay Byrne** chatting with contestants who had to rustle up a meal, talk about their husbands, and finish off with a party piece. The show was cancelled in 1990 when a sixty-three-year-old lady from Carlow shot ping-pong balls out of her orifice across the stage at the horrified judges.

Actually, that last bit's not true. If it had been, RTÉ could have hired her to write *Leave It To Mrs O'Brien* instead of the other housewife who was doing it. It would have been a hell of a lot funnier.

Going Strong was also a hoot. It was a show for the much older, hanging-on-by-their-fingernails generation, fronted by a man named after a toy motor vehicle used in the Duracell commercials – Bunny Carr. Bunny used to ask members of the audience probing questions like 'Do you take jam on your cornflakes, missus?' or 'Tell us about the last time you lost your slippers' or 'Would you like your medication now?' or 'Are you still breathing there, Sister Philomena?' The most memorable thing about

> **Bunny [Carr] hosted the quiz show, *Quicksilver*. It should have been called '*Quickcopper*' as prizes started at 1p. Or '*Quick! Get The Quicklime And Throw It In My Eyes So I Don't Have To Watch Any More Of This Crap*'.**

Going Strong is that it inspired the 'what's got forty legs?' gag template. (What's got forty legs and smells of pee? Answer: the front row of the *Going Strong* audience.) Bunny also hosted the quiz show, *Quicksilver*. It should have been called '*Quickcopper*' as prizes started at 1p. Or '*Quick! Get The Quicklime And Throw It In My Eyes So I Don't Have To Watch Any More Of This Crap*'. The truth is that the country loved Bunny and *Quicksilver*, in part for it's sweet decency, in part for the belly laughs: on one occasion a contestant was asked, 'What was Hitler's first name?' and replied, 'Heil!'.

None of these above-mentioned shows had killer material however. Not on the same level as 1979's *The Spike,* Ireland's first brave attempt to use TV drama to highlight awareness of social problems. It was an abject failure in this regard as it was taken off after five of its ten episodes. The reason for this was two-fold: boobs.

The Spike was set in a tough, working-class Dublin secondary school and its last aired instalment concerned the night classes being held there. Three classes, in particular, were the focus of the night's entertainment: the confidence course, the know-your-fur class and the cleaning science class. There is some intentional humour here as we see a teacher whiskeying himself up to get the confidence to face his new confidence class. Later, his pupils, who were too shy to speak to each other at the start of the session, are rampaging through the corridors feeling up total strangers. The principal even gets what's described as a 'friendly crotch touch' (as opposed to an 'angry crotch touch'). To add a little spice to these saucy shenanigans the art teacher then proceeds to call for a naked female model for his class. Up steps a member of the shy class who begins to disrobe and come on to him.

It was at this point that all hell broke loose.

Prior to this scene RTÉ had never screened a naked Irishwoman before. Foreign, French and American hussies yes, but not decent Catholic Irish ones. The scene, lest you be thinking 'Debbie Does Darndale', was extremely restrained. Actress **Madeleine Erskine's** naked body was first seen side and front-on from behind a screen. When she is posing for the class, her lithe womanliness is shot from behind from the hips up, then full-on sideways in long shot followed by a long shot of the full body finishing off with a medium shot from the hips up. It was hardly *Deep Throat* (1972) but it was the proverbial camel's straw and the moral people of Ireland rose up (no pun intended) to denounce it. Prior to this, the show had been under fire from all quarters over its content. Fermoy Urban Council said it was vulgar and suggestive while Waterford County Council had called it a slur on teachers.

The hysteria was so bad following Madeleine's boob display that the founder of the League of Decency suffered a heart attack after watching it. The unfortunate man got so angry while phoning the papers that he had a coronary. We're not making fun of him as he at least stuck to his convictions, but as a result of this sad occurrence *The Spike* is definitely The Best TV Show For Giving You A Heart Attack.

Or a Granny Attack. *Spike* actor Joe Fitzpatrick, sporting a plaster on his head, later told reporters he had been beaten up in the street by an enraged ould one wielding a handbag.

Worst Way To Get Put On Hold

If you're forever grumbling about baggage handlers' strikes putting your holiday plans on hold then please spare a thought for one who literally got put on hold himself.

On 28 December 2005 **Air Traffic Control in Dublin Airport** received a telephone request from a staff member aboard a plane which was revving up for take-off: 'Get me the hell out of here!'

You may think they might have been a bit disgruntled with the fact that the staffer was using his phone on board but he was forgiven, as he was phoning . . . from the locked cargo hold.

During a breakdown in communications the handler had got locked into the hold as he was leading two teams of loading crews for the Airbus flight to New York. Minutes later, the plane began taxiing towards the runway and it was only the handler's mobile phone that came between him and a trip across the Atlantic to New York.

According to a spokesperson, this wasn't the first time a loader had been inadvertently locked in a hold. A few years prior to this a handler was loaded with the cargo and spent an uncomfortable two-hour flight from Philadelphia to Chicago.

Whatever about the horror of being trapped in a jet plane's hold, surely getting trapped in the boot of a Bus Éireann coach is much worse.

In January 2007 a passenger found herself trapped in the luggage hold of a moving bus. The woman got locked in the baggage compartment after she tried to retrieve her cases when the Athlone bus stopped at **Heuston Station**. As she climbed into the hold to pull her bags out to the front, the door was inadvertently closed behind her, trapping her in the cramped bowels of the bus. To make matters worse, the coach pulled off from Skanger Central and continued on its way. The sound of the petrified woman calling for help and pounding on the doors of the hold were drowned out by the engine and it wasn't until the bus pulled into Busáras that her scarifying journey ended. Her fellow passengers probably left a few skid marks when they opened the hold to get their bags and discovered the dishevelled woman inside.

Happily she was uninjured and later received an apology from CIE over the accident. If you think it's miraculous that she was unharmed on that horror bus trip, may we draw your attention to the following . . .

Best Ever Miracle On The 7A

It's not every day that you come across a bus driver with the Gift of Healing. You'll meet a few with the Gift of Being A Pain in The (Bus)áras and a few with the Gift of Being Grumpy, but none like the driver of the 7A bus to downtown Sallynoggin in County Dublin.

An average of 600 items a month are left behind on the city's buses by absent-minded passengers. For some reason this halves during the month of December, which is surprising considering the number of locked people being ferried home from Christmas parties.

From 2006 to mid-2007 the usual boring items were found – mobile phones and baby rattles – but in amongst the commonplace were a few curiosities. These included a hearing aid, a doctor's blood pressure kit, several wigs, golf trolleys and a glass eye.

Dublin Bus are still scanning their CCTV footage for a bald, deaf, half-blind doctor, with a passion for golf, rushing to an emergency by bus. Come to think of it, it's just as well he took the bus.

Whatever about blindness and baldness being cured (that's the other theory for the glass eye and the hairpieces), in December of 2006 the aforementioned driver of the 7A featured in a mystery that endures to the present day. After turning in his bus for the night he arrived in the depot with a fully-working wheelchair.

'Someone left this on the bus,' he told his stunned colleagues.

As no-one has ever come forward to claim it, *Erindipity Rides Again*, like the driver and his workmates, can only conclude that the Lord was doing overtime that night. Another unusual find was discovered on another Dublin Bus in March 2007. Gardaí investigating a complaint arrested a passenger when they found him drunk in his seat, holding a plastic bag full of urine. This pathetic story is absolutely true and there are no gags attached to it.

And no, he wasn't arrested for taking the piss.

Best Reason For Being Told To Hump Off

Christmas is a time for sharing; for having detested relatives around for a sherry and a mince pie; for giving and receiving; and for watching re-runs of *Some Like It Hot* (1959). But most importantly it is for stuffing your big fat face – preferably at someone else's expense, like the hero of this tale to whom we will come presently.

Thanks to the greed of the nation's business folk, the build-up to 25 December now begins in June when the major department stores open their Christmas shops so the public can stock up early on baubles and candles and scented pine cones. In the Golden Age of Consumer Ireland this is now considered a shopkeeper's civic duty. Imagine the horror of waking up on Christmas morning to screams of 'Mum! Mum! You've forgotten to buy festive napkin holders!!! You've ruined Christmas! I hate you! Boo-hoo-hoo'.

Ten years ago Ireland's curmudgeons were cranking on about how Christmas decorations were going up the day after Hallowe'en. Now the tinsel is going up before 31

October. This is because Hallowe'en has become a fully-fledged festival in its own right with its build-up beginning at the start of September. American-style Hallowe'en is now fighting Christmas for our attention and money. The summer holidays are barely over when the trick-or-treat bags and wizard outfits appear in the aisles, illuminated by the twinkling lights of the shopping arcade Christmas tree. What else are the shopkeepers of Ireland to do but to keep pulling the start of the festive season back earlier and earlier? Eventually the run-in to Jesus' birthday will begin on Christmas Day and the January sales will be thronged with shoppers eager to get the best bargains on baubles and tinsel. It's not that far-fetched; some shops in Ireland already sell off their left-over decorations at a knock-down price at the start of the year.

Our merchants are not the only ones making the year seem shorter – the innkeepers are at it too. In July the first of the Christmas party ads appear in the entertainment pages of the tabloids:

> Enjoy our SENSATIONAL Christmas Party nites only at the Finglas Ritz Hotel with the Legendary Val Ocean and the Las Vegas Sound. Guest starring by the [sic] outrageous comedian Dick Bonehead (Winner of Courtown's Got Talent Best Newcomer Award). But don't bring your mother-in-law! Gala Dancing with the FABULOUS AbbaDabbaDoo Tribute Band. Book early to avoid disappointment!

One group of people who weren't buying into this claptrap were the employees of the **Mullingar**

Equestrian Centre who, sensibly, organised their own party at their workplace in December 2006. The centre's twenty staff stocked up on goodies and booze and were looking forward to having a nice, Val Ocean-free knees-up, unaware that an unwelcome guest had invited himself to the party.

On the afternoon of the appointed date the workmates decked out the main hall with tables groaning under the weight of mince pies and cans of stout, much in the same way one does on Christmas Eve for the arrival of Santa. Unlike that venerable old gent, the aforementioned guest did not come bearing gifts. The staff then fed the centre's animals and headed off home to get scrubbed up for the evening's festivities. When they returned they saw that all hell had broken loose, with the food and tables strewn all over the hall. Wobbling in the middle of it was a drunken eleven year old. It was a sight, everyone agreed, you didn't see every day, especially given that the cross-eyed pre-teen was . . . a camel.

Snout covered in mincemeat, **Gus the camel** was only too delighted to disprove that a ship of the desert can go for ages without a drink by swigging on six cans of Guinness. We'd like to think that he also gave a little hiccup and burped.

Greedy Gus had arrived in Mullingar only a few weeks earlier for the centre's 'Santa's Animal Kingdom' show. According to one of the centre's workers Gus – described as 'really a little sweetie' – had probably spotted the food when his door was ajar while someone was giving him some hay. Noting that hops are much nicer than hay, the thirsty dromedary planned his escape and – probably fantasising that he was Steve McQueen – later made his dash for freedom. Well, if not freedom, then free food at least. Next thing, he was using his sharp teeth to break open cans and snaffle the two hundred pies before him. Gussie well and truly dispensed with the orchestrated build-up so beloved of Ireland's business folk and, for him, Christmas really came early.

Zebras, emus, donkeys, piglets and reindeer – his fellow 'Animal Kingdom' mates – looked on, drooling, as he munched and glugged before being caught in the act and shown the door. Happily, it seemed he didn't have a hangover the next day. Neither did the staff for that matter, one of whom pointed out to a reporter that the camel was 'acting as if nothing happened'. Which raises an interesting point: what was he supposed to act like? Embarrassed? Furtive? He's a CAMEL.

Gus was, and still is, the first camel gatecrasher in Irish history, which is the Best Reason For Being Told To Hump Off at a Christmas shindig.

He's some party animal though.

INTERESTING FACTS

- An Irishwoman made legal history here after she was head-butted by a camel in 2002. The Dublin woman took a €38,000 damages claim against two travel firms after the brute nutted her on a holiday excursion in the Sahara. She suffered deep cuts and scarring to her face and claimed she spent the remainder of her holiday in her room. The defendants had denied her claim and eventually an out-of-court settlement was reached. Unlike gentle Gussie, the camel was not drunk at the time of the loafing.

• In September 2005, traffic was held up on the Ring Road in New Ross, County Wexford by a runaway camel. The beastie had escaped from Tom Duffy's Circus and was rescued before it could be bartered for someone's sister.

Worst Kiddies' Treat

In October 2005 a Dublin mum accidentally stumbled on a novel way to stop kids gorging themselves on chocolate in between meals. Mum-of-two Jackie Mitchel[17] from Sallynoggin had bought her children a box of sweeties with walnuts and marshmallows as a special treat. After doling out the goodies she went on about her daily business until her young son came to her and said he didn't want his treat. Jackie took it from him and was shocked to find 'fluffy stuff' inside it and creepy crawly things in the packaging.

The fluffy stuff turned out to be a moth and the maggoty creepy-crawlies were larvae. (Hope you're not

[17] This is not her real name. We've changed it and the names of the kids to spare them any embarrassment – not that they have anything to be ashamed of. The events are real and can be easily verified, so stop being so suspicious. Can we get back to the story now?

about to sit down to your tea). Horrified, she took the other treats from the children and checked them, only to find there were more larvae inside and the walnuts had been eaten away. Her son was sick and vomiting after the incident and had to see the doctor. Thankfully, he suffered no permanent damage.

Jackie rang the manufacturers, but she wasn't impressed with their attitude and decided to take a case on behalf of her children for anxiety suffered during the consumption of the sweets. The firm settled out of court and agreed to pay the children €2,500 each.

It will come as no surprise to learn that Jackie's little ones don't eat walnuts or marshmallows any more.

While the appearance of a sugar-coated moth in your chocolates is by all means disgusting, it did give rise to the following Sallynoggin joke: Two heads in the Noggin Inn are having a pint and one asks the other:

'How's de mot?'

The other replies: 'She's at home working her way through a box of chocolates.'

Best Poet For Getting Away With Being A Spy

'Come friendly bombs and fall on Slough.'

Britain's beloved poet laureate, **John Betjeman**, is probably best remembered for the above lines, satirically calling on the Luftwaffe to destroy that dull English town. Most poetry fans on either side of the Irish Sea will recall this master of light verse as a seemingly bumbling, archetypal Englishman; the kind of decent old duffer who would make a perfect favourite uncle. What most don't realise is that John Betjeman was a formidable spy.

During the early years of the Second World War Betjeman worked as a press attaché in the British embassy in Dublin planting propaganda in the newspapers and trying to negate the work of his German opposite number, a dastardly chap named Petersen. This was just a front however, and Betjeman was in fact a valued spy and political analyst. He had an unrivalled understanding of Eamon de Valera's attempts to maintain Irish neutrality, while Winston Churchill was throwing shapes at Westminster and waving his fist across the Irish Sea. Betjeman was so good at reading the situation here that he eventually attracted the attention of the IRA. His prying into their affairs earned him a death warrant, but in one of the most remarkable examples of the pen being mightier than the sword, he was given a reprieve – because they liked his poetry.

Diarmuid Brennan, the IRA army council's head of civilian intelligence, wrote to the poet laureate telling him how, in 1941, he had been spared a gunman's bullet. In that year Brennan had been approached by two gunmen from the second battalion of the Dublin IRA who were looking for a photograph of 'a fellow called Betjeman'. The second battalion men were known internally as the 'Edward-Gees' of the IRA, after the actor Edward G Robinson, who specialised in playing the role of gangsters.

In his letter, posted in 1957, Brennan wrote: 'I got

communications describing you as dangerous and a person of menace to all of us. In short, you were depicted in the blackest of colours.' Luckily Brennan had read some of Betjeman's work and decided to throw them off the trail, thus saving the poet's life. Betjeman's biographer, Bevis Hillier, believed the IRA man had liked *Continual Dew*, his 1937 book that contains poems about Ireland and one about Oscar Wilde. It also featured his best-known poem, 'Slough', which opened this piece.

'I came to the conclusion,' wrote Brennan, 'that a man who could give such pleasure with his pen couldn't be much of a secret agent. I may well be wrong.' He was, in fact, very, very wrong, as the cuddly Betjeman was exceptionally good at the 007 business (although he didn't get to kill anyone or cavort with ladies named Pussy). He knew more about the set-up of the IRA than a lot of its own members and had correctly concluded that the outlawed organisation was actually more anti-Dev than anti-Churchill because he had interned most of their leaders without trial. His estimates of their numbers and his reports of their internal feuds were bang on the mark in many cases and pointed to him as having a number of high-level contacts in the organisation. He even managed to get hold of an anti-fascist declaration signed by 140 left-wing IRA members interned in the Curragh. He relayed it back to England along with precise figures about how many prisoners were communist, pro-German and anti-British.

According to documents discovered in 2000, Betjeman had committed heresy by telling his handlers in London that the only way to get Ireland involved in the war was to put an end to partition. He proposed a 'defensive union of the whole of Ireland' and asked them to stop attacking Dev – who was a hate-figure in Britain – in the media. Dev, he wrote, was convinced the Bosch would win the war but there was 'no doubt that he and most of his ministers feel that the better interests of Éire will best be served by a British victory. For this reason Mr de Valera is Britain's best friend in Ireland'. He was also damning about the Unionist leaders of the devolved Northern Ireland government and their 'stupid anti-Irish remarks'.

So in actual fact, Betjeman was actually the best ally the IRA had in achieving their objective of a united Ireland.

Apart from the Edward-Gees, Betjeman was popular with just about everyone he came into contact with during his stay here, especially the writers who populated the Palace Bar beside the former *Irish Times* offices. These would have included the genius, Flann O'Brien, and rowdy old Brendan Behan, who was involved with the IRA himself around that time.

Betjeman's stock rose even further when he persuaded Laurence Olivier to film *Henry V* (1944) in Ireland. The yeomen who lined up against the French at Agincourt were actually Irish farmers, and paid extra if they had brought their own horse. The film put stg£80,000 into the Irish economy and was a great propaganda coup here for the British.

Betjeman's reports back to London were, unsurprisingly, witty. Pressed on whether there was a serious chance of Hitler launching an invasion from

Ireland, he wrote that Dublin pork butchers were nearly all German and that the Irish army bandmaster was also one.

> The Irish are not at all ideological . . . and not really interested in totalitarianism versus democracy. They are, however, intensely interested in Irishmen.
> Signed,
> Sean O'Betjeman.

INTERESTING FACT

- Professor Nicholas Mansergh, of St John's College, Cambridge, worked in the Colonial Office during the Second World War and read many of Betjeman's reports from Dublin. His son, Martin, is a TD for Tipperary South and a key formulator of Fianna Fáil's policy on Northern Ireland. He is credited with helping to persuade the Irish government to renounce its territorial claim on the disputed six counties.

How times have changed since Betjeman's day.

Longest
and Shortest

Longest Period Spent Thinking You Were Married

Forty years.

In March 2004 the *Irish Independent* published a story that was as bizarre as it was poignant. It told the story of an unnamed mother who was told by the Catholic Church that her marriage of forty years had never existed. The news came as something of a surprise to the woman who had lived, slept with and borne her estranged husband 'several children' over the four decades since their marriage in a Munster church.

'Sorry, you're not married any more and, in fact, you never were' was the message from the Cork Regional Marriage Tribunal which had made the decision to annul the marriage on psychological grounds. The woman told the *Indo* that the annulment was against her will and that she believed her marriage had existed for forty years.

Annulment, should you be considering it, differs from divorce in that it announces the invalidity of a marriage that was void from the start and not just terminated at a certain date. This can be on a variety of grounds such as the mental incompetence of one of the partners or bigamy. The decree attempts to leave the parties in the same position as they were before their big day.

The regional marriage authority told the paper that a respondent is always invited to personally appear before the tribunal to give evidence, but if they decline to cooperate the court has a right to proceed without them. That said, they did understand that many people would be shocked that a marriage could be null and void after so many years.

Not least, one presumes, the woman who woke up one morning after forty years in a marriage 'coma' to find out that she was never married in the first place.

One is reminded of the infamous shower scene in 1970s TV show, *Dallas*, where a once-deceased Bobby Ewing emerges from the steam and his wife gasps, 'It was all a bad dream!' and they continue married life together. Except this time it's in reverse.

Longest-Serving Hotel Guest

The owners of the Shelbourne Hotel must have done several backflips after **Ian Nelson** checked into this fine establishment in March 2007. The wealthy American, who dubs himself a 'landless peasant', was returning 'home' after a two-year enforced absence. Mr Nelson holds the record for being Ireland's Longest-Serving Hotel Guest having spent seven years, from 1998 to 2005, holed up in the famous Dublin hotel. In March 2005 when the Shelbourne closed for renovations, Ian upped sticks and moved to the three-star McEniff Grand Canal Hotel in Dublin 4. The enigmatic Yank is believed to own luxury houses in France and Australia but prefers to move around between his homes in Dublin and Glasgow, where he has ancestral roots. His family is based in Tucson, Arizona where they own 5,000 acres of land. As he doesn't have the necessary visa, Ian can't work in Ireland, but his people help him out and he's believed to receive a substantial monthly allowance from the US. He eats dinner in his room and is rarely seen in public before 3 p.m., when he can be spotted wandering around Temple Bar, cutting a low-key figure in his tweed jacket and jeans.

So why does he choose to live in Ireland as opposed to the US of A? According to one newspaper Mr Nelson is not a fan of the socio-economic system in his homeland and is reported as saying he is into Abe Lincoln but not McDonald's.

If he ever chose to return and take up a new life attempting to affect political change, there is no doubt that he would be a great success. He could even start his own political party and call it The Hotel Lobby group.

INTERESTING FACT

- Richard Harris spent the latter part of his life living in The Savoy, which is entirely appropriate considering he earned his money out of movies.

Shortest Love Affair With A Donkey

In March of 2007 a story from the online edition of the *Galway First* newspaper shocked internet users and made headlines all around the world.

It reported that a Galway man, who was found handcuffed and dressed in latex, had brought a donkey to his hotel room because he was advised 'to get out and meet people'. The man, with an address in south Galway, had been charged with cruelty to animals, being a danger to himself and obscene behaviour when he appeared before a judge in the City of the Tribes.

A charge relating to the damage to a mini-bar was dropped when the defendant explained that it was the donkey's fault. The court heard that Mister X had been having a hard time of it since his wife had left him. He had been consulting a counsellor who recommended he should get out and meet people. 'Do interesting things,' the counsellor said – and he did. These included booking a hotel room for him and his donkey. Mister X, for the record, was also fixated with the *Shrek* (2001, '04 and '07) movies and was forever talking to himself at work, muttering phrases like 'Isn't that right, Donkey?' The court wasn't told whether Mister X's love-donkey bore any resemblance to Eddie Murphy or not. It did hear that he had signed in as 'Mr Shrek' and told hotel staff that the donkey was his pet. The receptionist, who was a foreign national with only a little English, didn't think anything was amiss when Mr Shrek told her that the donkey was a breed of super rabbit which he was bringing to a pet fair in the city.

The court then heard that the donkey went loopy-loop in the middle of the night, running amok in the corridor before Gardaí arrived to calm it down. The latex-clad Mr Shrek was discovered in the room, handcuffed to the bed. The donkey was believed to have swallowed the key.

Mr Shrek was fined €2,000 for bringing the sexy beast to the room under the Unlawful Accommodation of Donkeys Act 1837. The other charges were dropped due to lack of evidence.

When the story broke, hundreds of thousands of web-users rushed to get online, crashing *Galway First's* website. Within two days, more than a million people had read the article at www.galwayfirst.ie or shared it online, and many news organisations around the world had picked it up. It was an editor's dream story and the best column entry to come out of the West of Ireland in years.

It was also completely made up.

The 'case' had featured on the 'Galway Worst' satirical pages of the *Galway First*, but online readers of the periodical failed to notice this and were convinced that the donkey shenanigans had actually happened. According to *Galway First* the yarn was run as a true story on London's *Metro* paper as well as on various news sites in America and Germany. More than fifty affiliated TV stations in the US ran it as a true story in their light-hearted 'And Finally' section.

The *Galway First* office took over forty calls from newsrooms in Australia and Canada as they attempted to verify the story.

The asses.

Least and Most

Least Amount Of Money Paid For A National Anthem

Ireland's National Anthem, 'The Soldier's Song' (or *Amhrán na bhFiann*) was composed by **Peadar Kearney** and Patrick Heeney in 1907. Originally written in English, Kearney's lyrics were translated into Irish by Liam Ó Rinn solely for the purpose of confusing soccer players who have qualified to play for the Republic under the 'my granny was born in Ireland rule'. It is a little known fact that Ó Rinn's translation originally contained the lines 'UMMMM HI-HUMMMMMM UMM UMM – UMM UMMMM HI-HUMMMMMM UMM UMMM MM-MM' before Kearney insisted he change them to '*Sinne Fianna Fáil atá faoi gheall ag Éirinn*'.

In the lead-up to 1916 the Irish Volunteers appropriated it as a marching tune and it became internationally famous after Easter Week. In 1926 it was made the nation's signature tune, but only after a lot of classic messing.

In 1924 the Director of Publicity (DOP) at the Department of External Affairs advised the government to finally come up with a national anthem as 'God Save The King' was still being sung at some public functions by pro-British types. In fairness to the government, it had had other rather more pressing issues to deal with (for example, the War of Independence and Civil Wars) and hadn't got around to choosing one. The DOP thought the militaristic 'Soldier's Song' was unsuitable and suggested holding a competition to write new words for Thomas Moore's ditty, 'Let Erin Remember The Days of Old'.

The politicians' response was the first example of an 'Irish solution to an Irish problem' – be seen to do something even if that something is nothing. They rejected the competition idea and decided to have two anthems: 'The Soldier's Song' for home occasions, and 'Let Erin Remember . . .' for official occasions abroad. The *Daily Mail* then got in on the act and offered fifty guineas to the person who came up with new lyrics to Moore's song. The entries were to be judged by authors **James Stephens**, **Lennox Robinson** and **WB Yeats**. The three boys, however, refused to choose a winner on the grounds that all the entries were crap.

The dual song arrangement continued until July 1926 when President of the Executive, WT Cosgrave, was asked by one of his own colleagues in the Dáil to name the national anthem. Cosgrave replied by passing the question on to his Minister for Defence, Peter Hughes. After much bobbing and weaving, Hughes eventually admitted that the army preferred 'The Soldier's Song' and later that month it was made the sole national anthem.

In 1933, Cosgrave's government agreed to buy the copyright from Kearney and the estate of the late Patrick Heeney, after the former instituted legal proceedings. It coughed up the modest sum of £980, which was The Least Amount of Money Paid for a National Anthem . . . that it could get away with.

INTERESTING FACT

- Phil Coulter's appalling 1995 tune, 'Ireland's Call', which is sung before international rugby matches, has come in for some deserved criticism over the years. However, 'The Soldier's Song' had its critics when it was made the official anthem. Deputy Frank McDermot described it as a 'jaunty little piece of vulgarity' and a 'cheap music hall jingle'.

Least Irish Of Irish Words

The Irish are great craic altogether, aren't we? There's nothing we like better than to sidle up to someone foreign (especially Americans) and create confusion about the 'great craic' we had the previous night. 'Oh, Jaypurs, noooooo! Not crack, like crack cocaine, God no, craic is the Irish word for fun. I'm not a drug addict hohohohohohohohoho, you're an awful character hohohohohoho!'

Let's stop this here.

'Craic' is not an indigenous Irish word. It's actually an English word, originating from the north of that country, probably around the twelfth century and it made its way here through Scotland. There are written examples of it being used in the Ulster Scots dialect.

So you're not great craic. And neither is your mot, or your gurrier brother. This is because mot is probably Dutch and gurrier is French.

The former, which is slang for girlfriend, may be derived from the Irish *maith an cailín*, or 'good girl', but most reckon it's from the middle Dutch word for prostitute – quite the opposite of good girl. Gurrier – or troublemaker – comes from *guerrier*, or' little warrior'. Don't be too disappointed though, there are plenty of words the English think are English but are, in fact, Irish, so let's rush headlong into the next section which is concerned with the . . .

Most Irish Of English Words

'I say, dear boy, don't forget to take your britches off when you go to the loo.' That sounded English, didn't it? Positively donned a bowler hat and umbrella and marched off to the Tube, did that phrase. Loo is sooooooo quintessentially English. It's like cricket, strawberries and cream, afternoon tea and scones pronounced without the 'e', the delicate clink of china . . . actually, it's more of a clunk of ceramic toilet bowl, Paddy-style. One of the most famous toilet scenes in literary history took place in **James Joyce's** *Ulysses*. It involves a Jewish gent named Leopold Bloom taking his morning dump. Elsewhere in the book Mr Joyce (who may or may not have been bottom-fixated) describes a toilet as a loo, by corrupting the word 'Waterloo'.

The word caught on and the English picked up on it. There are those who say that, plausibly, the word comes from the French *l'eau* (water) and that in the eighteenth century when the citizens of Paris were throwing buckets of pee onto the street they would shout *garde l'eau*, which means 'mind the water'. Then again it might come from the French *lieux d'aisances* or 'places of ease' picked up by British servicemen in France during the First World War. In any case it's not English, and Joyce was the first author to use it in print. Britches is not an English word either, it comes from the Gaelic *bristí* (trousers). Smithereens is from *smidiríní* (small pieces), whiskey from *uisce beatha* (water of life) and galore is from *go leor* (plenty). So if an Englishman ever tells you he fell over in the loo with his britches around his ankles, smashing the bowl to smithereens, after drinking whiskey galore, tell him to hump off and use his own language.

Here's a few other examples you may not know are from Irish: baloney (*béal ónna*, stupid talk); beak, as in magistrate (*beachtaí*, judge); beef, as in to have a beef with someone (*b'aifirt*, accused or complained); bees' knees (*béas núíosach*, new style); bunkum (*buanchumadh*, nonsense, rubbish); cantankerous (*ceanndánacht ársa*, aged

225

stubbornness) and cheesy (*tiosach*, cheap, second-rate).

And if you dig all that, man, then it might surprise you to learn that the word 'dig' is also an Irish word. It comes from *tuig/dtuigean*, to understand.

Who would have thought that Irish could be so (Finn Mac)cool?

Least Gaelic Of Gaeltacht Ministers

Note to **Eamon Ó Cuív TD**, Minister for the Gaelteacht: the author and his contemporaries were forced to endure the interminable ramblings of that mad ould one, **Peig Sayers**, for two years of our adolescent lives. We had to read about her never-ending hardships, the rain, something called 'the Sea Cat', more rain, some muck and a load of other stuff we didn't bother to remember past the Leaving Cert. Get this opening line for a party-starter: 'I am an old woman now, with one foot in the grave and the other on its edge . . .' Good God, someone drop that woman a few 'E's. Yes, we were sorry for her plight, but what spotty, hormonal sixteen-year-old with sex on his/her mind wants to imagine a moany old biddy with her legs straddling anything, let alone the grave.

On top of that, Minister Ó Cuív, there was the poetry. Sean Ó'Riordáin was all right with his '*Oiche Nollaig na mBan*', but what was the Department of Education thinking of when it decided to put on that one about the woman bearing her breast to the soldiers as they were about to skewer her baby? '*Ancrith an Mháthair* fe something something something', by Anonymous (we think). That gave us nightmares for years AND we couldn't even understand all of it.

The one thing, Minister Ó Cuív, that we do remember is that there are no 'Js', 'Ws', 'Xs', 'Ys' or 'Zs' in the Irish alphabet. And there is definitely no bloody 'V'. So either change your name or go to the back of the class.

We feel much better after that. Let's hurry on to the next bit . . .

INTERESTING FACT

- Senator John Minihan said the following in the Seanad in 2006: 'No matter what our personal view of the book might be, there is a sense that one has only to mention the name Peig Sayers to a certain age group and one will see a dramatic rolling of the eyes, or worse'.

Most Annoying Song Ever

If there is one word that is synonymous with Irish music and musicians, it's Gloria.

It must be to do with our religious nature. Holy rockers **U2** hit Number 55 in the British charts with the song 'Gloria', the second single and opening track from *October*. Its Latin chorus came from the liturgical 'Gloria

in Excelsis Deo'. (Dig that crazy Latin beat, man.)
Another glorious man (named after a small lorry) for
using 'Gloria' in a rock context is **Van Morrison.** His
ditty of the same name was recorded by his band, Them,
in 1964 as the B-side of 'Baby Please Don't Go', which
reached Number 10 in Britain and Number 71 in the US
charts in 1966. It is considered to be one of the most
perfect rock anthems and – consisting of an
undemanding three chords – is one of the easiest to play.
Someone once said that if you dropped a guitar down the
stairs it would play 'Gloria' on its way to the bottom. The
song is so revered by rock aficionados that it was inducted
into the Grammy Hall of Fame in 1999.

Neither of these two tunes are the Most Annoying Song
Ever. That distinction may well go to another Gloria, this
time a Country and Western singer by that name. The song
is called 'One Day at a Time', written by Marijohn Wilkin
and Kris Kristofferson, and on 18 August 1977 it reached
Number One in the Irish charts, where it stayed for the
next ninety weeks. It wasn't always in the Number One
position, but was never far away from the top slot. This
meant that every long-distance truck driver and lonely
farmer could request it on Irish radio at virtually any time
to torture the minority of the populace who hadn't bought
the record.

It still holds **The Record For Commandeering The
Charts For The Longest Period** ever by any song. It's
not possible to describe the utter awfulness of this tune.
It was like having hot slurry poured into your ears. It was
the musical equivalent of being given aversion therapy by
Fu Manchu. It was the application of a thousand

fingernails to blackboards in waltz time. It was Edvard Munch's painting, *The Scream*, vocalised. Thousands ran shrieking out of their houses or from moving taxis or buses or down lift shafts when the first notes started up: 'Oimmm only humannn/I'm just a wuhmannnngg . . .' If you got through that without reaching for the lithium then you had to endure the chorus:

Wannnnnn day ad a dime, sweet Jesus,
Dat's all ahhmm asking from yeouuu!!!!!!

I have to stop here. Too many flashbacks.

If Gloria's song was muck then fill up the old spreader with anything by **Brendan Shine**. This is the man who gave the world 'I'm a Savage for Bacon and Cabbage'. Leonard Cohen, Paul Simon, Macca, Bob – are you listening? Of course not, but unfortunately most of rural Ireland was and Brendan spent thirty-seven weeks (Number Seven in our Longevity List) in the charts with 'Do You Want Your Old Lobby Washed Down' from 24 May. It peaked at Number One.

Then, of course, there was the entirely appropriate vision of **Foster and Allen** on *Top of the Pops*, dressed as hairy leprechauns rueing the loss of their virginity (represented by the word 'thyme') as follows:

Once I had a bunch of thyme
I thought it never would decay
Then came a lusty sailor
Who chanced to pass my way
And stole my bunch of thyme away.

SWEET JESUS, to use the words of the immortal Gloria. Instead of getting a bunch of fives, Foster and

Allen's 'Bunch of Thyme' hit Number One in Ireland in October 1979 and refused to get the hell out of the charts for forty weeks. It's still not as annoying as Brendan's Lobby or Gloria's Time, though.

So what is the Most Annoying Song Ever? As Gloria spent the longest period getting up people's noses with her countrified warbling, she takes the gong. However, she can't hold a candle to the. . .

Most Politically Incorrect Song Title

Linda Martin, the former singer with showband Chips and regular contributor to RTÉ's *You're A Star* has had many successes over the years, most notably in that wolfpit of a competition, the *Eurovision Song Contest*. Linda took part in the *National Song Contest* four times with Chips, four times as a soloist and once more as part of Linda Martin and Friends. This is a record, should you ever want to impress your friends with your encyclopaedic knowledge of Eurovision statistics. She also represented Ireland twice, coming second in 1984 with Johnny Logan's 'Terminal Three' and winning it with another Logan classic, 'Why Me?' in 1992.

Linda's mantelpiece may be laden with awards, but if the Political Correctness police had their way she would be stripped of all her honours because of one song she recorded back in 1978.

Incredible as it may seem, the ditty was called 'Liffey Tinker'. Imagine the furore now if RTÉ put it back on its playlist, given that Travellers find the term grossly offensive. Whereas it was common back in the 1970s for settled people to call Travellers 'Tinkers' and not mean to be rude, today it is almost akin to using the 'N' word for Black people. *Erindipity Rides Again* has tried (admittedly not very hard) in vain to source the lyrics, but can recall that the song's heart was in the right place. It may or may not have told the poignant story of a poor Traveller girl begging on O'Connell Bridge over the Liffey. Then again maybe she was merely looking into the Liffey, or perhaps, again, she was named 'Liffey' and 'Tinker' was her surname. It really doesn't matter as – and let there be no mistake about this – it was a craptastically cloying, sentimental piece of sludge, dredged from the bowels of that formerly eggy fart-smelling river. It should have been named 'Liffey Stinker' (which it was around our way, at any rate).

Linda's song would raise a few eyebrows today if re-released but it pales into PC insignificance compared to a song by actor **Patrick Bergin** which was premiered on *The Late Late Show* back in 2003. The composition, titled 'The Knacker' was listed for eight weeks in the Top 50. The Most Politically Incorrect Song entered the chart at Number 16 on week forty-five of 2003 and its last, sorry, appearance was on week one of 2004. Its apotheosis was Number 11, where it stayed for one week.

Mr Bergin is best known for starring alongside Julia Roberts in *Sleeping With The Enemy* (1991), which seems sort of appropriate ('not tonight love, I'm knackered').

There are many people who would like to slip him an enema for writing 'The Knacker'.

INTERESTING FACT

- Captain's log, Season Two, Episode 18, Star Date 22/05/1989. 'The crew of the *Starship Enterprise* has encountered a strange new race . . . and they look like Irish Travellers . . .' Please do not adjust your sets. On the aforementioned episode of *Star Trek: The Next Generation* (titled 'Up the Long Ladder'), the ship encounters a society called the Bringloidis that was founded by Irish Travellers who left Earth centuries earlier. *Brionglóid* is the Irish for dream, by the way. The writers stopped short of including an Interstellar Flying Caravan in the storyline. Maybe they were afraid *Wanderly Wagon* might sue.

Least Eye-Catching Headline

The Irish Times is a fine newspaper, but sometimes the reader could be forgiven for believing that its sub-editors are secretly working on a cure for insomnia. On Monday 23 April 2007 they found it.

The Most Boring Headline ever written in an Irish newspaper stretched in two decks (lines) across eight broadsheet columns, the full width of the paper. It read:

Commercial Reality of Tractor Sale
Included Implied Term That It Was Free
From Dangerous Defects.

Sadly, they do not write them like that any more. Now compare the above to . . .

Most Eye-Catching Headline

During the run-up to the 1932 General Election the newly-founded *Irish Press*, determined to gain readers, ran the following headline:

WATER FAMINE

followed in much smaller type by

UNLIKELY

The intro read: 'Dublin readers need have little fear of a water famine despite the abnormally low rainfall since Christmas . . .'

Most Indecisive County Council

How hard is life as a county councillor? You turn up once in a while, hang up your coat, go to the pub, get a brown envelope stuffed with cash, go back in the chamber, have a row with somebody, then vote to knock down an orphanage for blind children and build a twenty-storey block of luxury flats. And then you put in for expenses. Easy. So easy, in fact that any simpleton could be a county councillor.

Bearing this in mind, it takes a special kind of simpleton to council the county of **Dun Laoghaire/Rathdown** which, in January 2007, was dubbed the Most Indecisive County Council in Ireland after it emerged that not a single motion had been debated there in more than seven months. Some of the eighty motions waiting to be discussed had been so long on the agenda that they were no longer relevant.

The reason the council gave for the backlog was the number of planning decisions that they had to deal with. By contrast, members of Dublin City Council debated fifteen individual motions at its January meeting.

The DLR Chairperson defended the council's operations, saying that there was too much talking during the debates (seriously).

'With all the talking during council meetings we haven't made the motions in a while. People don't want to prolong meetings,' he explained, adding: 'The councillor who proposes a motion can introduce it for six minutes and then everyone else is entitled to speak for three minutes so it can take a long time.'

The Dun Laoghaire–Rathdown County Council held a special meeting to deal with the outstanding motions at the start of 2007. The first item was aimed at providing a facility for the disposal of garden waste during the summer months. It had been waiting for a hearing from the previous summer.

The most enlightening topic debated was a motion about 'motions'. Specifically it dealt with

> . . . not a single motion had been debated there in more than seven months. Some of the eighty motions waiting to be discussed had been so long on the agenda that they were no longer relevant.

whether or not the council should introduce a financial incentive for families using bio-degradable nappies. The chamber heard that every child uses around 5,000 nappies between birth and potty training. Based on the number of births in 2006, that meant roughly 308,420,000 will end up in landfill sites before those children reach their fourth birthdays. Parents who used environmentally friendly nappies (on their kids, not themselves) would be able to reclaim some cash on their waste charges.

The motion was not passed, but it did provide a valuable insight into the workings of the council. It hadn't debated anything in seven months and when it finally did, it wound up talking crap.

INTERESTING FACT

- Ireland's local authorities send, on average, over a million tonnes of rubbish to landfill each year. This is the same weight as 2,000,000 cars. About 84% of a household's bin waste can be recycled and 32% is compostable. 46% is recyclable paper, made by chopping down 8,653,000 trees.

Most Culchie Of Paddy Wagons

Laois may be a small county, but it certainly knows how to grow suspected criminals. In January of 2007 the long arm of the law was dwarfed by the length of a suspected robber. Simply put: he was too tall to fit in the Garda car. **Fine Gael Laois/Offaly Deputy Charles Flanagan** voiced his dismay at the state of law and order in the county when it emerged that Gardaí didn't have a paddy wagon to transport the man to the local station. Indeed, it was revealed that there was not one single paddy wagon in the whole of the county. Tiny Laois, to put this in perspective, has two prisons, Portlaoise and the Midlands with a combined criminal population of 703 inmates. The amount of people who are not behind bars is 67,000 which means that 1.1% of folk living in the county are convicted criminals.

AND THERE'S NOT ONE PADDY WAGON!!!!!

Faced with the problem of ferrying this 1 metre 9 cm (6 ft 3in), 120 kg (19 stone) giant to the cells (perhaps he was actually lifting the shop when he was caught), the hard-pressed Gardaí came up with a novel solution – they hired a farm trailer. The suspect was tied in to the vehicle (pronounced 'veh-i-cul' in Garda speak) and driven through Portarlington as the locals watched in silent stupefaction. The extraordinary scene unfolded outside Deputy Flanagan's legal practice in the town.

The good people of Portarlington shouldn't have been all that surprised as the FG man had previously raised the issue of Garda underfunding when he claimed that the 120 officers stationed in Portlaoise had only one bulletproof vest among them.

This led to the suggestion that whenever there's a shootout in the county the Gardaí should line up and take cover behind the chap wearing the vest.

If prisoners being hauled through the streets in The Most Culchie of Paddy Wagons and Gardaí forming queues to fight crime isn't odd enough then we offer you the following as an example of how best to surprise a criminal.

In 2006 Deputy Flanagan reported that, due to the unavailability of any patrol cars, two officers had been forced to speed off to a crime scene . . . in a taxi.

'Suspect Arrested by Cab' the headlines (should have) screeched the following day, completely getting the wrong end of the stick and causing the Criminal Assets Bureau to issue a clarification. They didn't though, as the Gardaí have a hard enough time of it already.

INTERESTING FACTS

- The CAB, which was founded in 1996 to seize the ill-gotten gains of Ireland's criminal fraternity, collected €89million in its first ten years.
- Gardaí having to hire a farm trailer because they don't have a paddy wagon is bad enough, but having to rent out a firing range to practise shooting seems a tad unfair. Early in 2007 the Association of Garda Sergeants and Inspectors (AGSI) said it was 'totally unacceptable' that their members had to use a private range at Courtlough

in Balbriggan because the two ranges at Templemore and Garda HQ had been closed down. The latter, by the way, was shut in 2005 for health and safety reasons, including a few incidents involving ricocheting bullets. They also, understandably, complained that borrowing Defence Force ranges was no longer a runner. They backed this up with pictures of armed Gardaí blasting away while wearing wellies to stop them sinking into the ground at some army ranges during wet weather. Shortly after the AGSI statement, Garda top brass shelved their plans to issue the force with pitchforks to go with their wellies and farm trailers.

Most Embarassing Line For An Actress

You know how it is. You're an actress, you're well known on TV but you're looking to break into movies – big-time. Along comes the perfect script, with you acting alongside a buff young Leonardo di Caprio on a paradise beach, surrounded by other lovelies.

It's the kind of opportunity/experience you'll never forget, right?

Possibly not if you're Irish actress, **Victoria Smurfit**.

Young Vic got her chance to shine alongside Leo in the blockbuster movie, *The Beach* (2000) – but there was a trade-off. She got to utter what is possibly the worst line in a movie ever (apart from Mickey Rourke wailing 'dare'll be no more kallin' in *Prayer for the Dying* (1987)).

In the scene where Richard (Leo) is about to go ashore to get rice with community leader Sal he is inundated with requests for sundry items.

'New shorts and a new hat,' says one hairy chap.

'Bleach,' says a dyed-blonde siren.

'Toothpaste and a toothbrush,' says another hirsute islander.

And then it's Victoria's turn. 'Aspirin, paracetamol and,' she requests breathlessly, 'six boxes of tampons.'

Interestingly, the movie was never billed as a 'period drama'.

Most Amount Of Bridges Named After Artists

In the first *Erindipity* we published a section under the heading **Most Difficult Question To Answer If You're A Dubliner** that ended up perplexing the nation. It ran thus: 'In a straw poll on Grafton Street in May 1973, 85,000 Dubliners were asked the following question, which no one could answer:

Name the five places in Dublin that end in an 'O'. Phibsboro is not one of them as it is an abbreviation of Phibsborough. Neither is Monto (Montgomery Street).'

(Here's a clue: some of them have a Latin feel to their names while one is so wild the inhabitants have been known to eat their young.)

The answer was: Rialto, Portobello, Marino, Pimlico. The last one is Dublin Zoo.

During the course of an interview on Derek Mooney's splendid show on RTÉ Radio One, the author posed the question again. The response was phenomenal, with hundreds of Dubs ringing in to say that Phibsboro should be included. The controversy spilled over into the following day when Derek and his team got absolute confirmation that Phibsborough is spelt with 'ugh'.

In keeping with the spirit of that enjoyable row *Erindipity Rides Again* will now publish the second question from that Grafton Street poll. Hopefully it will irritate everybody again. And here it is:

Which Dublin waterway has the most amount of bridges named after creative artists (which includes visual artists, writers, musicians and the like)? Ninety-eight percent got it wrong and one man wearing bicycle clips and a duffle coat (in July) replied 'Melanie' before wheeling around and goosing a passing cleric.

Answer: The Tolka with three: John McCormack (singer), Luke Kelly (singer) and Dean Swift (writer) Bridges. The Liffey has only two: James Joyce Bridge and Seán O'Casey Bridge.

The amount of city centre bridges over the Liffey currently named after people is thirteen. They are: James Joyce Bridge, Seán O'Casey Bridge, Talbot Memorial Bridge, Butt Bridge, O'Connell Bridge, Grattan Bridge, Essex Bridge, O'Donovan Rossa Bridge, Fr Mathew Bridge, Mellowes Bridge, Rory O'More Bridge, Frank Sherwin Bridge and Seán Heuston Bridge.

And finally the last part of the bridge question:

Which Dublin waterway is spanned by the Hamilton Bridge? No one got this right.

Answer: the Royal Canal. Broom Bridge was changed to Hamilton Bridge by the Taoiseach Éamon de Valera in 1958 when he was laying a plaque to commemorate the mathematician Sir William Hamilton (see Best Royal Graffiti Artist, page 195). Typically, Dublin City Council either chose to ignore his directive or didn't read the morning papers reporting his announcement. Since then, few have known that its official name is Hamilton and not Broom.

Most Well-To-Do Beggar

A vagrant made legal history in March 2007 when he successfully legalised begging in Ireland. The thirty-three-year-old Blackrock, County Dublin man challenged and overturned the 1847 Vagrancy (Ireland) Act after he was arrested in 2003 while sitting outside a shop. Facing a mandatory month in jail the University graduate sought a judicial review, saying the law breached 'freedom of expression'. High Court judge Éamon de Valera agreed and upheld the challenge.

We're not printing his name to protect his privacy, but we will say that his current state of affairs is a lot different to his life in leafy suburbia, where his parents live. They are said to be strong, supportive people who have become estranged from their son, who is a highly clever man with problems. According to one source, Vagrant X was down on his luck and didn't want to resort to crime so he started begging which led to his arrest. In what would appear at face value to be the law making a heartless ass of itself, Vagrant X had just foiled a robbery when he was lifted by the Gardaí. He prevented a theft from a shop in the city centre and the grateful shopkeeper rewarded him with a sandwich and a coffee. He was sitting outside with his meagre meal when the Gardaí arrived to investigate the shoplifting incident and took him away for begging.

You would think after his harsh treatment by a heavy-handed law that Vagrant X would have celebrated his legal victory in some small way. However, due to his vagrant lifestyle, his solicitor was unable to contact him to tell him he had won.

Most Bizarre Kidnapping By Barney The Dinosaur

Who invented purple? It's a truly horrible colour. It's the colour of exertion: the shade your face turns when you're dancing like an idiot. It's the colour of embarrassment.

It's the colour of the title of the film *The Color Purple* (1985) starring that arch-irritant, Whoopi Goldberg. It's the colour of the jumper your granny gave you for Christmas and the one you have to wear whenever she calls over. It's the colour of your eye after the bigger lads on the road spot you wearing your granny's jumper ('It's dark red!' 'No it's not!' Thump, thump, smack). It's the colour of the pairs of knickers (with white piping) your mum keeps posting to your student digs with the message, 'Always wear clean knickers in case you get run down by a bus'. If you ever see a bus hurtling towards you at great speed be assured that your knickers won't be clean for long. Which is just as well, as who would want a nurse to see you wearing purple knickers?

Purple, purple, purple, purple, purple. It even sounds manky, like the kind of noise a pimple would make if it could talk. 'Purplepurplepurplepurplepurple'.

Priests aside, nobody wears purple – except for that tosspot king of children's entertainment, **Barney the Dinosaur**.

> 'Always wear clean knickers in case you get run down by a bus'. If you ever see a bus hurtling towards you at great speed be assured that your knickers won't be clean for long.

In 2006 a student walked into a Dublin Garda Station and claimed that he had just been kidnapped by Barney, or more precisely, two men disguised as Barney. The victim had been in his car at the University of Limerick when he was approached by the knife-wielding dinosaurs, who forced him to drive to Dublin. Bizarrely, they tipped him €700 for his trouble. (Presumably, the affair was all a bit of a purple haze.) The student's claims sparked a major hunt for the brutish Barneys. The Gardaí contacted their counterparts in Limerick while the student availed of counselling services. Investigators at Henry Street station studied CCTV footage from the campus and reported that there were no robberies in the vicinity at the time that the Barneys struck. The UL Students' Union said the incident highlighted the need for more on-campus security, but officers reckoned there was a nasty whiff about the incident and believed the eighteen-year-old had made it all up. A file was subsequently prepared for the Director of Public Prosecutions.

But why would anyone claim to have been kidnapped by Barney? Surely the humiliation would have been quite hard to bear.

The Gardaí noted that the carjacking had taken place the week before a Rag Week event where UL students were due to compete to raise €500 for charity. One of the criteria for the competition was that the entrants receive national publicity. However, the publicity officer at the university's students' union said the incident had no connection whatsoever with the charity event.

Erindipity Rides Again believes in the presumption of innocence, but whatever the outcome of the investigation, someone's face – just like Barney's – is going to turn a deep shade of purple.

INTERESTING FACT

- The phrase 'having a Barney', that is, an argument, originates from an incident in 1927. Two neighbouring Waterford farmers (Myles Herlihy and Francie Pilkington) were having a row over the building of a Barna shed on the border of their lands when the cable of the crane carrying the shed snapped, depositing it on Farmer Myles' head. Farmer Francie got permission for retention and 'having a Barna' went into the slang lexicon. True story.

Most Desperate Reverse Getaway

On 25 January 2007 Reuters press agency reported on what rates as the most bizarre motor theft in Irish legal history. Wexford District Court gave a twenty-five-year-old man a six-month suspended sentence for stealing a car and a €300 fine for failing to provide a breathalyser test. The judge heard that the culprit had nicked the vehicle after falling asleep on the bus home and overshooting his stop.

What makes this case noteworthy is that the thief's home, on this occasion, was Shelton Abbey Open Prison in Arklow, where he was serving time for some unspecified offence. Could it have been car theft?

The criminal mastermind made his dramatic dash to incarceration after missing a weekend release deadline.

Slowest and Fastest

Slowest Getaway

The capital city has thrown up its fair share of characters over the years: Fortycoats, Bang Bang, Bob Geldof, Two-tone Tony The Shetland Pony' (actually, he may be from Cork) and Billy The Bowl to namecheck a few. The best-loved Dublin character of them all wasn't from the city but found fame on its streets. His name was **Thom McGinty**, known to a generation of Irish people as the performance artist, **The Diceman**.

Thom, who was born in Glasgow, arrived here in 1976 to work as a nude model in the National College of Art and Design. Sitting still must have come easily as this was how he would spend most of his time on Grafton Street during the late 1980s and early 1990s – the prototype 'human statue'. The monicker, Diceman, came from a shop that sold role-playing games and when it closed he was snapped up to advertise various other businesses, including Bewley's Café. Where London had the bear-skinned guards outside Buckingham Palace to annoy, Dublin had The Diceman, and it was commonplace to witness youngsters trying to break his attention by throwing things at him or pulling faces (theirs, not his). Sometimes he would chase them off in a playful manner, other times he just suffered on for his art. Then there were the occasional idiots who would throw lit ciggies at his feet, but Thom always stayed in character, earning his celebrity status the hard way.

He became so well known that in 1989 he was given a part in the Gate Theatre production of Oscar Wilde's *Salome*, directed by superham Steven Berkoff.

Thom makes an entry here for recording the Slowest Getaway from the Gardaí ever. During one of their periodic clampdowns on busking, members of the Fun Police attempted to make life difficult for The Diceman, claiming he was causing an obstruction (which he was, due to his popularity). The constant 'move along there' from the underworked Gardaí would have become a major source of irritation for a lesser man, but Thom used it to enhance his act. According to legendary entertainer Alan 'Mister Pussy' Amsby, The Diceman's solution was to walk at a painfully slow pace, moving his feet in almost slo-mo, sometimes taking over an hour to walk down the street. For a bit of variety he would occasionally leg it at great speed across the road and would then stop, standing stock still for minutes on end before winking or blowing a kiss or running after a group of shrieking schoolgirls.

Thom also did his act across Europe, in the US and

Russia and was one of very few people to perform on both sides of the Berlin Wall and in Red Square.

In 1990 he was diagnosed with AIDS, and he passed away in 1994. After his final send-off his coffin was carried in an appropriately slow procession down Grafton Street.

It was, sadly, his one getaway that wouldn't succeed.

Fastest Fingers

It has been said that the definition of a true gentleman is 'one who knows how to play the accordion, but desists from doing so in public'. That may be a bit harsh. Some people consider the accordion to be quite 'cool', what with it being a cousin of the harmonica. Others say it's the harmonica's idiot cousin. We say 'we're saying nothing'.

However, trendy or not, there is one Irishman who will make your eyes melt when he lays his hands on his squeeze box. In November 2006 **Liam O'Connor** broke the World Record for Fastest Fingers when he played to an admiring mob in Eason's of O'Connell Street, Dublin. The former 'Lord of the Dance' star clocked up an extraordinary 11.14 notes a second while playing the Latin classic, 'Tico Tico'.

Erindipity Rides Again would be content with just having achieved that benchmark and would have kicked back to enjoy a few sherries. Not Liam though. He set out the following day and broke the record again, with 11.64 notes per second. One imagines when he plays at céilís there's always a defibrillator nearby. *Erindipity Rides Again* has decided to challenge speedy Liam in the New Year and has spent the last number of weeks at home doing finger exercises. At least that's what we're telling the neighbours.

Fastest Walkers

It won't come as a surprise to learn that the capital's citizens are among the fastest walkers in the world. A survey conducted across thirty-two countries by California State University found that pedestrians around the world are walking 10% faster since 1994, the year the survey began. Shrinks say the findings reflect the way technology, such as the internet and mobile phones, is making us more impatient. (No it isn't. Yes it is. Just get on with the bloody writing, will you.) The most noticeable acceleration was in the Asian Tiger countries of China and Singapore where pedestrians walked between 20% and 30% faster than in the early 1990s. The latter, by the way, has the fastest walkers in the world, with Copenhagen in second place.

If walking speeds really are an indication of high stress levels then London is more laid-back than Dublin. The English capital finished twelfth in the league table, while the Dubs romped home in fifth place. The survey found that this was not due to high levels of stress, but to the high levels of skangers chasing after them.

Biggest and Smallest

Biggest Haul Of Diamonds Lost In The Post

Everyone has lost something in the post at some stage. It's normal. It's natural. It's generally a cheque to pay a bill.

In March 2007 something went missing in An Post's Swiftpost system that led to an unprecedented Gardaí investigation – diamonds. The uncut gems had been posted by a reputable jewellery manufacturer to an equally reputable dealer in two parcels. When they arrived at Andrew Street Post Office, staff saw that the packets had been cut open. They notified the sender, who told them there had been a small fortune in diamonds in the packages – €10,000 in each.

The Gardaí were called in to investigate and were satisfied that the €20,000-worth of stones were in the parcels when they were processed through Swiftpost, which is marketed as a secure way of sending mail quickly. Their disappearance happened before the empty packets had arrived at Andrew Street. A lot of people would have handled the parcels before they were delivered, but the fact that both packages were opened suggested that the diamonds' 'liberator' knew what he/she/they were looking for. It remains the State's Biggest Haul Of Diamonds Lost In The Post.

There is no truth in the rumour that, shortly after the disappearance, Postman Pat bought his black and white cat a 'bling' new collar.

Biggest Breakfast

James Joyce was a great man for the sausages. He also liked a bit of fried liver and black and white puddings, with a kidney on the side. Hold the toast, missus I will I won't I will have a cup of tea in the hanky hand it'll do you good I will then please God. He also wrote a couple of books. They're very good. Masterpieces in fact. There's *Dubliners*, which deals with all manner of things from paedophilia to suicide, *Finnegan's Wake*, which is a bit mad, *A Portrait of the Artist as a Young Man*, which does exactly what it says on the cover, *Pomes Pennyeach* (they weren't really a penny) and the extraordinary *Ulysses*. Set in 1904, the book follows the activities of one Leopold Bloom as he roams around Dublin City on 16 June. His passage traces that of Ulysses/Odysseus as he travels back home from the Trojan War. At least that's what most people believe it to be about, hogtied as the storyline is by literary techniques as numerous as the threads on

251

Penelope's spinning wheel. That last reference was to Ulysses' wife who is waiting for him to return. Its clever inclusion has turned *Erindipity Rides Again* into a literary masterpiece and has won the author the right to call for an annual Erindipity Day on which every citizen will be called upon to dress up in silly clothes and parade up and down outside his former home (just don't disturb my mum).

Perish the ludicrous thought. Who ever heard of a book causing people to root around in their attics for fancy dress attire that would shame a three-year-old raiding their parents' wardrobe? Or to stand around on a rainy summer's day eating offal? Or to snip the plastic nose and moustache off one of those Groucho Marx false-nose-and-spectacles sets to get the correct Joycean eyewear?

It is absolutely certain that the majority of people who turn out at **Joyce's Martello Tower** in Sandycove, County Dublin, to celebrate the writing of *Ulysses*, have never read, will never read, or simply refuse to read the book. They amble about, starting debates about Stephen Dedalus' status as 'Philosophy's Superman' with reference to 'Hegelian Ratiocinations' and 'Satiation Stopping Time' and then run off before anyone has a chance to ask them what they mean. Still, it gets the old dears out of the house for a while and is an occasion for harmless, old-fashioned snobbery.

Another topic of discussion is the extraordinary lengths people have had to take to avoid possible breaches of copyright of Joyce's work, due to the narrow interpretation of copyright protection adopted by his grandson, **Stephen Joyce**. This France-based scholar obsessively controls the Great Man's estate and is constantly asserting his right to exploit Joyce's writing and hunt down anyone who attempts to do the same. In 2004, the centenary of Bloomsday, he warned the National Library that a planned display of his grandfather's manuscripts violated his copyright. The Seanad had to pass an emergency amendment in order to thwart him. More warnings from the Joyce Estate on copyright meant there were no official public readings from his works at the ReJoyce festivities in the same year. The legal advice for Bloomsday, under the rules of 'fair use', was that unofficial readings from the book must be limited to three sentences only.

At one seminar attended by luminaries like Séamus Heaney during the ReJoyce celebrations, an American professor from Ohio joked that he had received a letter purportedly from the grandson forbidding the use of allegedly copyrighted phrases like 'coming down along the road', 'stately' and 'riverrun'. How everyone laughed. Ho, ho, ho.

The ReJoyce 2004 festival took place between 1 April and 31 August, and on the Sunday before 16 June, served the Biggest Breakfast ever (in peacetime at any rate) in the capital city. No one will ever know how many true Joyce fans were in attendance on O'Connell Street that day, but it didn't matter as the massed armies of hungover Dubs, excited tourists and Joycean scholars alike all happily queued together to jack up their cholesterol levels. Also there to be fed were numerous stilt-walkers,

Joyce look-alikes and a street performer with a huge papier maché head, although that may have been Senator David Norris.

The Denny's[18] Breakfast catered for 10,000 hungry mouths, and to speed service along the traditional plated meal was dumped in favour of a baguette stuffed with a sausage, a rasher, and slices of black and white pudding. 40,000 pork delicacies . . . never before had so many piggy wiggies given so much for so many. There is no truth to the suggestion that Stephen Joyce considered sueing everybody attending the event for breaching copyright of the words 'yes', 'I' and 'will' 10,000 times.

'Will you have breakfast?''

'Yes.'

'What?'

'Yes.'

'Yes.'

'I will.'

'YES.'

INTERESTING FACTS

- The first Bloomsday took place in 1954 when Flann O'Brien (Brian O'Nolan), Patrick Kavanagh and Anthony Cronin visited the Martello Tower in Sandycove for a liquid breakfast and a horse-drawn trek back into the city to go on a Joycean pub crawl. They made it

---

[18] Denny's is mentioned in *Ulysses* when Leopold Bloom watches a young girl in Dlugacz's butcher's shop buy a pound and a half of their sausages, as he waits to buy a kidney. Donor cards weren't in operation back then.

as far as the Bailey pub, across the road from Davy Byrne's where Bloom has a gorgonzola sandwich and a glass of burgundy in the book. ReJoyce 2004 began on April Fool's Day – thirty-eight years to the day of Flann O'Brien's death.

- Mel Brooks' movie, *The Producers* (1968), features a lead character called Leo Bloom, an accountant, played with aplomb by Gene Wilder. In the 2005 remake, in the scene where Bloom first meets oily producer, Max Bialystock, the wall calendar shows the day is 16 June – Bloomsday.

Smallest-Minded Playboy Fans

John Millington Synge's play, *The Playboy of the Western World*, famously caused riots involving the police in Dublin when it opened in 1907. Many were scandalised by the notion of a man becoming a celebrity by killing his father, but for most it was the inclusion of a line about underwear that caused most offence. Christy Mahon refers to a 'drift' of women 'standing in their shifts'. The latter is another name for slips, or underskirts. One hundred years on it seems a bit of an over-reaction and its prudishness seems almost quaint.

Unbelievable as it may seem, the play almost caused a similar reaction in China in 2006.

Beijing audiences were upset by the sexuality of a Mandarin-language version of the play when it was performed featuring an actress wearing a short skirt. Instead of the West of Ireland, the innovative play centres around a foot massage and hairdressing parlour in the old part of the city. In place of red shawls the cast wear boob tubes.

As a result of a complaint about the length of the actress's mini-skirt, glimpses of knickers and cleavage, two policemen were dispatched to attend the performance at the Beijing Oriental Theatre. One of the show's producers said the country's arts and culture bureau had approved the Chinese version of the play, but wasn't taking any chances and would be lengthening the Sarah Tansey character's dress. The disreputable scene involves Chen Junnian as Christy being forced to disguise himself in a blonde wig and mini by the hairdressers. Sha Sha, who plays Sarah, has to manoeuvre the little skirt over Christy's thighs and with all her wiggling about she exposes a bit of booby and a hint of knickers.

In China, immodest displays are frowned upon and the complaint was taken very seriously. The criticism led to a headline writer's field day: 'The Actress's mini-skirt is too short – call the police!' cried the *Daily Mail*. 'Pegeen Mike evokes a blush in Beijing' whispered *The Irish Times*. The hands down winner was *The Sun*, however.

'Chinese Cracker in Stage Storm: An Irish Play has Sparked a Sex Storm in China – because one of the cast shows her KNICKERS', it joyously declared, under the banner headline of the year . . . 'PEKING AT YOUR KNICKERS'.

We love it.

Biggest Tea Party

The Irish have always been known to be fond of a drink. The irony is, of course, that we live in the wettest part of Europe and yet still have a raging thirst. So what is the nation's favourite beverage? Is it Guinness? Whiskey? Lager? Wine?

It's none of the above. Our favourite drink is . . . tea. In fact, Ireland is the biggest per capita consumer of tea in the world, beating China, India and Japan to the tea caddy with an average of 3.2 kg of brew swirling down our gullets each year. That equates to four cups of tea a day.

A little history: in 1835, **Charles Bewley** (of Grafton Street fame) sailed a ship carrying 2,000 chests of tea to Dublin from Canton. This was the first time that tea had been directly imported to Ireland after the ending of the East India trading company's monopoly on tea distribution in 1833. Merchants all over the world followed suit and tea was soon on its way out of the upper-class salons and into the humbler kitchens of Ireland.

Prior to the Second World War, most Irish companies – in the absence of a native merchant fleet – continued to buy most of their tea through British suppliers. However, when our nearest neighbours became embroiled in another ruckus with Germany, Westminster elected to ration its stocks of tea to all its client countries. When de Valera's government declared neutrality, the British struck back by drastically reducing Ireland's rations. Dev was fit to be tied. First they'd the set the Black and Tans on us and now they were going to take the mug of tea out of our hand – and Dev loved his cup of tea. Or 'tae' as he was wont to call it.

He established a private company, Tea Importers (Éire) Ltd, to restock the country's pantries, but it had some initial difficulties – what with not having boats to transport the tea here. Dev was no Admiral Nelson.

After the war was over new laws were passed, requiring Irish companies to import their tea directly (that is, not from Britain) and in 1958 the Tea Act was passed, setting up Tea Importers Ltd as the only authorised importer into the Republic. The firm was co-owned by fifty separate tea companies and its monopoly was broken only after Ireland entered the EEC in 1973.

Enough history. There are three basic types of tea: black, green and oolong. Irish tea blends favour the first type of leaf, which has the strongest flavour. Weak tea has always been synonymous in this country with meanness or poverty ('de tae was so weak it could barely get up and out of de spout'). Most Irish teas now come from East Africa and Sri Lanka. Whether any citizens from these parts of the world have ever travelled to Donegal solely for a cup of tea is unknown. What is known is that the Best and Biggest Tea Parties in Ireland were held annually throughout the 1990s at **Daniel Francis Noel O'Donnell's** castle in Kincasslagh, County Donegal. The Dark Lord of Country and Irish milked and poured for tens of thousands of grannies at his home, as a 'thank you' for the success he has enjoyed since striding onto the music scene in 1983 with the hard-rockin' 'My Donegal Shore'.

His get-togethers were legendary with all sorts of strange rock rituals going on, from putting the milk in after the tea to overindulging on sugar lumps. They do say that if you stir a cup of Daniel's tea anticlockwise you'll hear a secret message ('I love my mammy/I love my mammy/I love my mammy'), but that might be just rumour.

Although the slick Dublin media are quick to snigger, Daniel has sold five million albums to date and there are few other acts in the land that can command such a massive fan base. The old Queen Mother was even a fan and used to sing along to his records. Not even Bono can claim to have grannies and queens in his fan club.

> They do say that if you stir a cup of Daniel's tea anticlockwise you'll hear a secret message ('I love my mammy/I love my mammy/I love my mammy'), but that might be just rumour.

The irony is that although Wee Daniel – he's 1.7 m (5 ft 10 in) – used to host these massive tea parties, he doesn't drink tea himself. It's altogether possible that he got the above nickname after serving one of his fans a weak cup of tea – 'that's like wee, Daniel'.

If the total population of the Republic is 4,239,848 (which it is) and 864,449 of us are under the age of fourteen and probably (if the health fascists had their way) shouldn't be drinking tea, then the amount consumed daily is 3,375,399 multiplied by four.

That's 13,501,596 cups every day. That figure may have risen slightly on 3 August 2000 when 5,000 thirsty people descended on Kincasslagh for Daniel's last official bash, making it the Biggest Tea Party ever held in Ireland.

INTERESTING FACT

• Daniel O'Donnell's favourite food is mince and potatoes.

Biggest Consumers Of Pizza

Let the French eat cake – the Irish have the most adventurous taste buds on the planet. While our Gallic cousins have been stuck in a rut for centuries eating boring old sheep's anuses, stuffed tadpoles and snails, we have been experimenting with the culinary delights of the Orient (Chinese takeaways), the Sub-Continent (Indian takeaways) and The New World (burgers and chips). The cuisine of one country in particular has found a warm place in the hearts and bellies of this Green Isle, and that place is Italy.

Consider the delicacies the Italians introduced to Ireland – ice cream, Alphabetti Spaghetti, fish and chips and, of course, pizza. The latter was such a hit that we are now the biggest per-capita consumers of pizza in the world.

Nowhere on the planet will you find bigger fans of the cheese-encrusted pie than the residents of Tallaght in South County Dublin. In 2006 **Domino's Pizza chain** announced that their outlet in The Square shopping centre sells more pizzas than any of the other 8,000 outlets around the world, baking 200 pizzas an hour – that's three pizzas a minute – totalling 2,400 pies a day. Not even the notoriously hungry Yanks can out-eat the Tallaghtfornians, who spend €2.45million a year on Domino's Pizzas.

While the killjoys will insist that fast food like pizza contributes to obesity, this is clearly not the case in Tallaght which boasts the most athletic youths in Ireland. Indeed, at times The Square looks like Santry Stadium because of the amount of healthy people in tracksuits wandering around it.

INTERESTING FACTS

- According to health experts, the average, generic, medium-sized Irish pizza contains 900 calories – that's nearly half the recommended daily calories intake for a woman. Walking to the front door to take delivery of it burns off one calorie. So it's not all bad news then.

Biggest Contract Taken Out On A Dog By The Mob

LASSIE pulling its owner from a burning log cabin, Beethoven the St Bernard slobbering all over a slushy American family, Laughing Gravy playing the doggy clown with Laurel and Hardy, Scooby doing the Doo with those pesky kids, Toto having a gay old time with Dorothy in Oz . . . Since Hollywood was a sapling, doggies and the movies have gone together like a lamp post and a cocked leg – until the Irish got in on the act. While the aforementioned bowlers have all earned mega-spondooligs for their movie makers, **Paddy pooches Flo and Lucky** have made it their business to ruin as many would-be film moguls as possible.

Instead of destroying their snouts searching for 'Tinseltown Talc' (cocaine, dear), the Labrador chums made a name for themselves using their sense of smell to bust illicit film piracy rings in the Far East.

In 2006 our canine Cagney and Lacey angered movie pirates in Malaysia by helping the authorities there uncover 1.3 million discs and burners worth about €2.43million. On 16 April of the following year the pair made the headlines in The Philippines when they sniffed through steel doors and located stacks of bogus movies during a raid on the Makati Cinema Square Mall in Manila.

'SUPERBITCHES,' screamed the *Manila Times* (probably). The doggies – who sit down or freeze when they smell polycarbonate, which is used to manufacture optical discs – led government agents through the mall, wearing neon-yellow vests and sniffing glass cabinets, boxes, bags and the occasional crotch. The dogs, that is, not the government agents. The latter didn't sniff anyone's crotch that we know of.

As the local traders scattered, the police seized more than 300,000 pirated discs and arrested eleven people on copyright and pornography charges in the first hour alone. The police were delighted with their new partners in crime-busting. The Mob were not, however, and offered a bounty of more than €9,286 on each of the dogs, whose arrival in Manila was kept top secret until the mall raid.

'They are the Starsky and Hutch of the Motion Picture Association,' said the dogs' Irish trainer, David Mayberry, raising several cross-gender issues. The girls' next job was in India where they made such a name for themselves that they named a city after them – Madras.

INTERESTING FACTS

- In August 2007 newspapers reported that a senior crime figure in Limerick had put out a contract on Rocky, the Garda drug sniffer dog. One source speculated that as this villain had offered €10,000 to murder a certain prison officer this would probably be the going rate for a sniffer dog. As it was the newspaper silly season, and as the figure was only speculative, and as the author has been responsible for many 'fliers' in his journalistic career, this should be taken with a pinch of something white and powdery. Salt, that is.

- In February of that year, Gardaí in Drogheda were shocked to find porn videos hidden inside Disney DVD covers during a raid on a market stall. They had been expecting to see various characters fooling around with Mickey. Which, in a way, was what they got.

Last

Last *Erindipity*

We hope you've enjoyed *Erindipity Rides Again*, the second – and last – of the *Erindipity* books. It was a pleasure to talk at you while you went about your ablutions or got the train home or had your haemorrhoids attended to.

The author is now embarking on an intensive self-training course for the World Squat Jump championships in Helsinki in 2008. Perhaps someone will be kind enough to mention him in a similar book to this one should he squat his way to the title.

Erindipity

The Irish Miscellany

DAVID KENNY

Ever wondered:

- how many teeth Richard Harris lost to get nominated for an Oscar?
- when an Enya record was used in a multi-billion dollar heist?
- where's the place most likely to get a puck in the gob?
- how long it takes to re-feather a chicken in Dalkey?
- where's the really smelliest-smelling place?
- what's the largest amount of ice cream lost at sea?

It's all here, crammed into 125 rambling 'essays' – the good, the bad, the extremes of Ireland – that will amuse, educate, annoy and misguide you in equal measure.

'I loved this book' *Rick O'Shea*

'Answers a lot of questions that you would never even have thought of asking' *Sunday Tribune*

'Ingenious, informative, witty and hilarious and downright daft in places' *Dave Fanning*

'Provides the best laughs by far', 'an excellent tome' *Irish Independent*

'Very witty' *Sunday Tribune*

'I particularly liked the bit about the best place to keep cheese' *Joe O'Shea (Seoige and O'Shea Show, RTE 1)*

Beyond the Pale

The best of Ireland's local news stories

DONAL HICKEY

The stories you <u>won't</u> hear on the 6 o'clock news!

We've all read articles in local newspapers that make the mind boggle – the type of story that when repeated to family and friends is greeted with outright disbelief. Stories so outlandish, so strange, so downright weird that you have to re-read them just to check you didn't imagine them in the first place. Well, they're all in *Beyond the Pale*. A collection of stories from regional newspapers that proves beyond any doubt that the 'characters', the chancers, the rogues, the naïve, the gullible and the just plain insane are still out there causing havoc in all parts of Ireland.

From checking with an undercover cop to see if he'd be on for murdering your wife to the Casanova bull whose passing was mourned by thousands of cows in Ireland to the tongue-tied councillors who were too shy to list how many of them took part in a 'fact-finding' mission to New York for St Patrick's Day – as the fella says – read all about it!

Up the Poll

Great Irish Election Stories

SHANE COLEMAN

Up The Poll gathers together all the comical, tragic and farcical moments from Irish election campaigns from 1917 to 2007.

- Michael McDowell's shimmy up a poll in 2002, which kick-started the PDs' campaign and landed them in government. Surely the most profitable poll-dance in Irish history?

- The senior Fianna Fáil politician seen assembling a machine gun in a phone booth in Dáil Éireann after the 1932 election.

- The clash of the titans – Charlie v Garret in three RTÉ television debates. Would Garret's hair get any wilder? Would Charlie postpone dinner at Mirabeau's?

- Bertie's run-in with Vincent Browne about spending *his* money how *he* wants. So there.

. . . and many more.

Foot In Mouth

Famous Irish Political Gaffes

SHANE COLEMAN

Foot In Mouth – Famous Irish Political Gaffes recounts the gaffes that rocked governments, shocked public opinion and mocked accepted uses of the English language.

Containing over 70 cringe-inducing gaffes, including:

- Pee Flynn's musings on the *Late Late Show* on life on a measly income (how will he pay for that third housekeeper?)
- Jack Lynch's memory loss concerning two British agents
- *That* Fine Gael Ard Fheis
- The PDs' excessive housekeeping (let's dump these sensitive financial records in this skip!)
- De Valera's notorious response to the death of Hitler

. . . and many more.

The Great Irish Bank Robbery

The Story of Ireland's White Collar Villainy

LIAM COLLINS

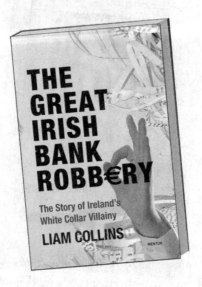

In this mesmerising book, Liam Collins weaves a fascinating tale of the biggest financial scandal ever witnessed in Ireland. Ten years after uncovering the shocking conduct of AIB Bank, Collins explains in clear, concise language the web of deceit involving some of Ireland's most prominent business figures, the banks they ran, the greed of their customers and the negligence of the tax authorities. A fast-paced saga of financial avarice that tainted almost every village and town in Ireland.

Great GAA Moments 2007

FINBARR McCARTHY

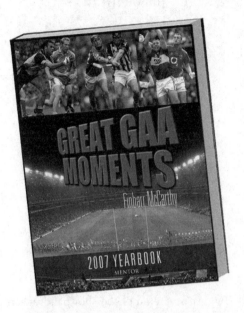

Sports journalist Finbarr McCarthy serves up another action-packed book chronicling the ups and downs of the 2007 GAA season. Kicking off with the first floodlit game in Croke Park in February, the season's most spectacular moments are captured in eye-catching colour photos. The Allianz Football and Hurling Leagues, the club finals on St Patrick's Day, the sublime and the best-forgotten moments of the Championship season are all covered in this book, along with many other GAA-related events. A perfect gift for any GAA fan.

Are Ye the Band?

A Memoir of the Showband Era

JIMMY HIGGINS

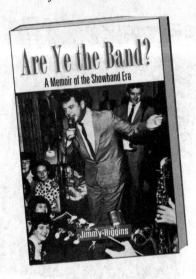

Jimmy Higgins, a veteran of the showband era, recalls the heady days of life in showband Ireland. As an innocent 14-year-old from Tuam, Co Galway, Jimmy started out as a trumpet player in the Paramount Showband. In this book, he recounts the many untold tales from this golden era in Ireland's social history. The characters, the clothes, the managers, the groupies, the near-hits and the close calls are all recounted in this nostalgic trip down a musical memory lane. Packed with photos showing the movers and shakers of the time – a must for anyone who ever danced on a Saturday night in an overheated ballroom to the music played by the 'pop idols' of the day.